Murder

in

Mount Pleasant

A JOURNAL THROUGH TIME MYSTERY

SARAH M STEPHEN

WZE PRESS

WZE Press
Vancouver, B.C.
https://wzepress.ca

Edited by Janet Fretter
Cover by ebooklaunch.com

Library and Archives Canada Cataloguing in Publication
Murder in Mount Pleasant / by Sarah M Stephen
ISBN: 978-1-7778330-5-3 (paperback)
ISBN: 978-1-7778330-6-0 (e-book)

This is a work of fiction. Names, characters, places, and incidents are of the author's imagination and used fictitiously.

To Nan. I think you would have liked this.

A Note about Language

This book is set in Canada and written in Canadian English (which is very similar to British English). If you're unfamiliar with the differences, we use our instead of or in "colour," "favour," and "neighbour" and double the l in "travelled."

CHAPTER 1

Jack (1898)

DETECTIVE JACK WINSTON slammed his fist on the cluttered shelf, sending a cascade of folders and papers to the floor. How had the file room returned to disorder so quickly? Hadn't Thomas reorganized it? He rubbed his hand. In truth several weeks had elapsed since Winston had assigned the constable the task, and in that time the other members of the constabulary had resumed their bad habits.

While Chief Constable Lawrence Philpott was away, Winston would reinstate order in this room. Thinking of his uncle spurred another thought: perhaps he needed to reinstate order in his life. Winston closed his eyes and inhaled deeply. He pushed the notion from his mind with a slow release of breath. Lowering himself to the floor, he began to collect the files. He would start with this space— order elsewhere would follow.

He stacked a neat pile of documents against the file room door and turned his attention to a collection of evidence. A knife. A child's shoe. A bloody handkerchief. He cast his mind back and couldn't place them as belonging to the same case. They must be from several. How would he ever know which ones they belonged to? He slammed his fist again, wincing at the impact. He was pondering this question when the door swung open. Pages scattered again.

"Damnation!" The word escaped Winston's lips before he could stop it.

Constable Thomas Miller stood in the door opening, eyes wide with surprise. "Sir?"

"Thomas." Winston clipped the word to prevent saying something he would later regret. He rose and took an exaggerated stride over the strewn papers.

Miller cleared his throat. "I did rearrange this room a while ago. I guess it's just—"

Winston held up his hand. Was it quivering, or was a flicker of the lamp's flame playing a trick on him? "Thomas, with our records in such disarray, we will never be able to identify whether two cases are connected."

Miller looked from the pile on the floor to the shelves. "Connected? Like the missing men, you mean?"

The first case they'd worked on together. The first he'd worked on with Riley. Important to Jack for so many reasons. "Yes. Like that one." His fondness for Miller wasn't enough to quell his anger. "We need to—you need to sort through those papers." He turned back to point at the evidence pile. "And match these items with the cases they belong to. Update me on your progress at the end of today. And continue working on this until it's done."

Winston rubbed the back of his neck as he left the younger man gathering the pages. If his tone had been sharp, it was Miller's fault for failing to maintain order in the file room. The beat of his own footsteps on the hardwood floor quashed any further thought for Miller or his new task.

Winston retreated to the chief constable's office, which he'd taken to working in during Philpott's absence. The sounds of the station died away as he closed the office door. Just as the chaos of the storage room had done, the files on the chief's desk taunted Winston. How many of the open cases could he solve before his uncle returned from his trip?

As he stared at the stack of pages, Winston tried to ignore the passing notion that perhaps he should have stayed behind with Uncle Larry in Ontario. They'd both made the journey east a few weeks earlier for the wedding of Winston's brother George. Detectives in the Toronto police force had contacted the chief constable the day before his scheduled return to Vancouver with news of a break in a case he had worked while he was a member there. They appealed for his help, requesting that he stay behind to provide the expertise and guidance to finally solve the case.

His uncle had given Winston two choices: stay in Toronto and work with him on the reopened case or return to Vancouver and manage the constabulary in his absence. Winston had chosen the latter. He didn't want to turn down the opportunity to lead the constabulary, if only temporarily. He welcomed the challenge. But if he was being completely truthful, he also didn't want to prolong his time with family.

His chest tightened.

Family. His brother Ellis. Not missing—dead. He placed his hand on the papers and took a calming breath. He could do nothing about his family's decision to keep the death a secret from him for nearly two decades. Solving a few cases? He could do that.

He would do that.

His chest eased slightly as he read through the first file. Two men, each accusing the other of stealing tools. Not a particularly challenging case, but it could be a good chance for Miller to lead an investigation. He imagined the junior officer speaking to the men, searching their homes, and finding the tools in one of the residences.

Yes, he would give Miller this opportunity. The gesture would be useful to demonstrate his faith in his constable. Perhaps they needed to dedicate someone to maintaining the file room. Miller's talents were better used speaking to suspects, not sorting documents. He'd relieve the man of his task in the file room shortly—reward him with his own easy-to-solve case. The idea softened the edges of Winston's mood.

Winston opened the next file. Another robbery. Another uninspiring case. Might this one be a better choice to give Miller? Winston weighed the two options and had nearly closed the folder when he caught the name of the robbery victim. Shuttleworth. He recalled the man he had encountered at the Vancouver Gentlemen's Club, picturing him as he'd last seen him: standing with a group of men congratulating themselves on a shared success. He recalled reading that Shuttleworth's wife had recently died. And now the insult of theft? Grief upon grief.

He sat straighter and began to read the case notes carefully. The constable who had taken them had been thorough. At least someone had heard Winston's pleas that his colleagues take care when documenting crimes. It was so much more efficient to prepare information such that another officer might review a case and provide insight. He relaxed into his chair as he read through the file again, this time jotting down his own observations. As thorough as the officer's notes were, Winston decided to visit the Shuttleworth house the next day. Nothing beat examining a crime scene in person. And he rather liked the idea of stepping away from the station.

Shuttleworth's name warranted greater attention than sending Miller on his own, though the constable would no doubt find it valuable to be involved. Winston could bring Miller to this crime scene, then brief him on the case of the tool theft and offer to let him lead that investigation. Surely that would repair any damage from his earlier outburst.

Winston closed the file and gave its cover a pat, satisfied with his decision. He cast his gaze around the room. Perhaps he should move out of his uncle's office as well. The space harboured sour memories of his family and their betrayal. Even walking past the office door and spying his uncle's desk brought back the moment Winston had learned of their lies.

Winston rubbed his dry eyes to clear away his indecision. Riley. Writing to her would help. He pulled out his journal and gathered his thoughts. Not only was her advice sound, she also had good investigative instincts. If they lived in the same century, he would ask her to consider becoming a detective, even though women were not permitted to be members of the police.

Dear Riley,

With my uncle away for at least another week, I continue to be in charge of the constabulary. We need to find a better system of organizing evidence. Perhaps you can offer some suggestions simple enough that my colleagues can follow them. Our caseload has been quiet of late, so this is a good time to reintroduce good file management to them.

Would she be drinking a cup of tea? She had shared that it was her preferred beverage. He flipped to the back of the journal where he stored the photograph she had sent him. Although the workings of the journal still baffled him, he was grateful for its gifts. Riley's charming face, so familiar to him now, always lifted his spirits. Winston imagined her reading the note while settled into her own chair.

Only if you're comfortable, of course.

Until later,

Jack

CHAPTER 2

Riley (2018)

RILEY FINCH FOLDED the last of the clothes from the dryer, piling them neatly in her laundry basket. She moved into the kitchen and flicked on the kettle, spotting the journal she kept with Detective Jack Winston at the other end of the counter. How fun would it be to share a cup of tea with Jack? More and more she found herself longing for a greater connection to him.

Riley picked up the journal and read Jack's latest message. His break from murder and malice on the streets of turn-of-the-century Vancouver would be short-lived, and soon enough messier crimes would overwhelm the city's fledgling police force, though she couldn't tell him that. It was her cardinal rule with him not to share something that would dramatically impact the future.

She jotted a couple of quick suggestions for him to help with organizing the station's files. Though it wouldn't be quick, she also suggested creating a catalogue of case details to make it easier to find information. She ended by promising a longer message soon.

Riley tucked the journal away and checked her phone. Her sister, Lucy, would be by shortly, fresh from her honeymoon and eager to share what she had cryptically referred to as a "new idea." She'd noticed the tremor in Lucy's voice. Had it been excitement or nerves? Excitement. Lucy had never been nervous about anything. Whatever had prompted it, Lucy's excitement would be short-lived. She was forever flitting toward the shiniest object.

Riley looked around the apartment they had shared until shortly before Lucy's wedding. A few minutes to wash dishes and change, and the place would be tidy enough.

Ten minutes later, Riley heard the key turn in the door. "In here," she called from her bedroom. Lucy stomped in, drenched and dripping onto the floor. "Luce! Take off your coat. You know where the closet is." Riley followed her into the hallway to supervise.

Lucy reached into the closet and pulled out Riley's coat instead of hanging up her own. "Take this. We're going out!"

"We are?" Riley looked down at her sweatshirt and jeans. "How 'out' are we going?"

"Just for a drink." She jutted her chin at her sister. "Actually, find something a little less 'studying at the library.'"

Tension pricked Riley's shoulders. Her sister could be so thoughtlessly offensive. "Give me a minute." She chose to roll with her sister's enthusiasm, trading her jeans for black slim-cut trousers and her sweatshirt for a black merino sweater. Lucy nodded in approval as Riley pulled on boots and jacket.

"Where to?"

"We're meeting a couple of friends. Jayne wants to talk about this week's gala. I thought you might like to get out for a bit." Lucy's clothing boutique had recently been discovered by local influencers, so she was regularly asked to dress them for events. She'd been invited to attend the next one. Lucy claimed she was going along with it because the exposure helped the business, but judging by her recent social media posts, she was enjoying her moment in the spotlight and seemed to harbour her own dream of becoming an influencer.

"Are you planning to rope me into some voluntold responsibility?" Riley asked.

"It's for a good cause, and you might enjoy yourself." Lucy pouted. "You don't have to commit to helping out at the gala. Just come out tonight. Maybe you'll decide you want to help on your own." She scrounged for something in her handbag. "Besides, you're always telling me you want to get out more." When she finished applying a coat of lipstick onto already perfect lips, she tilted the tube at Riley.

Riley shook her head. "I think you mean you're always telling me I should get out more," she said as she looped her arm through her sister's.

*

THE PUB LUCY'S friends had selected was a surprisingly low-key place for such polished people. Perhaps finding hidden gems was part of their role as influencers. A waitress ushered Riley and Lucy to a booth in the back, where two of Lucy's new friends scooted over so the sisters could sit.

After they removed coats, exchanged introductions, and placed a drink order, Riley chatted politely to the woman seated beside her. They'd met once before, and Riley had spent much of their conversation trying to understand how the woman was paid such jaw-dropping amounts to post a few words and a picture on a social media site. While the work didn't appeal to her, she could understand its draw. The woman tossed around the word "curated" in a way that irked Riley, but she thought better of taking the bait.

Eventually, Riley lost herself in the enthusiastic buzz of the conversation. For a few minutes she imagined what life as an influencer would be like. But her work at the museum was satisfying, and without it she wouldn't have met Jack. That was a life she didn't want to consider.

Before she noticed, two hours had passed. Riley was preparing to leave when Jayne, seated across from her, plucked something from a box that had sat in front of her the whole evening. "Isn't it gorgeous?" she gushed, flicking her long blond hair over one shoulder. She held a string of white pearls with a single black one at its centre. The necklace shimmered in the light cast from the canning jar chandelier hanging above the table. "I picked it up at a craft market last weekend. I saw it and thought of Lucy. She's going to shine in it," she said, passing the necklace to Lucy.

Riley squinted. "Someone made it?"

"No, it was at an antiques stall."

Riley straightened herself. It was easy enough for someone to claim a piece was older than it was when it had actually been produced in a factory. "Do you want me to get someone to authenticate it?" she asked.

Jayne dismissed the question with a flick of her wrist. "I've bought pieces from her before. She's genuine."

Riley sank back in the booth. It was getting late, and she was tired. She'd spent enough time with Lucy and her friends.

Beside her, Lucy uncoiled the necklace from Jayne's palm and stretched the strand into a straight line between her hands. She held one hand aloft and let the pearls coil again in her other palm. She switched hands and they spiralled into the other hand, like some kind of designer Slinky.

Riley lost herself in the shimmer of the beads in her sister's hand. "I've never seen anything like it. I'd love something similar."

"Well, if you ever decide to come out again, you can borrow it," said Lucy. "Do you think you would ever have occasion to wear something like this?" Lucy wagged one end of the necklace in front of Riley.

"You're right, Lucy. I don't get out much." Riley kept her voice light despite the sting of her sister's words. "But I do get invited to museum events and exhibit openings. I'm not as reclusive as you think, and I was just invited to something fancy event next week."

This elicited a laugh from the table. "It's spoken for that night. But you can wear it another time," said Lucy. "Right, Jayne?"

"It's for you, Lucy. Share it with whoever you want. As long as I can borrow it for my wedding."

"'Whomever,'" Riley said under her breath. Louder, she said, "It really is stunning."

The conversation turned to Jayne's pending nuptials, and the women passed the necklace around. When it reached Riley, she rubbed her thumb over the round beads. Lucy was going to look stunning in this. It appeared to be late Victorian or early Edwardian. Ladies dressed conservatively during the day, but their evening gowns revealed plunging necklines, and this necklace would have drawn the eye exactly where the wearer intended.

CHAPTER 3

Jack

WINSTON PEELED OPEN one eye and pulled his blankets to his chin. Temperatures in Vancouver were milder than in Toronto, but the dampness permeated everything, even as he snuggled beneath two down quilts. The fire wasn't going to start itself. He winced as his feet hit the floor and set about clearing the grate and laying a fire in his sitting room. The flame caught quickly, and Winston held his hands in front of it until his skin felt scorched. Perhaps Mrs. Bradley would agree to sending one of the maids into his room early to restart the fire. She might expect additional rent, but he would gladly pay it to avoid feeling so chilled each morning.

After washing and dressing, he descended the stairs and settled in the breakfast room. He nodded curtly to his fellow lodger, William Fisher, seated across from him. Mrs. Bradley emerged from behind the double doors carrying a bowl of her porridge, steam curling from the bowl. She poured his tea, perfectly steeped, and Winston—aware of Fisher's watchful eye—suppressed a broad, satisfied grin.

"What's wrong then, Jack? Ran afoul of a lady?"

Winston gulped down a mouthful of porridge and met Fisher's gaze. The man favoured his hair a little too long, and an unruly piece flopped over one eye. While Mrs. Bradley rarely asked personal questions—which was one of the reasons he remained her tenant—he couldn't say the same for Fisher, who had joined the household while Winston had been in Toronto. In the weeks since Winston's return, Fisher had peppered Winston with questions about his role with the local police. They had, it seemed, moved on to questions of a more personal nature. "Nothing of the sort, Mr. Fisher. I'm a little chilled after all this rain. You haven't been here long enough to have it settle in you." Winston set down his spoon and dabbed at his mouth with his napkin. "I'm not particularly pleasant once I get cold."

"You're not that bad, Mr. Winston," said one of the maids as she placed a plate of muffins on the table. "I've seen worse." She gasped as if only just realizing she had spoken her thought aloud and scurried from the room.

Fisher sniffed. "The impertinence. Unbelievable. I'll not miss it when I move into my own accommodation."

"Where are you moving?" Winston asked. "And Daisy is welcome to share her thoughts."

"Still . . . disrespectful. Will you speak to Mrs. Bradley about it?"

"Speak to me about what?" Their landlady's voice cut in from behind Winston, where she'd soundlessly moved to the sideboard to remove a serving dish.

Winston swivelled in his chair and said, "I wanted to speak to you about the fire in my room, Mrs. Bradley. Is there any way you could send in Daisy, or one of the other girls, in the mornings to light it—perhaps a few minutes before six? I find it dreadfully cold in the mornings." He shivered for effect.

The woman pursed her lips. "I'm not sure that's appropriate, Mr. Winston."

He held up his hand. "Not into my bedroom, of course. But the sitting room. I like to write correspondence in the mornings and my fingers take some time to warm, especially if it's been raining."

"Well then, I will ask the girls. They'll have to start a little earlier, you understand." Winston admired her stopping short of extending her hand to collect the extra pennies from him.

"I understand. You can add the payment for their time to my rent."

"As you wish, Mr. Winston." She shuffled from the room, running a finger along the mantel as she passed it.

"You're a smooth one, Jack." Fisher winked at Winston.

"You haven't been here long enough to know that with Mrs. Bradley, a few coins are usually sufficient to persuade her." Winston surveyed Fisher over the edge of his cup. "Tell me, Mr. Fisher, why did you look for your own house? Are you unhappy here?"

Fisher shook his head. "I've told you, Jack, you can call me Will. As for your question, I quite like it here, as a matter of fact. But it's time I move on."

"Where will you live?"

"I've acquired a small house in Mount Pleasant. Close to the action of the city, but not right in the centre of it, if you know what I mean."

Mount Pleasant, where the Shuttleworths lived. Winston hadn't spent much time in the neighbourhood, and yet here it surfaced in conversation on the day he planned to visit the area. Winston examined his acquaintance, realizing he knew little about the man. "Have you family here, Will?" The man's given name felt strange on his tongue.

"Not at the moment. But I'm expecting to marry within the year."

"Congratulations! I wasn't aware you were so close with a woman. Who is she?"

"Lovely lady, though I haven't met her yet."

Winston coughed into his napkin to mask his surprise. This man was quite something. "How is it that you know she's lovely?"

"She will be, Jack. She will be." Fisher puffed his chest and winked. If they had been standing beside each other, Winston was certain Fisher would have clapped him on the back.

Winston continued his breakfast, puzzling over Fisher's odd manner. Would it be more comfortable if the man were stone silent? Or would that bring its own awkwardness?

"What are you investigating today, Jack?"

As he reached for another muffin, Winston considered what to share. William Fisher likely had no qualms about repeating anything he heard. "A robbery." He flicked a crumb from his lapel. "As it happens, it's in your new neighbourhood."

"A robbery in Mount Pleasant, eh? What's gone missing, then?" Fisher reached for his own muffin. "I shouldn't be worried, should I?"

"I shouldn't speak about my cases. Let me just say it's something of sentimental value to the owner, and he wants it back."

"Let me know if you need me to put any feelers out for you, Jack."

Winston nodded, biting into the muffin to avoid saying a sharp word. When he swallowed, he examined the man's face. Instead of the arrogant smirk he was expecting, Winston was surprised to see Will's earnest expression. He truly believed he would be of assistance. Perhaps he'd been too quick to judge the man. "Of course, Will."

"I'd be a big asset with my connections."

Here was the boast Winston had expected. Crowing about his position, though Winston wasn't entirely sure whether Fisher truly possessed useful connections or simply wished it to be true. Winston kept his own connections private. He pushed himself from the table and wiped his hands with his napkin. "I bet you'll miss Mrs. Bradley's breakfasts, Will."

"You'll just have to invite me around every now and again," he replied with another wink.

*

"A ROBBERY, SIR?" Constable Miller asked when Winston explained the case. He had spoken the words calmly, but the flicker in his eyes betrayed his excitement.

Winston leaned back in his uncle's chair. "We'll work together on this, and I'll also give you a case to work alone. Another robbery, though it appears a little clearer who is involved in that one. It will be your case to make decisions about, but I'll be available should you wish to consult with me."

Miller inched forward in his chair and leaned his palms on Philpott's desk. "My own? And Shuttleworth. Why are you investigating that one? Aren't you acting as the chief while he's away? I've never seen him actively involved in anything before."

Winston shrugged. "Hard luck for Mr. Shuttleworth to have his home violated so close to the loss of his wife. And I am still a detective, Thomas, even in the Chief Constable's absence."

Worry clouded Miller's features. "How long will Chief Philpott be gone?"

"I've just received word from him that he expects to be away for at least ten days more, though perhaps longer. There's been a breakthrough on a case he worked before moving to Vancouver." Winston considered the reason behind Miller's question. "You can take as long as you need to solve the case. But I'm confident you'll manage it quickly."

Miller's jaw relaxed. Winston had guessed correctly. "These robberies are bound to be easier than the murders we've worked on, right?"

"Exactly. We'll have Shuttleworth solved before Philpott gets back, with time to spare, and I'm sure the same will be true for the other case."

"What about the files? The ones you wanted me to organize?" Miller tugged at the sleeves of his uniform.

"Those still need to be dealt with," Winston said as he ran his hand through his hair. "But for now, focus on these two cases." He willed Miller to accept this olive branch.

"Starting with Mr. Shuttleworth?" Miller pulled his notepad from a pocket.

"Good instincts, Thomas. Several people will have been through the house since the theft, but we should start there and see if we can find a clue left undisturbed by household members and visitors."

"When did Mrs. Shuttleworth die?"

Winston opened the case file. "A month ago."

When Miller's pencil finished scratching against the paper he looked up at Winston. "And the necklace. When did it disappear?"

Winston pulled his finger down the page. "It looks like it was discovered missing a week ago."

Miller frowned. "Why is it taking so long for us to follow up?"

"This report was only created yesterday. The man is in mourning. The theft may seem of secondary importance in the midst of his grief." Miller's observation was sound. Even in mourning, why would Shuttleworth have taken so long to report the theft?

Miller narrowed his eyes. "Is there anything else, sir?"

"Why do you ask, Thomas?" Winston heard the defensiveness in his tone, and Miller's face confirmed that he'd heard it as well.

"Pardon me for saying so, but you seem. . ." Miller tugged again at his sleeves. "You've been . . . different," Miller said. He shifted his gaze to the floor and continued. "You've seemed distracted."

The truth of Miller's remark brought a flush of warmth to Winston's cheeks. He bit back the reflex to snap at Miller. It wouldn't do to cause further damage to their relationship. His constable was right. Yesterday's outburst about the files was only one of several recent instances where he'd failed to rein in his temper. He inhaled deeply and deflected Miller's scrutiny. "Not at all, Thomas. The facts of this case seem rather straightforward. A necklace goes missing, accessible only to a dead woman and her maid. That leaves one suspect: the maid." He tapped the points out on his fingers, wiggling the one that represented the maid.

"I thought other objects also disappeared." Miller said.

"She likely took them to confuse matters." He wiggled the maid finger again.

"I'm a bit surprised, sir." Miller shifted in his chair, then met Winston's eyes. "You've always told me to keep an open mind."

Winston turned away, focusing on the painting on the wall to his left. Miller's observation—though accurate—stung. Surely there was nothing wrong with wanting to solve a simple case to demonstrate that Philpott had made the right choice leaving Winston in charge. Was Winston wrong to consider Miller for the other case? He brought his attention back to the constable. "Let's get to the house and see what we learn, Miller." They left the station in silence. Winston couldn't risk saying something unforgivable.

Although they could have taken one of the city's public electric streetcars across the bridge that traversed False Creek, Winston suggested they walk. He'd walked this same route when he'd first arrived in Vancouver, accompanying his uncle on one of his walking tours of the city's neighbourhoods. His uncle had explained that many of the residents of Mount Pleasant worked at the mills, lumberyards, and other industrial works yards that dotted the shores of False Creek. The inlet was nestled between Vancouver's Gastown neighbourhood, where the police station was located, and their destination: Mount Pleasant.

Winston's temper cooled as they walked, as did Miller's, judging by the affable manner in which he greeted residents as they acknowledged him in his constable's uniform. Winston let his thoughts wander to his breakfast conversation with Will and the man's search for a home—and then a family. No doubt Uncle Larry would return with unwelcome guidance from Winston's mother, encouraging him to settle down and start a family. His brother's marriage had not relieved Winston of the pressure to continue the family name.

He thought back to George's wedding, which he'd attended with great reluctance. During the long train journey to Toronto, Winston had dreaded reuniting with his family so soon after learning of their deception. George, he was certain, had no idea of the truth, and Winston wrestled with whether he should continue to keep the secret. Wouldn't that make Winston just as deceptive as their parents and uncle? He'd landed on a compromise, writing George a letter and sealing it in an envelope labelled "To George. Open only after your honeymoon." George and his new bride had embarked on an extended European tour the day after the wedding. Winston assumed George had followed the label's instructions as he'd not yet contacted him—which he surely would do when he learned what really had happened to their older brother, Ellis.

Ellis. Winston's hand reached into his pocket and found the stone Ellis had given him on the last family outing before he'd died—before his parents had woven the myth that their first-born son had simply vanished without a trace. Lies to conceal the shame of the truth, that Ellis had taken his own life. Winston's fingers squeezed the stone and released it.

Through difficult, deliberate manoeuvring, Winston had managed to avoid being alone with his parents for longer than five minutes, thereby avoiding any conversation about their lies. He had no desire to hear their excuses and had left them no opportunity to share them.

Miller cleared his throat and Winston shook himself from his reflections. Perhaps the cold air this morning had set his mood so sharply. Miller was right: he was approaching this case with a narrow mind before any actual investigation. He took a calming breath and smiled at Miller. He'd apologize to the constable on their way back to the station. He would not allow himself to be too proud to admit his failing.

Smoke rose from the industrial sites along the water. As they climbed the Main Street hill—a little steeper than he'd anticipated—the air cleared. The further they got from the water, the more the houses changed from simple structures to more elaborate homes similar to many found in the West End, the neighbourhood favoured by the city's wealthier residents. The Shuttleworth house, one of the largest on the street, faced Main Street and was situated just north of Broadway. With its occupants still in mourning, dark curtains hung in the windows.

Winston's heart rate accelerated. A new case was about to begin.

CHAPTER 4

Jack

INSTEAD OF KNOCKING on the larger front door, Winston approached what he assumed to be the kitchen door at the top of a small set of stairs at the rear of the house. A kitchen boy with sooty cheeks answered his knock. His eyes grew wide seeing Miller in his uniform. Miller lowered himself to the boy's height. "Were you expecting someone else? Perhaps a delivery?" he asked.

"Nothing's been ordered. No reason to." His voice faltered. "I'm just doing some cleaning. Mrs. Plum, she's not here."

"That's okay. We would like to speak with Mr. Shuttleworth, but perhaps we might chat with you first?" Winston asked.

The boy's eyes widened. He made no move to let them in.

For a moment, Winston thought perhaps he'd knocked on the wrong door. Then he remembered the curtains. "This is the Shuttleworth house, isn't it?"

The boy lowered his gaze. "Y-yes."

"Is Mr. Shuttleworth at home? Perhaps I should start by speaking to him," Winston suggested gently. Maybe the boy was nervous about speaking to an unfamiliar adult.

The boy pulled the door open to allow the policemen to enter and left the kitchen without saying anything further.

Winston and Miller exchanged glances. "They're mourning, Miller," Winston said, as if that excused the boy's odd behaviour. The coolness of the room confirmed that the kitchen had not been used recently. "The boy said it was cleaning day," he said.

After a few minutes, a man entered the room. His suit was half a size too large for his frame and his shoulders sagged, causing the suit to appear as though it was about to slide off its wearer. The man stared at Miller and Winston with expressionless eyes.

"Mr. Shuttleworth? I am Detective Jack Winston and this is Constable Thomas Miller with the Vancouver Constabulary. We're here about the theft you reported."

"It's taken you long enough," Shuttleworth said, his voice betraying deep fatigue.

Winston was hardly going to explain to the man that the police could only investigate crimes that were reported to them. Whatever his reasons, he'd only just informed the police of the theft. "We're here now." Winston shifted his hat and overcoat to his left hand and extended his right while Shuttleworth stared. The offer of a handshake went unanswered. Winston continued. "Mr. Shuttleworth, is there somewhere we could sit? I find it helpful to write, and—" He held up his coat and hat.

Shuttleworth shook his head. "Apologies. I find myself distracted and at a loose end since Penelope died. She would scold me if she knew I didn't show you through to the sitting room. It's this way."

Winston tucked his overcoat under his arm and followed Shuttleworth, who led them into a small sitting room furnished with two chairs and a sofa. Winston motioned for Miller to sit on the sofa and arranged his coat on the back of a chair. Shuttleworth noticed and started to reach for it. "Where's my head?" he muttered.

"Don't worry about my coat, Mr. Shuttleworth. It's dry and won't damage your chair. No need to concern yourself with formalities."

"Thank you, Detective. As I said, my wife looked after the household."

"Have you no staff other than the kitchen boy, sir?"

Shuttleworth stiffened. "We had a maid, but I dismissed her when the necklace went missing." Shuttleworth spoke the next words quietly. "I suppose she would have looked after guests."

"And a cook?"

"Oh yes, we still have a cook. Though there's no need for her to prepare elaborate meals when I'm the only one eating."

"Is she here today?"

Shuttleworth narrowed his eyes. "It must be her day off." This corresponded with what the boy had said and explained the unused kitchen. "You know, she was very fond of my wife." His voice had taken on a wistful tone.

Winston let Shuttleworth enjoy the memory. "When do you expect the cook to return? I'd like to interview her."

"About the necklace?" Shuttleworth seemed surprised by Winston's interest.

Miller edged forward in his chair. He spoke without seeking Winston's permission. "Yes. It's good to speak to all members of the household."

Shuttleworth crossed and uncrossed his ankles. "If you must. She will be working tomorrow."

Winston pulled a small notepad from his jacket. "Her name?"

"Mrs. Plum. A rather fitting name for a cook, if you ask me."

"Has Mrs. Plum worked for you long?" Winston asked.

"I've known her for years."

"And where does she live?"

"She has a room here." His brow furrowed. "I don't know where she's gone today."

"Do you know if she has family nearby? Maybe she's visiting with them?" Winston asked.

Shuttleworth pressed his finger into the space between his eyebrows. "She hasn't any family."

Miller smoothed the front of his uniform. "Mr. Shuttleworth."

"Edward, please."

Miller looked to Winston, who nodded. "Edward, then. Please tell us about your wife." Miller prepared to write the information in his notepad.

"She died. There's not much to say other than she grew ill and died. It all seemed so sudden. But what has that to do with her maid stealing her necklace? A valuable necklace, I might add."

Confusion clouded Miller's face. "I was hoping to learn a little about her to provide context to the case, sir."

Miller's voice had risen in pitch, which Winston knew meant he was growing nervous. "Mr. Shuttleworth, as Constable Miller says, it's helpful for us to understand more than just the item that was stolen."

"Items."

"Indeed, items." Winston leaned forward. "Looking more deeply into the environment can lead to a quicker resolution."

"It can? You've investigated thefts before?"

Winston nodded. "Lately I've been called into murder investigations, but we have solved all manner of crimes."

Shuttleworth passed his hand over his face.

Miller waited for Shuttleworth to compose himself. "Perhaps you could start by describing what was stolen."

"The necklace is a strand of pearls. It fell here on Penelope's neck." Shuttleworth indicated the hollow between his collarbones. "There is a black stone, round and polished, in the centre of a string of otherwise white pearls."

Winston stole a glance at Miller's notepad. He had sketched out a string of circles to represent the strand matching Shuttleworth's description. The middle circle was shaded. "Is the black stone also a pearl?"

"Yes, and it's larger than the white ones." Shuttleworth tugged at his ears. "The matching earrings are upstairs, in my wife's jewellery box." He pinched his eyes shut.

Miller tilted his head. "Were they in the same location in the box?"

Shuttleworth focused his gaze on the floor. "I don't know. I suppose you could ask the maid, though I let her go as soon as I learned the necklace was missing. She must have taken it. Nobody else had access."

"Not you?" Winston brushed at his moustache.

"To my wife's dressing room, of course. But to her jewellery box? No. That was hers. I assume she kept it locked."

Winston crossed his arms across his chest. "Where did your wife keep the key?"

"In her dressing room, I suppose." Shuttleworth's shoulders slumped. "You think I would take my dead wife's necklace, Detective, and then report it stolen?"

"Not at all, Mr. Shuttleworth," Winston said. "We simply want to understand the circumstances. What about the figurine that was stolen?"

"The figurine, as you call it, is from my first board game. The first one I created, I mean. It was a simple game piece, much like a pawn, but. . ." He scanned the room. "It represented so much."

"Was the game piece also in your wife's dressing room?" asked Miller.

Shuttleworth stared over Winston's shoulder for several seconds. He broke his gaze and pinched the bridge of his nose. Had something in Winston's question caused him to remember his loss? "Yes. We each have one—had one. Mine is in my study, sitting on a shelf."

"And when did you notice the items were missing?" Winston asked.

"I didn't notice. The maid. She told me they were missing." Shuttleworth shifted in his seat. They would not get many more answers from this man today.

Miller held his pencil in the air. "The maid you fired because you thought she had taken the items?"

"The same."

Winston leaned forward. "And when was that?"

"A week ago. Maybe ten days." He swatted the question away. "I've lost track of time."

And yet Shuttleworth only notified the police yesterday. Winston underlined the date in his notepad. "Is there a reason it took you so long to report the theft?"

Shuttleworth pursed his lips. "I have, as you can imagine, been rather unsettled by my wife's death." He edged forward. "Does the timing affect your investigation?"

Winston stood. "The investigation begins today. Mr. Shuttleworth, would it be possible for you to show us your game piece and your wife's dressing room so we might see where the items were kept?"

Shuttleworth lifted his head. "This will help you?" His voice had regained a steadiness.

"Yes. I believe so."

"Very well." Shuttleworth stood and made a small gesture with his hand for Winston and Miller to follow.

As they walked through the house, Winston noted the near silence of the space. Their breathing and footsteps were the only natural sounds. He couldn't recall a time when he'd been alone in a house. Even at Mrs. Bradley's, she or one of the maids was sure to be around. And his parents' house was filled with people—either the servants or his brothers. The steady presence of others, as much as the food, kept Winston living at Mrs. Bradley's.

Shuttleworth continued down the hall and ascended a set of stairs at the end of the hallway through an opening marked "Servant Access." He opened a door and pointed. "My wife's dressing room." He stood outside and let the policemen enter.

A dressing table rested against one wall, positioned in front of a mirror. A tall armoire stood to its right. Winston suppressed a shudder, remembering an armoire he'd encountered on an earlier investigation. Miller opened the door, revealing several dresses, all of which suggested a woman who was small in stature and clearly had attended formal engagements with some regularity. Winston turned his attention to the dressing table, which had a pair of drawers on either side of the area where Mrs. Shuttleworth would have sat. He tugged on the first one and found it locked.

"Is the key to the dressing table in here?" Winston called to Shuttleworth.

"I don't know. I haven't been in that room in some time. Certainly not since—" Shuttleworth's voice caught.

Winston turned to Miller. "Search for a key. I doubt she kept it too far from the jewellery."

Miller ran his hand along the top shelf of the armoire. After a moment he smiled. "I think I've found it, sir." He retrieved a small key and offered it to Winston. The interior revealed an ornate box that contained necklaces, bracelets, rings, and earrings, each stored inside its own compartment. The top two compartments folded out from the box, revealing a cavity below where more pieces were kept. Miller held up a pair of black pearl earrings. "These match the necklace?"

From the doorway, Shuttleworth nodded, his eyes glistening.

"Why wouldn't the thief take the entire box? Why take only the necklace?" Miller asked. "Look at what's here."

Winston's breath caught in his throat at the dazzling jewellery that glittered in the room's soft light. Miller's question was a good one. The thief had left behind a treasure trove. Very puzzling.

Winston left Miller to continue searching the dressing room to speak to Shuttleworth, who had remained in the corridor. "Sir, are you certain that only the necklace has gone missing? Your wife had quite a collection."

"She did, and she sparkled in it. The maid was confirming the inventory when she told me the necklace was missing. She reported everything accounted for, apart from the necklace."

"The maid you fired is the one who reported the necklace was missing? Why would she report it to you if she stole it?"

With a wave of his hand, Shuttleworth dismissed the question. "Who knows what goes on in the mind of a criminal? The maid and my wife were the only ones with access to the key."

"Miller found the key after a cursory search."

Shuttleworth blanched. "Are you saying anyone could have found it?"

"Anyone who came into your wife's dressing room, yes," Winston said.

"We've had several people stopping by to share their condolences." Shuttleworth drew the words out slowly, a hesitancy creeping into his voice.

"And you let them up here?" Winston asked.

"Well, I certainly didn't barricade off parts of the house. I didn't pay them much attention. Truthfully, I didn't much care." Shuttleworth straightened himself. "Still, I'm certain it must have been that maid." Despite his assertion, Shuttleworth no longer sounded certain.

Miller joined Winston and Shuttleworth in the hallway. "I didn't find anything else of interest, sir."

"Thank you, Miller. And thank you, Mr. Shuttleworth. I imagine being here has been difficult," Winston said.

"Do you still want to see my study?" Shuttleworth asked.

"Please. To see your game piece."

With a nod, Shuttleworth led the policemen down the stairs and into the hallway. He stopped in front of a closed door and rested a hand on the doorknob. "I have some private papers in here."

"We don't need to look at the papers. Just the game piece," Winston said.

"As you like." Shuttleworth swung the door open and led the policemen into the room.

A large desk dominated the study. On its surface, documents were organized into neat piles. Bookshelves lined the walls, and one shelf held a photograph of a woman—Mrs. Shuttleworth, judging by the woman's age and dress. Beside it was a copy of the game Finders and a small wooden game piece.

"Finders. We have a copy of that," said Miller. His face brightened with a sudden realization. "You invented it?"

Shuttleworth nodded. "It's in many homes, Constable," he said. His pride was clear.

Winston had seen the game at Mrs. Bradley's house but not played it himself. When he was growing up, his family hadn't spent their time on such pursuits. They were well beneath what his mother would have considered appropriate. "And you just have this piece on display? Not in a glass case?"

"I didn't dream that anyone would ever take my wife's, Detective. It holds no tangible value."

"For a collector?"

"I suppose that's possible."

Winston stepped closer. The carved piece was approximately two inches tall and an inch in diameter at its base. As he reached for it, Shuttleworth cleared his throat loudly. Winston withdrew his hand. "Do you have any idea why someone would have taken it?" he asked.

"It was there. Available to be taken," said Shuttleworth. "It has sentimental value only." The weariness had returned to Shuttleworth's voice.

"Right." Winston recalled the full jewellery box. What thief would leave the necklace's matching earrings and other valuable pieces? He looked more closely at Shuttleworth: first widowed, now robbed. Pain creased the man's eyes. Was he hiding something else? Winston sensed the answer would not be revealed today. "I'm satisfied we've seen enough, Mr. Shuttleworth," said Winston.

The policemen followed Shuttleworth out of the room. "Before we go, can you tell me the name of the maid? The one you fired?" Winston asked.

Shuttleworth frowned. "Her name?"

"I'd like to speak to her. Discover if she took the necklace, as you suggest."

"Kate. Or Susie." Shuttleworth scratched his head. "No, her name is Kate."

"Do you have her surname or address?" Miller asked.

"You'll have to check with Mrs. Plum when she's back. Tomorrow."

"Thank you, Mr. Shuttleworth. We'll do that."

As they prepared to leave, Winston heard voices in the kitchen. He looked at Shuttleworth, who shrugged. "Perhaps she has returned early."

They made their way to the kitchen to find the kitchen boy and a woman, evidently a maid, working side by side. They stopped their task and looked up at the men.

"Sorry, Mr. Shuttleworth. Were we too loud? Polly was telling me a story," the boy said.

Shuttleworth stared at the boy. "Who are you?"

The boy's cheeks flushed. "I'm Charlie, sir. The kitchen boy." He turned to look at Winston, his eyebrows knit in a mix of fear and confusion.

Did the man not remember Charlie fetching him to meet the policemen not thirty minutes earlier?

Charlie continued, his voice barely audible. "I help Mrs. Plum. And this is Polly. She's a scullery maid."

Shuttleworth considered this. "Hmm. . . Right." He turned to face Polly. "Scullery maid? Is that a different type of maid? I'm afraid my wife looked after the staff details. Did you just start? We no longer need you."

Polly folded her hands in front of her apron and kept her eyes low. "I've been working here a year, sir," she said in a careful tone. "I make your meals when Mrs. Plum is off." She spoke this last sentence as if it were a question, as if she wasn't sure if she had been doing as she said.

"Oh," he said, though he didn't seem entirely convinced. "Mrs. Plum will be back tomorrow. Mind you don't make a mess in here before then."

"We was—" Polly started to answer when Charlie cut her off with a hand gesture.

"As you like, Mr. Shuttleworth. We'll have your midday meal prepared presently. Cold meats and bread. The way you like it."

Shuttleworth, still looking confused, nodded. He led the policemen to the front door. "There you go, gentlemen. It seems I have been looked after without having realized it. Come back tomorrow and you can speak with Mrs. Plum."

*

INSIDE HIS RENTED rooms, Winston stoked the fire as he recalled the day's events. When they had returned to the station after interviewing Shuttleworth, he had briefed Miller about the other robbery case—the one he was assigning to the constable. Miller had spent the afternoon speaking to the men involved in that case, and he later returned wearing his pride as if it were a badge on his uniform. It was remarkable how buoyed he was by the confidence Winston had placed in him.

Winston returned his thoughts to Shuttleworth's puzzling manner, to the grief he'd expressed at the loss of his wife's necklace. No, not grief. Distress. His grief had been compounded by the theft. Losing the necklace and the game piece had reopened the man's still-raw wounds. Winston set the poker down and stroked his moustache, its hairs soft and sharp at once. Shuttleworth's behaviour had been odd, as if he were unbalanced. Grief was taking its toll.

He moved to his upholstered chair and leaned against its tall back. Winston studied the crown moulding framing the ceiling. The rich brown stain contrasted with the whitewashed walls and ceiling. Although the window was closed, a gust of wind fluttered the curtains so they grabbed at his feet. He stood to draw them shut against the damp late January evening.

Instead of returning to his chair, he sat at his writing desk and pulled out his journal. Perhaps Riley would have an observation about Shuttleworth's behaviour.

Dear Riley,

I have opened a new case involving the theft of a necklace and a game piece from a resident of Mount Pleasant. The necklace was his wife's—she died a few weeks ago— and the game piece is from a popular game that he invented and made his fortune from. It has sentimental value only. After speaking with the husband, I have some observations.

So much of Shuttleworth's behaviour was unusual. Why had he waited over a week to report the theft, then criticized Winston for taking his time to investigate? And how was it that he knew so little about the people who worked for him?

Whether he was distracted by grief over his wife's death or for some other reason, he seemed to be completely unfamiliar with his household staff. He couldn't remember names, other than that of his cook Mrs. Plum. I have met the man before. We were introduced through my uncle. He is much changed from our last encounter.

If you have the time, I would be grateful if you would be able to put your researching skills to use to look up Edward Shuttleworth and his deceased wife, Penelope.

As ever, with thanks,

Jack

Winston settled back into his chair and cast his mind back to the few social engagements he'd attended since arriving in Vancouver. His uncle, the chief constable, had dragged him to these occasions. When Uncle Larry had persuaded him to move from Toronto and join him in Vancouver's police force, Winston agreed to attend one or two social events to help acquaint him with the city and its inhabitants. Winston didn't share news of these events with his mother; she'd tried unsuccessfully for years to get him to dances and dinners with Toronto's wealthy residents and would have been disappointed to learn how quickly Winston had agreed to attend at her brother's urging.

When he had boarded the train heading west, Winston wanted to shed much of that life. By the time he'd snaked through the country's mountains and reached the rugged coast, Winston was certain he'd never again don evening attire. Changing his mind had taken surprisingly little prodding from Uncle Larry. It served the police to be friendly with the decision makers in the city. Winston was also convinced that building relationships with other citizens, regardless of their social standing, would prove useful.

Winston had seen Shuttleworth on one of these occasions. "Gatherings of the great," Uncle Larry had called them. Shuttleworth hadn't seemed quite so absent-minded then. Perhaps his wife had been his tether. With her gone, making sense of things was another level where he felt her loss so deeply. Winston cleared his thoughts with a sigh. Regardless of Shuttleworth's behaviour, he was committed to solving the robbery.

CHAPTER 5

Riley

RILEY PULLED OFF her boots and carried them to the closet. It was a relief to be back in the quiet familiarity of her apartment. Sometimes she longed for the ease with which Lucy seemed to navigate social occasions. Riley only felt truly comfortable at events where she knew everyone. Even then, she liked to prepare in advance and think about something to say to each person, though in the moment she often forgot what it was she had planned.

Changed into her comfiest pyjamas, Riley opened the journal and read Jack's latest note. She could certainly research Shuttleworth. She pulled her laptop toward her and entered the name into a search engine. It yielded few results. The family could have moved away, or if they didn't have any children, the branch of the family could have ended with Mr. Shuttleworth. This wasn't surprising, and she had many other places to look.

She logged in to the city archives. These results were more fruitful, with pictures of men dressed in evening wear, each with a glass of something in their hands. Whisky, likely. They stood in front of an ornately carved mantel hung above a fireplace. The caption read "Celebrating Finders' Success—VGC." VGC must be the Vancouver Gentlemen's Club. What was Finders? Had the caption misspelled "founders"?

She opened another image result from the archives. This time it pictured a man and a woman. Riley always had a hard time gauging the ages of people in photos from the 1890s, but she guessed they were between twenty-five and fifty. The photo captured them from the waist up, standing stiffly next to each other, again in evening attire. The caption read "Mr. and Mrs. Edward Shuttleworth." She rolled her eyes at the convention of denying married women an identity by not naming them. She saved the image to a folder on her computer and opened the next image. It was also captioned with the Shuttleworths' names, but the woman pictured looked quite different from the one in the first photo. Edward Shuttleworth appeared to have aged about ten years. She revised her first estimate of his age in the first image to between twenty-five and forty. Their clothing was also more Edwardian than Victorian in the second photo. An image of the back bore a handwritten date: 1935. This must have been when the archive acquired the photo, clearly not when it had been taken. She made a mental note to make sure she didn't make similar mistakes—omitting key information—when cataloguing documents she received at the museum.

She increased the size of the faces in both photos of Mr. and Mrs. Shuttleworth. The second was definitely a different woman. Is this his second wife, one he married after his first one died? She made a notation in the notebook beside her. *Remarried when?* Her fingers tingled with the excitement of starting a new case with Jack.

A quick search of the provincial archives revealed Mrs. Shuttleworth's death certificate from 1898, showing her death as the result of illness and Mr. Shuttleworth's death certificate issued thirty years later. The second Mrs. Shuttleworth had died another five years after her husband. Riley noted her name: Susan.

Riley checked the dates again. How awful for Mr. Shuttleworth to be the victim of a burglary so soon after his wife's death. She typed a few words into the newspaper archive search to see whether any other thefts had been reported in the Shuttleworths' neighbourhood around the same time. She scrolled through the results but found no mention of any two weeks before or after the theft. Not part of a string of robberies.

Riley turned her thoughts to the victim. Could he have been targeted? As a member of the Vancouver Gentlemen's Club, he likely had a nice home filled with nice objects, which would have been tempting to a thief. But why Shuttleworth and not his neighbours?

Another thought struck her. Surely the home would have been open to mourners following Mrs. Shuttleworth's death. Could one of these visitors have taken her necklace? How would they have had access to her dressing room? Presumably, they would have been restricted to the sitting room or dining room? No doubt Jack would ask Mr. Shuttleworth for a list of recent visitors. She'd ask him to share the list. Perhaps she could find something in the archive about them. She wrote *Who visited house?* in her notebook.

Riley reread the note. Should she really ask him that? Jack hadn't mentioned whether there had been visitors. Would asking this be overstepping? What if he hadn't thought to ask Shuttleworth for that information? Would he be insulted if she suggested it?

Riley shook her head. Why was she being so foolish? Jack was a good detective. And he'd been clear that he appreciated her help. Why would he tell her about this case if he didn't want some of her suggestions?

She closed her laptop as her phone buzzed with a text from Johnny.

What are you up to?

She flushed. They hadn't had a formal conversation about it, but she had begun thinking of him as her boyfriend. She smiled, remembering their first meeting and how she thought he looked so much like his great-grandfather. She placed her hand on the journal. Its cover felt warm under her hand. Was Jack touching it too? What would he think of her dating his great-grandson? What would Johnny think of her corresponding with his great-grandfather? She gave her head another shake, baffled again by this inconceivable reality—having a foot in two worlds, separated by more than a hundred years.

Riley opened the journal and started writing.

Dear Jack,

Your case sounds like a perplexing one. Was the necklace genuine? Was there a significance to the necklace other than its monetary value?

You wrote that the game piece had no value, but could it have been meaningful to someone else?

I haven't found much yet about the family. Is the game Mr. Shuttleworth's sole income source? Who has visited the house since Mrs. Shuttleworth died? Perhaps I could check some of those names for information that might help.

I have so many questions!

Riley set down her pen when her phone buzzed with another text from Johnny.

> Hey, haven't heard back from you. Are you already asleep?

Riley flushed again. As much as she loved spending time with Johnny, when she and Jack were exchanging messages, she found it difficult to switch between them. But, thanks to text-message apps, Johnny could tell whether she'd read his messages, so she had to respond now.

> Sorry! Was out with Lucy and her friends. I'm beat and heading to bed in a minute. Can we catch up tomorrow?

Of course. X.

She picked up her pen again.

Must sign off now. I'll keep looking into Shuttleworth.

R.

The screen of Riley's phone lit up when she plugged it in to charge. Johnny's text reappeared and she smiled. She liked seeing Johnny, but the more time she spent with him, the less time she would have to help Jack.

*

RILEY ARRIVED AT work early the next morning and stole a moment to reread Jack's response.

Dear Riley,

Thank you for looking into this case. I am certain any information you are willing to share will be useful. You asked about guests in the house. I will ask Shuttleworth about visitors, though I would be surprised if he had seen anyone recently. He truly looked adrift.

When we spoke, he informed me that he had fired the maid he suspected of stealing the items. This is the same maid who reported the necklace missing, and I'm not sure why she would report her own misdeed, unless it was to misdirect attention. Regardless, Shuttleworth terminated her employment. I will speak with this former maid as well as with the family's cook to glean details that I hope will give me more direction in the case.

Finally, the necklace is valuable, according to Shuttleworth. The game piece held sentimental value to him alone.

Keep well,

Jack

Jack's observation about the value of the game piece struck her. If it had come from the first edition of a popular game over a century ago, it would hold some value now to collectors, more so if it was accompanied by other game pieces and the game board. She doubted anyone in Jack's time would be thinking of that. Was the theft more of a personal attack? A targeted act to harm Shuttleworth? Riley picked up her pen.

Dear Jack,

I'll keep searching for information here. I did find a photograph of the couple. There may be more in the archive. If the game piece held no value, why was it taken?

R.

As she finished writing her note, Nick Blume entered the archive. Seeing the journal, he grinned. "Writing in your diary again, Riley?"

She closed the book and slid it into her bag. Heat rushed to her ears, a reaction she deeply wished Nick did not elicit from her. "Not a diary. Just collecting my thoughts using analogue technology."

"Your generation. So unpredictable."

She crumpled a scrap piece of paper and threw it at him. "You're two years older than me, remember? Same generation."

Nick grinned and settled onto the stool beside her. "What are we working on this week?"

"Claire sent me an email asking me to look into domestic workers and how their roles have changed since the city's early days."

"There's nobody better for that than you," Nick said. "Did she mention having me work on this too?"

Riley's cheeks tingled at Nick's compliment. But he was right. Since she had started at the museum, Riley had become known for her expertise in a specific era—the early recorded history of the city of Vancouver after European settlers had first arrived. "I think that's her plan, but she didn't explicitly say so in the message." Riley bit her lip. "We've been working well together. Why wouldn't that continue?"

"Where is she going with this? Did she talk about a specific exhibit idea?"

"Nope. No details. Just the request to look into it."

Nick sighed and swivelled on his stool to face Riley. "So how have their roles changed?"

"Fundamentally, they haven't, really." Riley settled into the subject. She could happily talk about her research niche all day if Nick gave her the opening. "They clean, provide childcare. . . some might cook. But circumstances have changed. I don't know anybody with a live-in maid or live-in cook. But that wouldn't have been unusual a hundred and twenty years ago."

"Do you know anyone with a live-out maid or live-out cook?" Nick flashed her a cheeky grin.

Riley laughed. "Not personally, but I know people who have a cleaner come in every week or twice a month. Does that count as a maid?"

"The cleaner wouldn't be solely devoted to them, though, right?"

"Exactly. A cleaner might be part of a service or could be a nanny who's picking up extra money by cleaning on her days off."

"What about live-in nannies?"

"Those still exist, but I bet they aren't as common, especially when people are living in condos." She thought of her own apartment. Perfect for one or two adults, but add in a child and it would get crowded quickly. And there certainly wasn't enough room for another caregiver. "The security of this kind of work would be more precarious today," she said. "Most people only really need a nanny when the kids are preschool age. Once they're at school for most of the day, the nanny needs to find a new placement. So they might be looking at three or four years, maybe a few more if the family has a couple of kids a few years apart."

Nick pulled a notebook from his bag and started writing. "Have the working conditions improved?"

Riley gave him a bit of an eye roll. "Well, yeah, I would hope so . . . as they have for most types of employment over the last century." Nick didn't return the tease, so she offered some facts. "They are entitled to minimum wage now, but when it was introduced around 1920, it didn't apply to domestic workers. Beyond that, I'll have to look into how the broader conditions compare. We have rules about how many hours someone can work in a day, but I imagine that line gets blurred if an employee is living in your space."

"What about their responsibilities? How do they look different now?"

Riley couldn't tell if Nick was asking these questions to help her improve her idea or to distract her from her earlier question about working together. She didn't recall him ever taking notes during their conversations, either. She decided to go with the flow until he revealed his agenda. "In the city's early days, larger households would likely have had at least a maid and a cook. Today some nannies likely do a bit of tidying or meal preparation, but I have no idea when they'd fit these extras into their days. Have you ever babysat? Kids need a lot of attention."

"I don't have kids, but my sister does, and she's always complaining about not having time."

"Right, and your sister probably works, which wouldn't have been common then." Riley waited, but Nick didn't confirm her assumption. "Anyway, your sister's needs would be the same whether she were a parent now or a hundred years ago."

Nick threw his hand into the air. "Are you sure Claire wants a full exhibit about this? Who is going to find it interesting?"

Riley tilted her head. "Don't you think exploring the lives of ordinary people is interesting?" She glanced over her shoulder at the rows of boxes. "Everything we have in here is because someone thought it was interesting. Besides, Claire's email doesn't give specific direction, just her initial request. If, after I spend a bit of time on this, it's clear that there isn't enough for a full exhibit, I can point that out and either suggest a way to expand it or to incorporate the information into another show." Claire had advised Riley to think about the next step when responding to a research request—to assess the "so what" impact of what she unearthed.

"I suppose." Nick returned his notebook to his bag. A signal his interest had waned?

She narrowed her eyes. "What's with you? Rough weekend?" They didn't always get along, but this attitude was unusual for him.

Nick ran his hand through his surfer-style hair. "Weekend was fine. I'm just trying to figure out some stuff."

"Like what? Anything I can help with?"

He looked away. Riley did the same so he didn't feel like she was staring at him. Out of the corner of her eye, she saw him check his phone. "I don't think so. But thanks for offering."

"Let me know if you want to talk, any time." Riley thought about putting her hand out to grasp his arm, but he stepped away and pocketed his phone. Something was definitely up.

"Sure."

Riley watched as her colleague grabbed his coat and left the room. What had she said to send him away? She started to return to her task when her phone vibrated with a message alert.

> Hey, sister. Not feeling so great today. Can we reschedule dinner?

Riley's heart leaped as she realized she'd forgotten about making plans with Lucy.

> Of course. Feel better. When is the gala?

> Wednesday.

> XXOO

Riley fired off another text, this time to Johnny.

> Ended up with an unexpected free evening. Do you have plans?

> Just to see you.

Riley refrained from replying with a heart emoji. They hadn't quite reached that stage of their relationship, though her heart fluttered at his response the same way it did when his great-grandfather Jack wrote to her.

She leaped off her stool and began pacing. Neither man had a clue about her relationship with the other, which made her feel weirdly deceitful. She'd run through it so many times—how she might one day broach the subject with Johnny: "To you, your great-grandfather is an image in a family photo album, a character in your family's history. To me, he is alive. We're partners. We correspond, lean on each other for help. I trust him, and he's as dear a friend to me as anyone in the twenty-first century." She stopped mid-step and put her face in her hands. Who was she kidding? Even if Johnny accepted that this inconceivable situation were true, he might not take too kindly to the competition—her pouring out her thoughts to his great-grandfather through their journal and becoming giddy when he replied.

She rolled her eyes and took a deep breath. Couldn't she just appreciate what she had, whatever that was?

When she returned to her laptop, there was a new meeting request from Claire. Unusual. She would normally just pop down to the archive. The subject was vague: "update". That could be about anything, really. Is Claire expecting her to update her on the progress of her work on this potential exhibit? Likely not, given Riley only started working on it this morning. Even more unusual was the meeting being scheduled to start in fifteen minutes. At least Riley wouldn't have to wonder about Claire's topic for long.

CHAPTER 6

Jack

THE DAY STARTED with clear skies and the promise of sunshine, judging by the first rays of sun brightening the sky over the distant mountains east of the city. As Winston walked toward the station to meet Constable Miller, he thought again about the Shuttleworth case. It wasn't much of a case, really. A straightforward theft, the most likely culprit a disgruntled former employee. Miller should be able to continue working on his own case—the other robbery—after they'd paid Shuttleworth's cook, Mrs. Plum, a visit and tracked down the maid who'd been let go. Winston had a spring in his step. Maybe they could wrap up both cases within the week.

The night before, Winston had examined a copy of Shuttleworth's table game, Finders, in Mrs. Bradley's parlour. It was simple enough. Four players each tried to get around the board, seeking treasure. They rolled the dice to move forward. On some squares, they picked up cards that let them advance further or acquire a tool to use in their treasure hunt. On other squares, they encountered obstacles—a broken tool, for example—that hindered their advancement toward the treasure. The clever part of the game was the strategy portion, where players could choose to collaborate with others or work independently, laying their obstacle cards in opponents' paths or freeing opponents from obstacles they encountered. He and his housemate William Fisher had played two surprisingly pleasant rounds of the game, and Winston quickly saw that choosing to collaborate yielded greater success.

Miller met Winston outside the station, on time and ready to go to the Shuttleworth house. The constable's uniform had been freshly pressed, a sign of the man's obvious enthusiasm for the challenge of leading his own investigation. After they boarded a public trolley, the younger man turned to Winston. The smile that reached his eyes suggested he had forgiven Winston's harshness of the day before. "I was wondering," he began. "Do the Shuttleworths have any children?"

"Why do you ask, Thomas?"

"It's only that I wonder if one of them might have taken the necklace . . . to remember their mother."

"A good thought. I didn't see any sign of children yesterday, but let's remember to ask that question today." A bubble of satisfaction warmed Winston. Thomas had been developing his detection skills.

The trolley made quick work of the distance they'd walked the day before. They climbed off in the Mount Pleasant neighbourhood and briskly walked the remaining half block to the Shuttleworth home. Edward Shuttleworth answered Winston's knock, unshaven and wearing a rumpled shirt. Winston—reluctant to draw attention to the man's state of dress—was certain this was the time they'd agreed on. He pulled his watch from his pocket. "Have we come earlier than you were expecting us, Mr. Shuttleworth?"

"I slept poorly last night, yet what little sleep I got was deep. It took me longer than usual to rouse myself." Shuttleworth brushed his hand across his stubble of beard.

"Would you like for us to come back in an hour?"

"No need," said Shuttleworth, sighing the words. He stepped back and signalled with a sweep of his hand that the men should enter.

The widower's grief hung in the very atmosphere of the house. Winston silently reaffirmed his commitment to find the necklace, if for no other reason than to bring some small comfort to this man. "Before you show us to the kitchen so we might speak to your cook, perhaps you could answer one question," he said. When the man nodded, Winston continued. "Do you have any children?"

A wave of pain crossed Shuttleworth's face. "I'm afraid we were not so blessed. It is a source of sadness for my wife." Shuttleworth looked deeper into the house, then down at his sock feet. "Was a source of sadness for her," he said toward the floor. When he turned back to Winston, colour had risen in his cheeks. "I'll show you to the kitchen and introduce you to Mrs. Plum now."

The policemen followed Shuttleworth through his home. Before they reached the kitchen door, the soft lilt of someone humming a tune met them in the hallway.

As Winston stepped in, he found the kitchen warmer than the day before, now that the stove was lit. A woman he assumed to be Mrs. Plum turned from reaching for a container in the pantry, which slipped from her grasp. A cloud of white enveloped the woman. Winston stepped back instinctively, though he was well away from the powder as it settled.

"Oh dear. Look what I've done. I am ever so sorry for the noise and the mess, Mr. Shuttleworth."

Shuttleworth, who seemed to have regained his composure during the short walk down the hallway, waved her words away. "Mrs. Plum, do not worry about the mess. I've forgotten it already." He didn't offer introductions.

The woman's face bore an expression of bewilderment. Miller stepped forward and found a broom behind the door. He stooped to right the canister of flour and placed it on the counter. Then he got on with the cleanup.

The kitchen reminded Winston of the one in his childhood home, although there the atmosphere was bustling. The cook in his parents' house had several people working with her to feed the family and their guests. As a child, it had been a favourite place for Winston—warm and filled with appetizing aromas and delicious morsels of food. Winston had learned quickly to visit the kitchen if he needed a scraped knee tended to. There'd always be a delicious treat to follow Cook's attention.

Mrs. Plum watched as Miller dumped the dustpan's contents into a bucket by the sink. She rocked from one foot to the other, appearing to be torn between taking the broom from Miller and tidying her own appearance. She opted for the latter, smoothing her apron and tugging at her hair. She finished, her face flushing, just as Miller rejoined them, his freshly pressed uniform now covered in a fine dusting of flour.

Shuttleworth snapped out of his silence. "These are the policemen I mentioned: Detective Winston and Constable Miller. They'd like to ask you a few questions about my wife's missing necklace."

Her hand flew to her neck. "I didn't take it."

"Of course you didn't." Shuttleworth smoothed his shirt, a flash of surprise flickering in his eyes when he noticed he wasn't wearing a waistcoat. "If there's nothing else. . ." The kitchen door swung as he scuttled from the room.

Mrs. Plum motioned to a large table occupying a corner of the room. Winston and Miller each sat in one of the six chairs surrounding the table, and the cook chose one opposite the policemen. "Thank you for your help with tidying, Mr. Miller."

"Not at all, Mrs. Plum. I've spent time working in a kitchen, and I know how important it is to clean up right away. Do you have any help in here?"

"I did. Before. . ." Tears welled in her eyes. "Before Mrs. Shuttleworth died. She and Mr. Shuttleworth entertained regularly, and this space was filled with laughter as we worked together, me and the kitchen help. We needed more hands then to feed more mouths." Winston waited as she lost herself in a memory. "Never mind the two maids who kept the rest of the house."

"But you have no help now? We saw the kitchen boy, Charlie, yesterday. And a maid, Polly," Winston said.

"Yes, Charlie still comes, and he cleaned everything yesterday." She crinkled her nose. "And Polly, though she hasn't arrived today."

"You are expecting her, Mrs. Plum?"

"I am."

Miller pulled his notepad from his pocket. "Where does she live? We can check on her."

Mrs. Plum wiped her hands on her apron. "I'll have to look it up." She reached into the pantry and returned with a small notebook. She bit her lip as she thumbed through the pages, landing on a page and reading out an address.

"It sounds like this once was a full and busy house. What about children?" Miller kept his voice soft, so Mrs. Plum had to lean toward him. He already knew the answer, of course, but by asking the question, he gave Mrs. Plum the opportunity to share a little about the nature of the household. Another excellent example of his progress as an investigator.

She shook her head. "There were none. If they had a family, Mr. Shuttleworth wouldn't be quite so alone now." She produced a handkerchief and dabbed her eye before returning it to a pocket in her apron. "Still, they seemed happy enough with each other. Not that it's my place to say."

Winston retrieved his own notepad and flipped it open. "You said there were two maids? Mr. Shuttleworth spoke only of one yesterday. The one he thinks took Mrs. Shuttleworth's necklace."

"That'll be Kate. She was Mrs. Shuttleworth's maid. Her sister, Susie, worked here too. She kept the rest of the house tidy. When Mr. Shuttleworth fired Kate, Susie left as well." Mrs. Plum clasped her hands in front of her. "Kate didn't spend much time in here with me, but Susie often lent a hand when we prepared for a big party. You know, I always wondered if Mr. Shuttleworth didn't realize there were two of them. They look rather alike." She covered her mouth with her hand. "Now, listen to me. I've just said more than I should."

"Do you know how to reach Kate or Susie? What is their surname?"

"It's Pegg." She searched through the address book again, furrowing her brow after flipping between several pages. "It's not in here. I'm sure they told me that they live down the hill. But not on Main. Try Quebec or Ontario."

"Thank you, Mrs. Plum. Most helpful. We will pay them a visit today." Winston made a note of the intersections. "Do you know why Susie left when it was her sister who was fired? I assume they both need employment?"

Mrs. Plum shrugged. "I'm sure they do, but they'll find work in this city without trouble. Mrs. Shuttleworth's friends were always asking me or the girls to work for them."

Miller cleared his throat. "Why have you stayed, Mrs. Plum? If you regularly received offers to work elsewhere?"

She stared past the policemen. "It didn't feel right to abandon Mr. Shuttleworth. He's always paid me fairly, and, well. . . He has nobody else."

"And before? When Mrs. Shuttleworth was alive?" Miller leaned on his forearms to bring his head closer to Mrs. Plum.

"Oh, I couldn't have left them. I know just how to do their tea and their pudding. And like I said, they treated me well." She dabbed at her eye again.

"I admire your loyalty, Mrs. Plum." Miller gave her a warm smile. "And I'm sure Mr. Shuttleworth appreciates it, especially now."

Mrs. Plum tucked her handkerchief into her sleeve. "You don't think one of those girls took Mrs. Shuttleworth's necklace, do you? It's hard to imagine one of them doing such a thing."

Winston shook his head. "I don't think anything yet, Mrs. Plum. I'm still looking for facts."

"Those girls, Kate and Susie. They were a little silly, but they would never steal. Not from here, at least."

Miller raised an eyebrow. "Might they steal from someone else?"

"I don't think so. They were raised well. And they're young enough and pretty enough that they're as likely to be given something if they ask for it. Even if—" Mrs. Plum clapped her hand to her mouth. She focused her gaze on an invisible blemish on the tabletop, then dropped her hand to work a finger back and forth over it.

"You were saying, Mrs. Plum. Even if. . ." Winston gestured, encouraging her to continue.

She brought her hands together and entwined her fingers. "Well, you know how girls can get silly notions in their heads. I overheard Kate saying that she was owed something."

Winston nodded his encouragement. "Owed what? Do you know?"

"I don't. She was talking to Susie, though. She might know."

In his notepad, Winston underlined Kate's name. "Mr. Shuttleworth told us that he thought Kate had stolen the items. That was why he fired her," he said.

A knot formed in Mrs. Plum's brow. "He never told me that directly. It isn't my place to inquire after his reasons."

Winston leaned forward. "But your impression is that you don't think she would have done it?" Household staff had a way of knowing everything about the house, even if they weren't directly involved. And this woman's posture signalled she knew more.

Mrs. Plum stared at her hands, still clasped. "I don't know. The woman was fond of her. I'll give you that." The cook pointed a finger at Winston as she spoke. "She gave Kate little gifts on her birthday, or around Christmas. Little things, like a book or a comb."

Winston read a hint of satisfaction in Mrs. Plum's face. She enjoyed being privy to these details.

"Mind you, Mrs. Shuttleworth didn't give me anything, other than praise for my scones." At this, she stood and swatted a path to the oven with a tea towel, where she lowered the door and pulled out a steaming tray. "Here. These might be a little hot to the touch yet, but if you'd like to try one in a few minutes. . ." She tilted her chin toward the ceiling. Almost as if in response came the muffled sounds of Shuttleworth preparing for the day. "He won't mind."

Winston's mouth watered as the scent of the scones wafted toward him. "Those smell delightful, Mrs. Plum. You make them daily?"

"I used to. Mrs. Shuttleworth loved them. Now that she's gone, I only make one or two batches a week. Mr. Shuttleworth nibbles one, then throws the rest of it into the garden. The crows enjoy his leftovers." She busied herself preparing a plate of the scones and pouring hot water into a teapot.

Winston watched her practised motions. She had likely performed them hundreds, if not thousands, of times. This kitchen was her domain, and from here she would know everything about everyone in the house.

She brought the scones and tea to the table. "Doesn't he mind the waste? Don't you?" Miller asked.

Mrs. Plum's eyes grew wide. "I don't ask. He hasn't said to stop making them. I assume they must remind him of her. Our nose is a funny thing, to give us such a strong memory when we smell something."

Winston bit into a still-hot scone. As Mrs. Plum predicted, the memory of his family kitchen flooded in. His heart clamped. His family. Ellis's stone lay in his pocket and he wanted to hold it, to hold on to the memory of his brother. He concentrated on chewing. After he swallowed, he said, "I can't believe Mr. Shuttleworth throws any of these away. They are incredible. You could sell them."

Colour rose to Mrs. Plum's cheeks. "How lovely of you to say so, Detective."

"People would line up for these." He moved the plate toward Miller. Had he not done so, Winston was certain Miller would have grabbed the scone off Winston's plate. Miller closed his eyes and chewed.

"You're right, sir." Miller turned to Mrs. Plum and wiped a crumb from his mouth. "You could do quite well if you ever left Mr. Shuttleworth."

"Oh, I couldn't leave him. He'd have nobody." She wiped her hands on her apron. "Do you have any more questions for me? It's only that I should get back to this." She tilted her head in the direction of the pantry.

"Thank you, Mrs. Plum. I think we've taken enough of your time."

"You're welcome." She handed Miller a warm bundle. "Here are some scones for your day." She gave Winston two smaller bundles, patting the tops where she had labelled them. Gentle heat radiated from the packages. "And this is for the girls. Be well."

Winston made sounds of protest and Mrs. Plum raised her hands. "It's nothing, Detective. I recognize a man who doesn't get as many scones as he would like. Does your wife not make them?"

Winston dodged the question. "We really must get going, Mrs. Plum. Thank you." He and Miller left through the kitchen door that led to the back garden. As they descended the steps to the path, a younger woman approached them. "Hello, Polly," Winston said.

The girl's eyes lit with a spark of recognition. She gave the briefest of nods in answer.

"We were just speaking with Mrs. Plum, and she'd expressed concern that you hadn't yet arrived for work." He stepped aside and she continued toward the house. "We were here yesterday, speaking to Mr. Shuttleworth," he said as she passed him. "Charlie introduced us."

The girl paused, turning. "I remember."

"Do you know what happened to Mrs. Shuttleworth's necklace? Did someone take it?"

The girl's cheeks flushed. "Nobody I know. They'd never do such a thing." She crinkled her nose. "Maybe Mrs. Shuttleworth gave it to someone."

"Have you any ideas who she might have given the necklace to?" Winston kept his voice soft to avoid causing alarm. He didn't want the girl to flit off.

"She gave Kate gifts. Kate showed me. But she would never have taken anything."

Kate again. They needed to move on, track down Kate and her sister, Susie. Miller cleared his throat from the bottom of the steps, as if he could read Winston's thoughts. Winston gave him a slight nod but wanted to keep Polly engaged just a little longer, see what she might add to what they knew so far. "What is it like working in the house now, with just Mr. Shuttleworth?"

"Mrs. Plum is there too. It's much quieter. But Mrs. Plum said Mr. Shuttleworth just needs a little more time, then he will feel better. That's why she has kept me and Charlie on. She said that soon the house won't be quite as sad anymore."

"Did she say why?"

"No. I hope she's right, though. She's started to show me how to do more in the kitchen, and I like working with her. I want to keep learning from her. She said maybe I can be the cook in a house one day."

Winston thanked the girl and she answered with a half-curtsy, then entered the house. Winston's hand brushed the journal as he opened his satchel to slip in the bundles of warm scones. "Well,

Thomas. What did you think of Mrs. Plum?" Winston took the last couple of steps to join Miller on the pathway.

"A fine baker, she is," Miller said through mouthfuls. "How can you stop eating these? I could eat ten more."

Winston gave him a broad smile, fishing his notepad from his pocket. "We need to find these maids, Kate and Susie Pegg." He checked his notes. "Mrs. Plum didn't have a specific address for the sisters. You can eat as many scones as you like while we knock on a few doors." He winked at Miller. "Just be sure to keep your uniform clear of crumbs."

Miller brushed at the front of his jacket. "And if we don't find them?"

"We will keep knocking until we do."

"Then what, sir?"

Winston tugged a corner of one bundle out of his satchel. "As she said, the sense of smell draws memories. And if you can resist eating all of these, the scones should serve as a useful trigger of memories for those maids."

Miller frowned, confusion clouding his face. "I don't understand."

"You saw Mrs. Plum give me scones for the Pegg sisters. It's her way of introducing us as safe to speak to."

"That's thoughtful of her." Miller scratched his temple. "If she cared that much about them, wouldn't she know more specifically where they live?"

"Not if she didn't look after paying their wages," Winston said. Adopting a gentler tone, Winston continued. "Now let's find those maids and that necklace."

✳

WINSTON AND MILLER walked the short distance to where Mrs. Plum had suggested Susie and Kate Pegg lived. As they trudged against the steepness of the hill, the homes around them grew smaller. Screeches and squeals from lumber mills and shipbuilders grew louder. The Shuttleworth house was among the few grander homes in the neighbourhood. But most residents occupied these simpler homes, built for workers at the nearby mills and other industrial sites along the False Creek shore.

Winston had been mulling over Miller's words. He stopped mid-stride and turned to his constable. "You asked why Mrs. Plum didn't know where Kate and Susie live, supposing that if she cared for them she would know." Winston held Miller's eyes. "If you believe that, then I must admit I'm embarrassed I don't know where in the city you live, Thomas. Please don't think it means I don't care about you."

Miller pointed in the direction they'd come from. "I live further up the hill, closer to the Shuttleworths." He shook his head. "I don't expect you to know where I live, but I thought because women often attend to such detail, Mrs. Plum would be more likely to know."

"Still, I had no idea. And you've been to my rooms." Winston thought of a recent case, where they had spent a few days working from his rooms at Mrs. Bradley's house. They'd have no need to do the same with this case. And if they did, it would be difficult to keep William Fisher from asking questions. Though perhaps he wouldn't be a concern for long if he found a house quickly.

Winston gave his chin a rub. Having one's own space would certainly afford more privacy. Maybe he should consider it too. "Do you like living around here?"

"I do. The houses are new, ours is clean, and everybody works hard." Miller surveyed the street. "It's quite a good community, actually. People look out for each other. It's nice."

The men resumed walking. Winston reflected on Miller's description. A community. It did sound nice. Then Winston realized what he might mean. "Do you know the maids? Kate and Susie Pegg?" he asked.

"I don't know everyone who lives around here. And our house is a few streets away. Don't have much occasion to spend time at the bottom of the hill. There are more shops and businesses further up." Miller pointed with his thumb over his shoulder.

A mechanical whine suddenly whirred and Winston winced at the noise. It continued for several seconds, then finally faded. "Do you know how long this noise carries on? Into the night?"

Miller shrugged. "The shipyard and mill close at six o'clock in the evening."

"That's not too bad, Thomas. You would be away from it most of the time. If you weren't, though, this constant hum would be distracting." Winston quickened his pace. "Now let's find those maids."

"Let's start at the corner grocer," Miller said, indicating a building ahead of them. "The shopkeeper will know who lives in the area."

Winston followed Miller through the door into the small shop. Jars of preserves and dried meat lined the shelves, with a few loaves of bread on the counter near the front of the store. A man stood behind the counter, the top of his apron crisp and white. "How can I help you, gentlemen?" He waved to a customer passing by the window behind them.

Winston cleared his throat. "We're with the constabulary, and we're looking for a pair of sisters who live nearby. We think they might have answers to some questions we have."

The shopkeeper's face betrayed nothing.

"They're not in trouble," Miller said. He stood with his hands clasped behind his back and offered the man a reassuring smile.

"A fair number of sisters live around here. Brothers too. Fathers, mothers." The shopkeeper laughed. "We've got all sorts."

"These girls were maids at a house on Main Street."

"Many around here are. The girls you want, do they have names?"

"Kate and Susie Pegg." Winston waited for a glimmer of recognition in the man's face. The grocer glanced toward the door of his shop before returning his gaze to the men in front of him. "Do you know them?" Winston asked.

The shopkeeper rubbed his chin. "I do. You're sure they're not in trouble?" Bells above the door chimed as another patron walked in. The shopkeeper smiled and lifted his fingers in a partial wave. "Let me help this customer, sirs. I'll be back directly." He stepped from behind the counter and assisted an older woman carrying a basket on her arm. She handed him coins in return for a loaf of bread.

After placing the coins in a drawer behind the counter, the shopkeeper returned his attention to Miller and Winston. "They're good girls." He paused, and only after Winston nodded did he continue. "The Pegg girls live on Quebec Street, near Sixth Avenue. Second house from the corner."

"Thank you, sir."

"You're not likely to find them home at this hour, though. As you say, they are maids and will be at work."

"Thank you all the same." Winston tipped his hat at the man and motioned Miller toward the exit.

The racket from the mills and workshops was louder here, closer to the water. "I suppose the neighbourhood is more pleasant when the millwork is over for the day. And if residents are working themselves, they're unlikely to be much disturbed by this." Winston raised his voice and leaned closer to Miller. "Still, it's too much for me. I'm not sure I could live here."

Miller set his mouth to a firm line. "Some people have no choice, sir."

"But these girls must, if they're working as maids."

"How much do you think maids earn, sir?"

Winston shrugged. "I don't know. I don't have one. Surely they get enough to secure a warm bed in a quieter neighbourhood?"

"Maids are paid little, sir. They often live with their employers, which means they are paid even less but, as you say, have a warm bed. These girls likely live with other members of their family—their parents and siblings, no doubt. I live with my brother and our parents. Our sister is married and lives in her own house with her husband and children." Miller passed his hand through his hair. "Have you never been to a home outside the West End?"

Winston bristled. He and Miller had never discussed his family background, so the younger man would have no idea of the household he'd grown up in when he had lived in Toronto. And though he chose to live at Mrs. Bradley's house, it was more out of convenience, and he didn't have a wife or family who would need larger accommodation. "Of course I have. We just left one. I've just never thought of the costs of maintaining anything more than rooms."

"Don't you pay rent to live with Mrs. Bradley?"

"I certainly do."

"And she must use that to pay for the food she feeds you, the wages she pays to her staff, and for her own needs. Do you think you pay her enough for all that?"

Winston raised his hands in defence. "I must, or else she should charge me more."

"If she charges you too much, you might decide to leave. Then what would she do?"

"She could find a new tenant. Her house is well kept and clean, and the food is good."

"Sir, not everyone has the connections you have."

Winston's jaw tightened. This was beginning to feel like an assault. "Whatever do you mean, Thomas?"

"I mean your uncle. Your father."

Miller's reference to his father surprised him. Though perhaps it shouldn't, given Miller's developing detection skills. He'd undoubtedly observed that his uncle, the chief constable, made no effort to hide his appreciation of the good—and expensive—things in life. It was not a leap to think Winston came from a similar background. "This is not something I wish to discuss further, Thomas."

Miller said nothing more, but the slump of his shoulders spoke of his mood as they neared the maids' house.

CHAPTER 7

Riley

RILEY RAISED HER hand to knock on Claire's office door but dropped it again when she heard Nick's voice from within. She started to step away then thought better of it, leaning closer to listen.

"Thanks, Claire. I won't let you down. I really appreciate the opportunity."

When chair legs scraped on the floor, Riley skittered back a few steps so it appeared as if she were just arriving. Nick opened the door, avoiding Riley's eyes as he slipped past her.

"Come on in," Claire called.

With a glance over her shoulder at Nick disappearing down the hall, Riley entered, forcing a smile.

"Hi, Claire," Riley said as her boss motioned for her to sit. "I didn't prepare anything. I wasn't sure what you were expecting."

Claire exhaled and clasped her hands on the desk. "I'm not expecting anything from you. I wanted to update you on some changes here."

A pit formed in Riley's stomach. "Changes? Am I fired?" Her underarms grew damp. Why was "about to be fired" always her first assumption?

"Not at all," Claire said with a wave of her hand. "I'm really pleased with the work you've been doing." Her smile was genuine. "No, it's me."

"*You're* fired?" Riley covered her mouth with a hand. Had she really just blurted the question? She shoved her hands under her thighs as if sitting on them would slow her mouth down.

"No. Nothing like that. But I am taking some time off. A six-month sabbatical where I'll be spending time in other museums around the world."

Riley leaned back into her chair. Nobody was getting fired. "That sounds amazing. When do you leave?"

"In about a month." Claire leaned forward, her face serious. "I wanted you to hear it from me. I've asked Nick to act in my place while I'm gone."

Riley tried to process what Claire had just said. She opened and closed her mouth a couple of times, but didn't have a ready response. Nick was going to be her boss? Temporarily, but still. He only had a few more years' experience than her. She swallowed and at last said, "Nick. That's great. Keep it in the department." Was that why he'd been acting so strangely? Would Nick's preference for sexier exhibits put the new research she'd been assigned in jeopardy?

"You seem to work well together, and honestly, I didn't want to go through the hassle of posting the position and interviewing some-one when I know he can do the job," Claire said.

Questions flooded Riley's mind, but she couldn't ask any of them without sounding jealous or hurt. She would never have dreamed of taking Claire's place, even temporarily. She had so much to learn. Didn't Nick have a lot to learn too? Was Nick going to have the power to make big decisions for the museum? Or was he just sup-posed to keep things going while Claire was away? Riley settled on a simple question so she could get away from Claire's office and process this news. "Do you need anything else from me? It's just that I should get back to work." Riley sat forward, palms pressed on her legs, ready to launch out of the chair.

Claire searched Riley's face, a look of concern pinching her fea-tures. "Are you disappointed? Nick is an excellent researcher."

Riley stood. "I know he is. We've worked together on several exhibits. It will be fine." She kept her voice flat and left.

*

"It will not be fine. I mean, I like Nick. He's a great guy, and like Claire said, he's a good researcher. But that doesn't make him a good boss. I get that she couldn't give me the job—I've only been out of grad school for a year. But he's just a few years older than I am. How can he be the boss?"

Riley threw her fist into the pillow beside her, and Johnny jumped. He reached over her and moved the pillow to his lap. "Let me get this out of your way," he said, his laugh cut short by Riley's stern frown. "Maybe it won't be that bad. You're good at what you do, and it's only six months. It's not like Nick can change a bunch of things in such a short time." He placed the pillow in her outstretched hands, and she returned it to its spot.

"It's not even that. I'm just frustrated she didn't even consider me. It never came up. At all. She could have at least let me compete for the job and learn something in the process." Johnny reached for her hand and gave it a squeeze. She squeezed back. "It's fine." It would have to be fine. She loved her job at the museum, and she wanted to continue working with Nick, even if he was occasionally arrogant.

She turned to the television, which was frozen on the selection screen for the mystery-suspense streaming service Unsolved. "Let's watch whatever we were going to watch." She sighed heavily. "It's fine."

*

AFTER JOHNNY HAD left, Riley was still stewing about Nick. She checked the clock. Jules would just be getting up to prepare for his workday. She tapped his name on her phone to start a video call.

He answered after the first ring. "Riley? Everything okay?"

"Hi, Jules. Yeah. I'm fine. How's London?"

He spent a few minutes telling her the latest about his elderly neighbour. "But that's not why you called. What's up?"

"I want to come visit," she blurted. Only once the words were out did she realize that was what she wanted. "I mean, if you're having visitors."

"Of course I am. I'd love to see you. When were you thinking?"

"Can I come next week?" Jules's face froze. Was it their connection? Or had she said something wrong? "Are you still there?"

"Steve and I have plans to get away next weekend. And the weekend after that." He looked away from the screen. "Actually, we have plans for weekend getaways the next six weeks. But you could come away with us."

"I don't want to be a third wheel on your romantic getaways. But I'm jealous."

"So many great places are just a two-hour flight away. Why don't you book your trip for a few months from now, then we can choose a destination for a city break for part of your stay here? Like a vacation within a vacation." He spoke quickly. "And that way, I can take time off too. Show you around a little."

"I'm happy to explore on my own, but I was hoping to see you sooner." She had never travelled without doing weeks of planning beforehand. Now that she'd decided that she needed to see him urgently, it felt pressing that she follow through.

Jules lowered his voice. "Riley, what's up? I haven't known you to ever book a trip on a whim. You need to plan, organize, reserve."

Of course Jules, one of her oldest friends, would sense her uneasiness, even though thousands of miles separated them. "My boss is going away for a few months, and she's leaving my colleague in charge."

"And?"

"And it's going to be a disaster. He's not ready to be in charge."

"Are you? Is that what's upset you?"

She turned his question over in her mind. "I'm not. But I wish I was."

"And coming to see me would help how? Don't get me wrong. I want to see you. But would it solve anything?"

"Maybe I can get a job in London too. There are so many museums there. Surely there's something I could find." As she spoke the words, her voice caught. Leaving Vancouver would mean leaving her family. And Johnny.

"I'd love for you to work here. But you can't just walk into a museum and ask for a job."

He was right. And if she left Vancouver, she wouldn't be as helpful to Jack without access to the archives of the Vancouver History Museum, along with its collection of old police files. "Yeah," she said, hearing the resignation in her own voice, "I suppose I'd need a visa or something."

"Make a plan, Riley. It's what you do best. Come here, speak to some key people—after you've made appointments to see them, that is—and then decide. I don't want you to rush into anything. Make sure it's something you really want."

She wrapped her arms around herself. "I miss you, Jules. Thank you." He was right. If she was really going to leave the city, she'd need more reason than pure impulse. "Now tell me, where are you going on each of your getaways?"

As Jules shared his weekend holiday plans, her breathing calmed. She stifled a yawn when he finished telling her about the short jaunt they'd planned to Paris. "Thanks, again, Jules. You probably need to get back to preparing for the day, and I need some sleep. Love you." He promised to send her an email with some museum ideas for her to consider.

Riley prepared for bed and climbed under the covers. She let her hand rest on the journal beside her and mulled over the conversation she'd just had with Jules. He was right. She needed to make a plan. But first, she'd help Jack with his case. She pushed the journal to the other side of the bed and turned out the light.

CHAPTER 8

Jack

THE POLICEMEN EASILY found the house that the grocer had spoken of. Winston let Miller lead them up the half-dozen steps to the porch and knock on the front door. A young boy, about ten years old, pulled the door open. "Hello," Miller said in a gentle voice. "Do Kate and Susie Pegg live here?"

The boy's gaze was fixed on the badge on the constable's uniform. Winston admired Miller's instinctive reaction to crouch and meet the boy's eyes. "My name is Thomas, and I'm a police officer. Kate and Susie aren't in trouble, but we would like to ask them a few questions. Can you help us find them?"

He pointed with a shaky finger over his shoulder into the house. "Susie is here."

"Would you get her for us?"

The boy turned on his heel and ran inside, leaving the door open.

Winston turned to Miller. "Nicely handled. You connect well with children."

"I have younger siblings. They're not hard to figure out."

"I doubt I would have persuaded him to find his sister," said Winston.

"Who is at the door?" a voice called from inside the house. A tall woman appeared, hair in a long braid over one shoulder. Winston put her at twenty years old. She stopped mid-stride and swallowed. "The police? For me?" She pulled her dark braid to her other shoulder.

Winston stepped forward. "I'm Detective Jack Winston, and this is Constable Thomas Miller. We are with the constabulary. You are Susie Pegg? You worked for the Shuttleworths?"

She nodded her head slowly. "I'm Susie and yes, I worked there for two years, cleaning and helping Mrs. Plum in the kitchen." Her hand flew to her face. "Is Mrs. Plum okay?"

"Mrs. Plum seemed just fine," he said, offering the package the cook had given him. "She spoke highly of you. And your sister, Kate. She also worked there, didn't she?"

Susie Pegg brought the package to her nose and inhaled deeply, then opened the door wider and ushered them into the hallway. "Yes. Kate was a maid. She was supposed to be a housemaid, like me, but Mrs. Shuttleworth treated Kate like her personal servant. Kate helped her dress, mended her clothes . . . that sort of thing." A tinge of frustration had crept into Susie's voice. "Why are you asking?"

"We have a few questions, Miss Pegg. Is there somewhere we can speak?" Winston asked.

She led them into a sitting room furnished with four chairs and a chesterfield. A low table occupied the centre of the room. "My father made this," said Susie, pointing to the table. "Well, he made all this furniture but is especially proud of this." Susie arranged herself on the table's smooth surface and indicated that the men should take a seat. They settled into chairs facing her.

Winston pulled his notepad from his pocket but left it closed on his lap. "Your father should be proud. The furnishings all look well made. Is he a carpenter?"

Susie nodded. "Though he works from time to time on the water. When the shipyard needs an extra pair of hands. He's there now. Do you need to speak to him?"

"No, we want to speak to you. And your sister, Kate," Winston said. "When did you leave the Shuttleworth house?"

Were he not paying attention, Winston would have missed how Susie drew her feet slightly closer together on hearing her sister's name. "Mrs. Shuttleworth died. We left after that." She said the words with little emotion. Had she been unhappy working at the house?

"You must know what we've come to speak to you about."

Susie's feet inched closer again, and she leaned slightly forward. "Mr. Shuttleworth thinks my sister stole a necklace from him." She spoke quietly, though her tone was harsh.

"Did she?" Winston asked the question gently.

She sank into her shoulders, rounding her back. "She said she didn't."

"Do you think she did?" Miller's question matched Winston's tone.

"I don't." Her voice rose. "She wouldn't. Even if she was mistreated. Kate has always been honest. This accusation. It means she'll have a hard time getting a new position."

"Was she mistreated?" Winston asked.

"Not by Mrs. Shuttleworth. And Mr. Shuttleworth didn't really mistreat her. He was in pain." She looked away.

Winston leaned forward, silently urging her to continue.

She gathered some of the fabric of her dress, as if gathering her thoughts. "He seemed different after Mrs. Shuttleworth died."

"Different?" Winston asked.

"Upset. Short-tempered."

"Was it because of his grief, do you think? About his wife?" Winston asked. Shuttleworth hadn't seemed angry. Lost in grief more accurately described his state of mind.

"He was sad, certainly, but it was more than that. He grew angry. Especially when he realized her necklace was missing. I heard him say something about 'it was never going to be complete.'"

"What did he mean by that?" Winston asked as he wrote a note.

Susie scrunched more of her dress in her hand. "I don't know. I thought he meant the jewellery set." She released the fabric.

"Did you discuss this with your sister?"

"Not recently. I haven't seen Kate for. . ." Susie's brow furrowed. "For a few days."

Miller and Winston exchanged glances. Was Susie angry with her sister? Had Kate fled with the stolen necklace? "Why is that, Miss Pegg?"

"She was very upset when Mr. Shuttleworth fired her."

"Did you leave the Shuttleworth house together?" Winston asked.

"We did, but she went to see her beau." Susie whispered the words.

"She didn't come home after that?" Winston asked.

"She's staying with him, but I can't tell my father. He would be so disappointed."

"Where does your father think she is?" Miller asked.

"Our mother died last year, after an illness. My father works long hours and isn't here much. Kate and I keep an eye on Jimmy, our brother. He answered the door. We take care of him as best we can. I just arranged for him to start as an apprentice baker next week."

As she spoke, Winston noted the fatigue in her voice. This young woman had taken on a lot. Was it too much?

"My father asked about Kate this morning, actually," she said. "I told him she's been working longer hours. He is not a curious man, my father, and the answer seemed to satisfy him. If he asks again, I'll tell him Mr. Shuttleworth asked her to stay at the house to help Mrs. Plum. But I expect she will be back before he notices she's gone."

"Where does your sister's beau live? Haven't you gone to check if she's there?"

"I haven't had time. As soon as I left Mr. Shuttleworth, I found a position with another family, and they have kept me busy. Today is my afternoon off, and I was about to take Jimmy to get a new pair of trousers before he starts his apprenticeship."

Miller sat forward. "Would you like us to check on your sister, Miss Pegg?"

Her eyes grew wide. "Would you? I just haven't had time to see her. I keep expecting her to turn up for dinner." Susie ran a hand along the edge of the low table. "With our mother dead, my father so rarely here, and now Kate staying with Clay, everything has fallen to me. And I need to work. We used to share the responsibilities. Now. . ." She tapped her chest twice.

Winston nodded. Susie's frustration with Kate had kept her away. "What is his name, and where can we find him?"

"Clayton Block. She told me he lives east of Main Street in a house he shares with his brother." Winston wrote the address Susie provided in his notepad. The neighbourhood was a short walk from the one Kate and Susie's family lived in.

"Is your sister planning to marry Mr. Block?"

"I think he's already asked her, or she wouldn't stay with him. She's not so foolish as that, Detective. Still, my father won't be happy if he learns she's been staying with him before they're official."

"Constable Miller and I can go check on your sister this afternoon, when Mr. Block should be home from his work."

Susie's face broke into a weak smile. "I appreciate it. You'll tell me after you speak to her?" She reached for the package Winston had given her. "Would you mind giving these to Kate? She always liked Mrs. Plum's baking more than I did."

Winston nodded his reply as he stood, tucking the package into his bag. She followed them to the hall, shutting the door behind the men as they descended the porch steps.

"Are we going to Block's house now, sir?"

"Let's find something to eat." Winston patted his bag. "If we don't, we won't have any scones to bring to Kate Pegg."

✳

AFTER A MEAL at a nearby pub, Winston and Miller made their way to the address Susie Pegg had given them. Rather than being a house, as she had suggested, the building contained several apartments. The debris of the tenants' lives littered the area: broken cartwheels, rusty tools, and weathered piles of cloth lined the low fence surrounding the building. "Quite a different space from Miss Pegg's family home, sir."

"That it is, Thomas. Mr. Block is likely young and not yet established, which is why he's living here. Adding her to his household, especially if she's not earning money, might be more of a burden than he can accommodate."

Miller set his mouth in a firm line. "I'm young and not well established."

"And you live with your family, correct? A sensible decision, especially if this is the alternative." Winston indicated the clutter with a nod of his head.

"Yes, I live with my family, sir. I would like to settle down but haven't found the right woman. What about you? Will you marry?"

The images of two women flashed through Winston's mind. Riley had given him a photograph of herself, placing it in the pages of their journal. Although he still found the properties of the journal an unfathomable puzzle, he treasured this gift. He kept it tucked in the back of the book, though recently he'd found himself pulling it out to look at her fine features. Miller's question also brought to mind Melodia Spectre—the confounding woman who had originally sold him the journal that connects him to Riley. She popped into his thoughts far more than she was invited. And into his cases. He shook his head, sweeping the images from his mind. "Like you, I haven't found the right woman to make a home with."

"It may prove difficult in this city, sir. So much of the population is male."

"I have made the same observation." Winston waved his hand. "Let's find Kate Pegg."

A man dressed in coveralls and carrying a tool box exited the building as Miller and Winston approached the entrance. When Miller asked the man for Block's apartment number, he frowned. "He in trouble, then?"

"What would he be in trouble for?" Winston asked.

"You tell me. You're the police." The man's gruff voice matched his features.

"I can assure you that Mr. Block is not in trouble," Winston answered.

"He pays his rent. He's quiet."

Winston considered the man's clothing and the tools. He couldn't be Block. He looked considerably older than he'd assumed Block would be. And besides, Block would still be at work at this time in one of the factories along False Creek. This man must be the building owner. "Do you own this apartment building, sir?" Winston surveyed the scene around them.

"This and the one across the street." He pushed his chin out to indicate the facing building.

"How many people live here?" Winston asked.

The man narrowed his eyes at the question, taking in Winston's shiny shoes. "Why? Are you looking for somewhere to live? It's not gentlemen's housing. No rooms for maids or anything like that."

A shiver passed through Winston as he looked at the building and the surrounding detritus. "I'm simply curious, sir, how many apartments and how many people occupy them. My father lives in Toronto and is involved in real estate. He's asked me to keep him abreast of potential opportunities in Vancouver." He sensed that the man would respond better if Winston addressed him as an expert.

The man stood taller and straightened his hat. "My buildings are simple and clean. Affordable for a workingman." He pointed at his clothes. "My regular maintenance man just quit, so I need to fill in." He patted the breast of his coveralls as if searching for something. "I have a contact card somewhere. In my suit, perhaps." He nudged a pile of old newspapers with his foot, then stepped back. "I don't know who these belong to."

"How many tenants did you say you have, sir?"

"I didn't say. But I'll tell you we have fifteen apartments in each building."

Winston and Miller exchanged glances. "Fifteen? That's impressive."

"Five per floor. Each has a bedroom, a kitchen, and a sitting area."

"How much is the rent?" Miller asked.

"You looking to move, son? Most of my tenants work down at the mills." The landlord jutted his chin in the direction of the water, a few streets behind where they stood. Winston noted that the noise level was louder here than it had been at the Pegg house.

"I might be. How much would it cost me?" Miller asked.

"Twelve dollars per month." The man stepped closer to Miller. "I haven't any rooms available at the moment, but if you're interested, I might have something coming free in the next little while."

Miller raised his hands. "I don't want you to put anyone out. I'm not even sure I'm ready to move yet."

"All right, then. You know where to find me if you change your mind."

"Thank you. Which apartment is Mr. Block in again?"

"Apartment 3B. I'll get the door for you." The landlord pushed open the building's door for Winston and Miller. They thanked him and entered.

As they climbed the stairs, Winston turned back to Miller. "That was nicely handled, Thomas. I'm not sure if you're seriously considering moving into this man's apartment building, but your inquiries certainly seemed to warm him to us."

"Thank you, sir. I have been thinking about it. But I think that right now, I rather prefer staying in my neighbourhood, closer to my family."

"I imagine your house, even with your brothers, is quieter than around here during the day. Might as well stay with them if that's the case."

Miller nodded. "I agree."

Winston stopped outside the door to 3B. "Here it is." He held a hand up to knock.

"The landlord suggested Mr. Block is still out, sir," said Miller.

"He could have slipped home without his landlord noticing. And we're really seeking Kate Pegg."

"True."

Thirty seconds after Winston's second knock remained unanswered, the policemen turned to leave. Both spun around at the sound of the door opening. The woman who stood in the doorway so closely resembled Susie Pegg that Winston almost thought she was playing some kind of trick on them. As he looked closer, he saw that this woman had dark shadows beneath her eyes and her hair held less shine than Susie's. "Who are you?" she asked.

Winston removed his hat. "My name is Jack Winston, and I'm a detective with the constabulary. This is Constable Thomas Miller. Are you Kate Pegg?"

"Can you come in? I would prefer not to have the door open." Without waiting for Winston to answer, the woman turned and shuffled into the apartment.

Miller and Winston followed her into a plain room with bare walls, save for a small curtainless window opposite the door they had just walked through. The space showed no signs of having been decorated with any thought, and certainly no evidence of what Winston thought of as a woman's touch. In a corner, atop a small round table, three flowers wilted in a vase. A pair of mismatched chairs sat opposite a couch in the style of a chaise longue. A blanket had been thrown over the couch, though the effect did little to soften the space. Beyond the couch was a closed door.

The woman spread her skirts around her and sat on the couch, leaning into its armrest for support. Even in the dimly lit room, her face appeared pale. She motioned for Winston and Miller to sit in the chairs facing her. "Why are you looking for me?" she asked.

"You are Miss Pegg?" Winston repeated the question, as she'd still not given a direct answer. As he spoke, he pulled his small notepad from his pocket and nodded for Miller to do the same.

She held out her hand to show a ring on her finger. "I'm Mrs. Block, formerly Miss Pegg." Winston glanced at Miller to see if he'd caught the note of pride in the woman's voice. Miller's subtle lowering of his chin suggested he had.

Winston glanced around the room. Surely this was not the home a newly married woman expected to stay in for long. If she had taken the necklace, its value would go some way to financing better accommodations, or at least better furnishings.

"Well, Mrs. Block." Winston scratched a note on the page. "We've come to speak to you about your former employer, Mrs. Shuttleworth, and the necklace taken from her house."

Kate Block touched her throat where the necklace would sit. "I didn't steal it."

"Do you know who might have?"

She cast her gaze around the room, as if seeing its simplicity for the first time. "It could have been anyone. Mr. Shuttleworth received many visitors after Mrs. Shuttleworth died. He was so sad and distracted, he didn't pay attention to how some wandered through the house. And people knew she had beautiful jewellery. It was in her dressing room, locked, but the key was easy to find."

Winston recalled the cursory search he'd made of the room. "We found the key with no trouble," he acknowledged. "Do you recall the names of any of these visitors?" It would be easy enough for Miller to confirm whether any of them had visited Mrs. Shuttleworth's chamber, though why anyone would, Winston couldn't imagine. She shared a few names as Miller wrote them on his notepad. When she finished, Winston continued. "Do you recall when you last saw the necklace?"

Kate bit the corner of her lip. "It wasn't with her jewellery before she died." She continued to nibble. "I didn't steal it."

Winston made a note about Kate's reference to when she'd discovered the necklace was missing. He'd return to it later. For now, he wanted to set her at ease, keep her talking. "Mr. Shuttleworth also reported a game piece was missing. Do you remember when you saw that last?" he asked.

"Mrs. Shuttleworth kept that in her jewellery box." Kate shivered. "Would you excuse me a moment? I feel a chill coming on." She stood and gestured for Winston and Miller to remain seated. Her shuffle into the room behind the closed door was measured. A few moments later, she reappeared with a shawl wrapped around her shoulders. "I find this place rather drafty, don't you?" She looked toward the window. "We'll move from here shortly, once Clay has enough funds." She resumed her seat on the couch, then stood with a start. Winston and Miller rose with her. "Goodness, I haven't offered you anything. Though I'm afraid I haven't much to offer. We're not really set up yet to receive guests." Her cheeks coloured as she spoke. "I can fix us some tea, if you'd like."

"There's no need, Mrs. Block," Winston said. She had quickly changed the subject. It might serve the case to leave the theft for now, let her think he hadn't noticed. He pushed his hand beside his leg to signal to Miller that he was ending that line of questioning. Miller replied with the slightest raise of his fingers to indicate he understood.

Good man. "We do have something for you from Mrs. Plum. She isn't aware of your recent marriage. Otherwise, I'm sure she would have also sent congratulations." He reached into his bag and produced the bundle of scones with Kate and her sister's names on them. "And no need to share them with us. Mrs. Plum ensured we didn't leave empty-handed." He pulled out a corner of his own wrapped package and tucked it away again.

Kate hesitated. "You said you ate some?"

Miller nodded. "Yes. They were delicious."

Hearing this, Kate squealed with delight. "Oh, thank you, Detective. These are welcome." She set them down on the kitchen table and returned to the couch. She studied her fingers, clasped in her lap, then suddenly asked, "What if the necklace wasn't stolen? What if Mrs. Shuttleworth was planning to give it to someone?" She spoke the words as if she was testing the idea.

Interesting that she was returning to the subject unprompted. "Do you know who she might have given it to?"

"It wasn't stolen. That's what I was trying to tell Mr. Shuttleworth. He made me check that all her jewellery was there. He had a list, but I didn't need it. I knew every piece that Mrs. Shuttleworth owned. Besides, I can't read, so the list was no good to me." With a bit of a gleam in her eye, she added, "But Mrs. Shuttleworth was teaching me. To read, I mean." Then she returned her gaze to her lap, as if the impact of the death of her employer was hitting her afresh.

Winston encouraged her to continue. "And what did you report to Mr. Shuttleworth?"

"I had to tell him that the pearl necklace wasn't with the others. He cut me off and fired me before I could say anything more. He refused to speak to me again."

"And what would you have said, if he'd given you the chance?"

"I would have told him that it hadn't been there since just before Mrs. Shuttleworth died." She looked away. "You know, she was generous. Always giving gifts."

Winston thumbed to an earlier page in his notepad. At the Shuttleworth house, Mrs. Plum and Polly had said something similar. "What sort of gifts?" Winston asked.

"Different things."

"Jewellery? Necklaces?" The woman shrank at this question, though she retained eye contact with Winston. "Did she give you the necklace?"

Kate sniffed. "She trusted me."

Not an answer, but perhaps as close as they would get her to admitting she'd received the necklace. "What did she trust you with, Mrs. Block?" He kept his voice quiet.

"She told me that there was more to her husband's games than people knew. I didn't know what she meant, and then she—" Kate broke off. "I think Mrs. Shuttleworth was scared." She squeezed a corner of the shawl in her fist. "I didn't want to work in the house after she died. That's why I didn't say anything when Mr. Shuttleworth fired me."

What had scared Mrs. Shuttleworth? Winston wrote the question for himself. Beside him, Miller's pencil scratched on his notepad. "What did she do after she told you about the games?"

Kate Block shook her head slightly. "She just told me to tell no one. Even if I did, no one would believe me." The words came out as a sigh.

Miller locked his gaze on Mrs. Block. "Do you know what she was scared of?"

"I don't. I didn't ask her. And if I had, I'm not sure she would have told me. She was friendly, but we weren't friends."

Was she hiding a secret for Mrs. Shuttleworth? Did it matter? Perhaps not, but it would help to have some proof of what Kate was saying for when Winston told Shuttleworth that his wife had given away the necklace before she died. Winston pressed on. "What exactly did she say?"

"Like I said, 'Tell no one.' That was it."

Penelope Shuttleworth must have been a remarkable woman to instill such loyalty in a servant. But why keep her gift a secret? Winston could ask Susie whether she had received secret gifts from Mrs. Shuttleworth. Such past behaviour would support Kate's claim. "And you told nobody about the necklace?"

Betraying nothing, Kate remained still. She was keeping to her word.

"Did you enjoy working for her?" Winston asked.

Kate's mouth turned upward slightly. "I did. I'm sorry she's dead." She dropped the shawl's corner from her hand. "I don't know if it matters, but I did hear Mrs. Shuttleworth say something else. 'It's time, Edward. You must let her go.'"

Winston wrote the words in his notepad. "Do you know who she meant?"

Kate shook her head "I don't. It was late. They'd just returned from a party, and Mrs. Shuttleworth had asked me to have a bath ready for when she returned."

"Thank you for your time." Winston slid his notepad into his satchel. "Before we go, Mrs. Block, we spoke with your sister today. She's rather concerned for you."

She stiffened. "I've been meaning to see her, but I've been busy . . . making our home. Though I don't expect we will live here long." Her eyes swept the small room. "We'd like to start a family, and this isn't a place for a baby."

Winston also surveyed the neat, sparsely furnished room. It lacked the little details—books, trinkets, personal touches—that marked a space as belonging to someone. But these were acquired with time as memories were made.

Kate Block continued. "I haven't been feeling well, but I'm sure I'll be better soon." She looked at the package of scones. "Mrs. Plum's baking always did the trick." The memory of the scone he'd consumed made Winston's mouth water.

"When did you start living here?" Miller asked. Winston would have to congratulate him on confirming what her sister had stated.

"With Clay? The day Mr. Shuttleworth fired me. Clay asked me to stay with him, which I refused to do until we married. We said our vows that day."

"Your sister doesn't know that you've married. You didn't invite your family?" Winston asked.

She waved a hand, rejecting the idea. "Susie quit when I was fired. I'm sure she's already found a new position, and I didn't want to trouble her. Clay is my family now." Winston noted the difference in perspective from how close Susie had claimed to be with her sister. Wouldn't Kate have wanted her sister present?

"What about his brother?" Miller sat forward. "Your sister, Susie, said that your husband lived with his brother."

"When Pauly heard I was moving in, he moved out. Wanted to be able to walk around in the buff and couldn't do that with me around."

Miller coloured at her reference to nudity. "He told you that?"

Kate winced and let out a raspy laugh. "Of course not. He knew we were getting hitched and gave us some space. We get along great, Pauly and me. He's moved across the street. Mr. Chance, he owns this building and another. He had an apartment come available and let Pauly move in." As she spoke, she rubbed her throat.

"Mrs. Block, how long have you been ill?" Winston asked.

She slumped on the couch. "I haven't felt well for a few weeks, though I started feeling a little better yesterday, and even more so today. I think it just takes getting used to, living with so many other people around. I was thinking to ask Pauly if he might trade places with us in case it's the air or something in here. He's not affected since he lived here before. But I—" She placed her hand on her chest, covering her collarbone. "I'm not sure what it is."

Winston stood. She was holding something back, but they were unlikely to get more from her today. "We won't trouble you any longer, then. Congratulations on your recent nuptials. As I said, your sister expressed concern for you." He weighed how to say his next thought. "It would help greatly if we could see the necklace."

"I'm awfully tired, Detective. Can it wait?" Fatigue had drained colour from Kate's features.

"Perhaps you can bring it to the station tomorrow. We will need to verify that it was not stolen." He took care to deliver the instruction so she didn't interpret it as an accusation. He could be firmer with her tomorrow.

"Thank you, Detective. I will speak to Susie." She gestured over Winston's shoulder. "I'm afraid I won't see you to the door."

"No matter, Mrs. Block. Please don't get up." He hitched his bag on his shoulder.

The policemen left Kate sniffling and leaning against the arm of the couch, adjusting the shawl. As they descended the staircase, Winston asked, "Well, Thomas, what have we learned?"

Miller counted his observations off on his fingers. "We've learned that Kate Pegg is now Kate Block and her sister doesn't know this. Kate claims she didn't steal the necklace, and that Mrs. Shuttleworth gave her the necklace shortly before she died. And what about what she said about Shuttleworth's business? Or Mrs. Shuttleworth being scared?"

"Yes, those last points are intriguing, though I'm not sure how much we'll need to follow up on them, now that we know what happened to the necklace. As I said, we will need to verify the necklace was a gift, which may be difficult. I will tell Mr. Shuttleworth, but I believe we need to consider the robbery investigation nearly closed."

He clapped Miller on the back, satisfied that they had come to such a swift solution. "Well done."

The two men exited the building. "It's been a long day. Let's leave anything more until tomorrow," Winston said. He started to walk away, then turned and called after Miller. "Since it's on your way home, please stop by Miss Pegg's house to tell her we saw her sister and ask her whether she too received gifts from Mrs. Shuttleworth. But best stay silent about her new marital status. That's a surprise her sister can share."

CHAPTER 9

Riley

AFTER HER CONVERSATION with Jules, Riley had been surprisingly untroubled by dreams about Nick or Claire or work. Instead, she'd had a dream about starting a new job as a researcher at a different museum. Throughout the whole dream, she'd been searching for something, but she'd been unable to articulate what it was. When she woke, she realized it was Jack's journal she'd been looking for. There'd been such a sense of emptiness in the dream. Was Jules right? Was she just trying to run away?

She walked to work to clear her head and arrived at the museum feeling refreshed. She started her day with a renewed resolve to demonstrate how good she was at her job. While Claire might not have selected her, she was still a good researcher and she would make sure the task Claire had given her to do was done well.

She'd compiled a list of several resources to search, and her first pass had yielded enough notes that she was certain she could build an engaging exhibit. She opened a document to begin a report to Claire—and Nick—suggesting they move forward with the idea. She could do this.

Just as she was finishing the document, her phone pinged with an alert.

I can't make lunch today. Still not feeling great.

Riley stared at the screen. She and Lucy were supposed to have lunch at their favourite place so they could plan a visit with their mother. This was the second time Lucy had cancelled on her. Maybe the stress of being an influencer was getting to her sister.

OK. But we need to talk about Mom's visit.

You can handle it. I'll make it up to you. Promise.

Riley rolled her eyes. It wasn't as if preparing for their mother to spend a few days in Vancouver required a lot of work, but Lucy would inevitably complain when whatever Riley chose for them to do wasn't what she was interested in, even if Riley took great care to find activities that suited their different personalities.

Their mother had moved to Victoria a couple of years earlier, after their father died. She'd needed distance from the city and its memories. But now she made a point of visiting Vancouver every couple of months to spend time with her girls, and Riley cherished these weekends. She and Lucy tried to find one new restaurant or café for them to visit, or maybe an art show or concert. The rest of the time they just enjoyed each other's company, simply reading or watching a movie, or—more often, lately—sharing memories. Each visit, the pain of his loss had become less acute. This visit would be the first one since the whole Educoin affair, and Riley wanted it to be extra-special.

Riley tapped out a terse reply, then deleted it before sending, knowing that her sister wouldn't respond well to it. She settled for a thumbs-up emoji. She would use the found time to research the Shuttleworth robbery for Jack.

When she did this kind of work for Jack, her connection with him, with the time in which he lived, grew stronger. But she'd never be able to tell anyone about it. She was afraid of how it would be used. Or misused. She could imagine the requests for her to ask Jack to send a message along to a relative—"Invest in Company X," or "Search for gold in this area!"—or propose schemes to alter a family's fortunes. Or anguished pleas to tell someone not to leave the house on the day they would be struck by a car. This last scenario, where she might help people avoid pain, held some appeal for Riley, but even such a wonderful gift would inevitably be corrupted. But worse than any consequence she could imagine, she dreaded losing her vital connection with Jack.

Riley began by pulling up the photos she'd found in her online search. She connected her laptop to a larger monitor and enlarged the image of the men at the Gentlemen's Club. She examined each face. According to the information accompanying the image, on one side of Shuttleworth was Jack's uncle, the chief constable. On the other was Charles Steele from the *Western Daily News*, one of the local newspapers. Also in the picture was Mr. Collins, whom she knew Jack had interviewed in previous cases. A frisson of excitement shot through her with a thought: these men had spoken with Jack.

She turned her attention to the other photo, the one of Mr. and Mrs. Shuttleworth. It had been taken about a year before Penelope Shuttleworth's death. The couple looked happy, at least as happy as anyone in photos from the late nineteenth century appeared. She couldn't tell the colour of Mrs. Shuttleworth's dress, but it was light—yellow or cream, perhaps. The bodice was narrow and the skirt was full, accentuating her waist. Gloves stretched past her elbows. Riley zoomed in, pausing to look at the jewellery Mrs. Shuttleworth was wearing. A pearl necklace rested at her collarbone and matching earrings adorned her ears. She looked elegant and beautiful. Riley could imagine the swish of the gown's fabric as the woman moved, though the dress itself must have been heavy.

Mr. Shuttleworth's fingers rested just inside the pocket of his evening jacket. The collar of his crisp white shirt looked stiff and uncomfortable. Yet he had a hint of a smile on his face. What sort of occasion were they attending? Riley entered a few words into the search engine. The city had a vibrant opera house at the time, owned by the railway as a draw to bring people to the city. Before long she had constructed a scene of the two of them stepping out of a cab in front of the Vancouver Opera House, the light cast from nearby street lamps making Mrs. Shuttleworth appear to glow. Did Jack attend the opera? He'd never mentioned it, and he was likely too busy solving crimes.

She brought her attention back to Mrs. Shuttleworth. Something about her image looked familiar, though Riley couldn't pin it down. Perhaps she had seen her in a photo for some other project. She stared at the photo a little longer, then began a new search.

CHAPTER 10

Jack

"**There's a woman** here who's asking for you. Says she spoke with you yesterday." When the desk constable spoke, Winston looked up from the notes he'd been reviewing. He sat up taller in the chief constable's chair and cast his gaze over the officer's shoulder toward the small entrance area behind him. This was the man's usual post, where he routinely stood at a tall desk, available to meet any members of the public who sought police assistance. Winston could see only the woman's arm.

"She said it was urgent." The desk constable stepped further into the room and added in a hushed voice, "She's been crying, sir."

It must be Kate Block with the necklace after reflecting on their conversation the day before. But why would she be crying? Had she actually stolen it and simply made a vague suggestion of having received it as a gift? If so, her tears may be evidence of her shame.

Shame. It led people to make bad decisions.

Winston reached for the stone in his pocket, then gathered the few pages that were spread on his desk. He rose and slid his arms into his jacket. If it was Kate Block waiting to speak to him, his plan to give her time to bring the necklace to the station had been effective. He nodded to the constable and walked to the desk at the front of the station.

He stopped as soon as he saw who stood at the desk.

Susie Pegg.

Had she stolen the necklace? Had she performed a desperate act, thinking that nobody would notice the necklace was gone, and then allowed her sister to be accused as the thief? Susie's face betrayed fear, and Winston's heart rate picked up. His thoughts raced before he found his focus. "Miss Pegg, how can I help you?"

"It's Kate." Susie wiped a tear from her eye, though her voice stayed strong. "I think she's been murdered."

Winston let his mouth hang open. Had he misheard her? Murdered? Surely not. He'd seen her only yesterday. "What makes you think she's been murdered?" He fought to regain his composure. Where was Miller? He caught the desk officer's eye and made a small gesture, pointing his head toward the entrance to the main room of the station, hoping he'd understand the signal to get Thomas Miller.

"Why else would she be dead? She's not yet twenty!" Susie's voice rose as she spoke.

"Come this way, Miss Pegg." He ushered her into the station's small interview room. Winston mused aloud as they entered the room. "She seemed to be recovering from an illness when I spoke with her yesterday. Perhaps her condition worsened and she died in her sleep." As soon as the words left his mouth, Winston knew they were a mistake. Susie Pegg was not a woman who would appreciate being told she was wrong. He changed his tack. "Please take a seat. May I get you a cup of tea?"

She looked at him, tears welling. "I'd rather you find out who killed her, Detective."

He sat down opposite her, pulling his notepad from his pocket. Miller slid into the room and sat beside Winston. The men exchanged quick nods. Winston would fill him in after they'd spoken with Miss Pegg.

"When did you find her? Where?" Winston asked.

The woman's tears flowed freely now. She couldn't seem to find her voice.

Miller surprised Winston by leaning over the table and resting his hand on the grieving sister's arm. "Tell me what you know."

She squared her shoulders and dabbed at her cheeks with a hand-kerchief, bracing herself. Her eyes moved from Miller's face to Winston's and back again. "After I learned you'd spoken with Kate, I decided to find her this morning before going to work, see if she'd come home." She spoke softly, hesitantly.

Miller spoke again, his tone encouraging. "You went to the apartment building where Clayton Block lived?" he asked.

"I did. I thought he lived in a house, and I almost turned around when I saw that it wasn't. Thought I must be mistaken." The words came out hoarse and she cleared her throat, but it made no difference when she spoke again. "The condition of the building was far below what I expected for her." She pulled her arm from under Miller's hand and began squeezing her hands, alternating between each one.

"Where did you expect him to live?"

The squeezing paused for a moment, then resumed when she spoke. Perhaps she needed stillness to gather her thoughts. "I expected him to have better accommodation. He's always smartly dressed." As if she realized something, she focused her gaze on Winston. "When you saw her yesterday, how was she?"

Winston cleared his throat. "As I said, she was recovering from an illness, maybe suffering from a chill. What did you do when you found your sister?"

"I came here immediately. I didn't know what else to do."

"You did the right thing. I will have the desk officer contact the medical examiner to arrange for him to meet us there," Winston said.

"What must I do now? Stay here?" Her shoulders slumped as she stared past him at the wall. "I'll need to tell my father."

"It's better if you go home and wait for Constable Miller and me. First, we will examine your sister and hear what the doctor says." He gestured for her to rise. When she did, Winston and Miller also stood. "Why is it that you think your sister has been murdered?"

"She just didn't look right." Susie stumbled to find the right description. "I mean, it wasn't like she was bleeding or anything. Actually, she looked quite peaceful, like she was asleep on the couch. But something about her looked unnatural. . . awkward, maybe."

"She was on the couch, not in her bed? Did you see Mr. Block?" Miller asked.

Susie shook her head. "No. I wanted to see Kate before I went to the house where I'm working. He wasn't there when I arrived."

"Do you know if that's usual for him? To be out of the house so early?" Winston asked. If it was murder, Block would be at the top of the suspect list.

She dropped her gaze to her feet. "I have no idea what hours he keeps. My sister. . ." Susie sniffed. "My sister would be able to answer that. But she can't." This sentence brought on another onslaught of tears. She returned to her chair and the policemen did the same.

Winston let her collect herself before he continued. "What about your father? Had you told him that we'd asked after Kate? Could he have gone to speak to her?"

She fixed her gaze on Winston. "My father would never hurt her." Her voice was clear, firm. She shook the idea away with her head. "As I told you yesterday, he wasn't even aware that Kate had gone. He works hard. The hours are long."

Winston sensed she would say more and waited for her to continue.

"When he finishes, he typically goes for a drink. He sits with men he knows from the mill or from other jobs. It's how he learns of additional work if he needs it." She wiped her eye with her handkerchief. "When we worked at the Shuttleworths', especially when they had a party, Kate and I would arrive home after him, and he was often already asleep. Other nights, we would retire before he returned. We tried to spend Sunday evenings together after going to church, though Kate, she hadn't joined us recently."

Winston scratched a note. "Was he ever angry with you or your sister?"

Colour drained from her face as she considered this. "My father? Of course. What parent isn't?"

"Has he ever been violent?" As soon as he'd asked it, Winston knew the question was ill-timed. Beside him, Miller stiffened. They had no idea how Mrs. Block had died, and Susie may be unwilling to answer openly if she thinks he suspects her father. Winston drew in a slow breath. He needed to be more strategic, and sensitive, in his questioning.

"Are you asking whether my father might have killed my sister?" She held Winston's eyes. "If you knew my father, you would realize how terrible that question is."

Winston extended his hand toward her arm, and Susie pushed herself away from the table. Winston leaned back in his chair to help her increase the distance between them.

As if sensing his cue, Miller motioned at Winston. "Detective Winston doesn't mean to offend you, Miss Pegg. If your sister was murdered, we have to ask questions about who would want to harm her. Sometimes the questions are uncomfortable." She nodded but remained behind the table.

Winston rose. He was thankful Miller was in the room and had righted the interview that Winston had nearly steered off course. What had he been thinking? "Now that you are recovered, Constable Miller and I are going to go to Mr. Block's to meet the medical examiner. You may return home, and we will find you there this afternoon." He narrowed his eyes. "Would you like us to send an officer with you? To make sure you get home safely?"

"I'll manage on my own, thanks." She exited the room and squared her shoulders. "Please tell me as soon as you learn anything." Her voice had gained strength since leaving the interview room.

Winston escorted Susie Pegg to the door of the police station. As they walked, he asked another question. "What about your new employer? You are expected there this morning?"

"I'll get a message to the house. I can't work today." She reddened. "I'm sure they will understand, and if they don't, I will find somewhere else to work. The city has many houses and few maids."

"I'm truly sorry to hear of your sister's death." Winston knew what the loss of a sibling felt like, though he couldn't compare his own pain with hers.

"Thank you," she said before turning on her heel to leave the station.

As he watched her, he fought the urge to call her back, thinking he'd omitted an important question about her sister. The thought would return, no doubt, when he saw Kate Block's body.

*

ON THEIR WAY to the Block residence, Winston and Miller compared notes about their conversation with Susie Pegg. "She didn't have clear evidence for why she thinks her sister was murdered," Miller said. "Only that she was too young to die. And that she looked 'unnatural.'" Miller made a face that revealed his skepticism. "But when we saw Kate yesterday, she complained of having been ill. Do you think perhaps Susie is overreacting? That her sister died naturally?"

"I share the same thought, Miller," Winston said as the streetcar jostled them back and forth. "Still, Susie is correct. Kate was young, and she did say she had been feeling better yesterday. She certainly didn't seem to be at death's door."

"Maybe a few steps away," Miller said.

"Let's see what Doctor Evans has to say when he examines her." Winston was mindful that other passengers might be listening.

"I did ask her yesterday about receiving gifts from Mrs. Shuttleworth. She said she'd never been given anything, but her sister received a nice comb. She thought there might have been something else small, but she wasn't certain."

"A necklace is a considerably grander gesture than a comb," Winston said as they stepped down from the streetcar. Was there meaning behind the gift?

They arrived at the apartment building to find Doctor Evans stepping out of his carriage. "Well, Detective Winston and Constable Miller. We find ourselves together again."

Winston nodded. "And Miller and I find ourselves here again." Confusion crossed Evans's face. "We spoke with the dead woman just yesterday."

"Did you?" The doctor's eyes widened with surprise. "About what?"

"A jewellery theft."

"Do you think this is a robbery gone wrong?"

"I doubt anything was stolen from here, but let's not shut our minds to the possibility." Winston led the way through the building to the Blocks' apartment. The door was unlocked. Inside, as Susie had described, Kate looked to be asleep on the low couch, her arm dangling toward the floor. A blanket covered the lower part of her body. Winston pulled out his notepad and wrote himself a reminder to ask Susie whether she had found her sister this way or had covered her up. As he stood closer to the body, Kate's face appeared wax-like, almost glistening.

Beside him, Miller's pencil moved quickly. Winston peered to see what he was writing and was pleased to see a sketch of the position of the body, including the other pieces of furniture in the room. Miller looked up, his eyebrows arched in an expression of uncertainty.

"Continue, Thomas. This will be very helpful. We should look into acquiring a camera for the station. I think it would soon prove indispensable."

"Chief Philpott has never seen the need, sir," Miller said.

"I'll address it with him. Better yet, let's just obtain one. He won't be able to argue with the results." Winston swallowed. "In fact, I'll pay for it." His uncle wouldn't be able to complain if the expense was not the constabulary's.

Winston turned to Evans. "What are your first impressions, Doctor?"

Evans bent over the body. With his stomach flipping, Winston stepped back, grateful that he didn't need to get as close to it as Evans. After a minute, Evans rose. "I don't see any obvious damage to her head or face but can't draw any conclusions until I examine her more closely." He tenderly removed the blanket to reveal her dressing gown tucked around her ankles. "Is she likely to have done this herself, Detective?"

"Her sister found her. I will ask her if she tucked Mrs. Block in before she came to the station." Winston was moved by this tender detail. "It looks like a final act of comfort." The words evoked an image of his dead brother. He knew very little about the circumstances of that death. Who had found him? Where? His anger and hurt had been so great when he learned the truth that he hadn't been able to ask those simple questions. He brushed the side of his pocket to feel for Ellis's stone.

Evans's voice broke through Winston's moment of reflection. Winston chided himself for his lapse as Evans tugged at the fabric of the gown, then brushed his hands over her limbs and torso. "I will preserve her dignity here," the doctor said. "Once I get her back to the morgue, I will be able to give you more precise impressions. But for now, I can tell you that none of her bones appear to be broken."

"What about her neck?" Winston asked.

"Her head is not at an angle indicative of fracture, but, as I say, I will know more later."

Winston turned away from the body. Miller had also taken several steps from the couch to continue his sketching. "Thomas, do you see anything different from our visit here yesterday?"

"I don't, sir. The few belongings that were here remain." Miller focused his attention on the apartment door. "Should I find her husband? Tell him?"

"He could be anywhere. But yes, we should try his place of employment."

"Didn't Mrs. Block say that her brother-in-law lives across the street? Shall I check to see if he's at home? He would know where his brother works." Miller avoided looking at the body.

He could hardly scold Miller for his uneasiness around bodies given his own discomfort. As much as he wanted to leave the room, Winston agreed that Miller should find the brother-in-law. "Yes, go. Meet me back at the station rather than returning here." Winston waved his constable away.

Miller made for the door. In the hall, the tread of his footsteps quickened in pace as he neared the stairs. Evans continued preparing hte body for its removal to the morgue. "Detective, your constable needs a stronger stomach if he's going to make this work his vocation."

"I know, Evans. This scene isn't in any way gruesome, so I'm surprised at his reaction." As he spoke, Winston noted a mild queasiness in his own stomach. Death, even bloodless, was unsettling.

"Not wanting to be in the room when I examine a body is understandable, but this—" Evans swept his arm in a low arc. "This could be a woman sleeping, were it not for the colour of her skin." He bent closer, bringing his face within an inch of the dead woman's face. "How long ago did you say her sister found her?"

Winston pulled his watch from his pocket. "We've been here twenty minutes, and it took us that long to get here. Susie was at the station, which would place her here, I'd say, at least ninety minutes ago. Why?"

"It's helpful to know when determining the time of death." The doctor placed the back of his hand on her forehead, then her cheek, then her forearm. After a minute he nodded. "Already her body is cooling." Evans lifted her arm and let it drop to her side. "Her death was within the last three or four hours, though. Rigor mortis is only just setting into her limbs."

Winston pulled on the chain of his pocket watch. "I wonder what time her husband left for work today. It's just past ten, and Susie said she didn't see him when she found Kate." Winston wrote his question in his notepad. "Do you need anything else, Doctor? Can we bring the body back to the station?"

"I have what I need." Evans looked out the window. "I see the wagon has arrived."

"Good. I'm just going to get a few notes down before I leave." Winston pointed to his notepad. "Can you let the men downstairs know they can take her?"

Evans slipped into his coat. "I will. I don't see anything unusual about this death. She may have had a heart condition or some other illness."

"When I saw her yesterday to ask her about a jewellery theft, she lacked energy. She said she'd been feeling unwell for a few weeks, but she certainly didn't seem on the verge of dying."

"Some illnesses have a period of remission. Did she share any of her symptoms?"

Winston searched his notes. He hadn't specifically written her complaints down, but recalling the conversation was easier if he had a point of reference. "She said she'd been tired. Thought it might be something in the apartment." He tapped his pencil on his book. "I'm out of my depth here, but what effect does a burden of guilt have on the body? If she had stolen something and then lied to everyone about it—including the police—could the guilt from all that deception lead to serious illness?"

"I am not sure there is a medical condition I could point to," Evans said. "But our bodies do react when uncomfortable. Think of how you feel when in the morgue."

Winston felt the colour rise to his cheeks, and Evans reached a hand to Winston's arm. "I know you're working on it, Jack. Nevertheless, at this stage I don't see anything that points to needing a police investigation. Her heart may have simply given up."

If that was the case, Susie Pegg had simply overreacted when she found her sister. Still, a persistent uneasiness remained with Winston. "Even so, I'd like to attend the autopsy, Evans. I'm still involved in the case of this missing necklace, and I feel I should follow your findings to their conclusion, as she was a primary suspect in the case." Evans agreed just as two men entered the apartment with a stretcher.

"Ah, good men. Yes, you may remove the body," Evans said, stepping aside to let them pass.

Winston watched them gently place the body on the stretcher and manoeuvre it out of the room. Evans tapped the brim of his hat, signalling a wordless goodbye to Winston as he followed the body out the door.

Finding himself alone in the apartment, Winston felt the need to collect his thoughts. He sat at the small table to write a note to Riley. A chill passed through him when he glanced at the now-empty couch.

Dear Riley,

Yesterday, I met the maid who reported the missing necklace. Today, I am sitting again in her apartment, only for a very different reason: to see her body. She was found deceased this morning. I am left feeling unsettled as I spoke with her so recently. She had been unwell but thought she was on the mend. With the death of her employer, Penelope Shuttleworth, just a few weeks ago, I feel ill at ease. She had also been a healthy woman until she had a brief illness.

Warmly,

Jack

CHAPTER 11

Riley

A **CHILL CREPT** down Riley's spine as she read Jack's note. As a police officer, he would encounter death regularly, but to speak to someone one day and see them dead the next must be unnerving. She set her hand on the journal to steady her thoughts. Jack hadn't shared the name of the maid, so Riley couldn't look up her name or death certificate. She jotted a quick note to him to ask for that information.

She opened the document she'd been working on for the exhibit. Claire had agreed that there was enough material to begin planning an exhibit about how the lives of domestic workers had changed since the early days of the city. Riley hadn't seen Nick to discuss it with him. She'd get as much done as she could while Claire was still officially the boss.

As she wrapped up work for the day, a sound pierced the usually silent archive. After a couple of rings sounded again, she realized it was her own cellphone, which rarely rang. She pulled it from her bag to see Alex's flashing on the screen. Why would Lucy's husband be calling? Riley's heart fluttered as she swiped with her thumb and brought the phone to her ear. "Hey. What's up?"

"It's your sister. She's pretty sick, and I think she should go to the hospital. But she's refusing. Can you talk some sense into her?"

Riley gripped the phone tighter, remembering in a flash the time her mother had phoned with news that Riley's father was being taken to the hospital. He never left. The phone slipped slightly as her palms grew damp. She wiped one, then the other, on her jeans. "I'm on my way."

"See you soon," Alex said.

Riley's thoughts swam. Lucy's gala was tomorrow night. There was no way she would miss that, but dismissing Alex's concerns wouldn't be helpful. And she was curious about why Lucy had blown her off twice this week. She grabbed her coat and headed out the door.

The apartment Alex and Lucy shared was about a twenty-minute walk through downtown Vancouver. Along the way, Riley picked up some soup and a bag of Lucy's favourite sweets. Alex buzzed her up to their floor and met her at the elevator. When the door opened, the worry pinching Alex's features made Riley shiver. "What's wrong with her, Alex?"

"She hasn't slept well for days. Last night she took a sleeping pill and hasn't gotten out of bed since," he said, his voice hushed.

"Why isn't she sleeping well? Does she have a cold? A fever? Nausea?"

"No, nothing like that. She says she's tired and her head aches. The last couple of days, she's also had some tremors in her hands."

None of these symptoms sounded pleasant, but they were hardly worth a trip to emergency. "Why do you think she needs to go to the hospital?" Riley asked. A few days of rest sounded more like what Lucy needed. Clearly Alex's concern for Lucy had blown up into an overreaction. Lucy had chosen a good partner, even if he was overprotective. Still, it was unlike Lucy to spend so long in bed.

Alex cocked his head. "Maybe you're right and she's just run down. She's been so busy with these new projects she's taken on."

"I'll talk to her, see what she says. Then we can decide what to do," Riley said.

Alex took Riley's jacket, and she stepped out of her boots and headed toward her sister's bedroom. Before she crossed the threshold, she shot a glance at Alex. He nodded, his face grim. He really seemed to be taking Lucy's illness seriously.

Lucy was propped against a pile of pillows. Only she didn't look anything like Lucy. Riley hadn't seen her sister without makeup on since Lucy had moved into this apartment with Alex. Riley stepped closer. The person in the bed looked drawn, with limp hair and sunken eyes. "Lucy?" Riley tiptoed forward tentatively. Her heart raced at the sight of her sister looking so unwell.

Lucy turned her head to look in her direction. "Riley? What are you doing here? I told you I had to reschedule."

"Alex invited me over." She held up the bag in her hand. "I got you some gummy bears."

Lucy scrunched her nose. "Do you know what's in those? I can't eat them."

"I thought they were your favourite." Riley set the bag down on the nightstand beside the necklace Jane had given Lucy the other night. She had never known her sister to refuse gummy bears.

Lucy shook her head. "They're filled with sugar and other things that wreak havoc on your body."

"Since when?"

"Since forever. But I've really been paying attention to my health lately."

"Clearly," Riley said, unable to avoid the sarcasm in her response.

"You don't understand." Lucy turned her head away. "Thanks for coming over. You didn't need to, though. I'll be fine."

Riley sat on the side of her sister's bed. "Are you eating? If you won't have these gummy bears, what about something else? I brought soup. Or I could ask Alex to fix you up some pasta. Spaghetti?"

Lucy turned her head again. "I don't want any pasta. But what's in the soup?"

"Vegetables. Broth. Soupy things," Riley said. "You need something to keep your energy up." Riley waited for her sister to respond, but she just picked up her phone and started scrolling. Rude.

Riley could see there was nothing to be gained by continuing to press Lucy. She stood and left the room, stopping in the bathroom. Lucy's side of the sink was cluttered with brightly coloured vitamin bottles, tubes of cream, and a jumble of makeup paraphernalia. What were they all used for? Moving out and getting married hadn't changed her sister's tendency to spread out the clutter of her life. Riley shuddered, thankful that restoring order from her sister's chaos was no longer her responsibility.

In the kitchen, she found Alex chopping vegetables. "You said she hasn't gotten out of bed, but she must be feeling awful. She refused gummy bears." She pushed her package toward Alex. "Keep these for when she's better."

"It's been a while since she's eaten anything like that," Alex said. "She's on this 'careful eating' kick." He paused his chopping to create air quotes with his fingers.

"What's 'careful eating'?" Riley mimicked Alex's hand gesture.

"The rules seem to keep changing, but each week, she is supposed to eat a certain amount of different nutrients. It's tracked through an app or something."

Maybe that's what Lucy was looking up on her phone. "Right. Lucy has gone through all the different diet and lifestyle options, so this isn't new. Do you know if she can eat soup?"

"I've tried. She won't eat anything out of a tin." He pointed at the vegetables. "That's why I'm making some from scratch."

Riley tried to remember when they'd last had a sister night. It must have been many weeks ago now. Was it before or after their mom's last visit? With their schedules—mostly Lucy's—and with Lucy no longer living in the same apartment as Riley, it meant they had to plan to spend time together. She couldn't remember anything that stood out about their last sister night. Riley had bought an assortment of treats. Had there been more than usual left over? "What else has changed with her eating, Alex?"

"She's completely eliminated sugar. A dessert every now and again wouldn't hurt, but she's firmly against them right now." At the stove, he swept vegetables from the cutting board into a stockpot, where they landed with a sizzle. "You know her. Eventually she'll find something else to embrace, and we'll be swimming in chocolate soon enough."

Alex was probably right. And with her influencer aspirations, Lucy was probably ahead of the curve. Maybe too much sugar wasn't a good thing anyway.

"Okay, well, I hope she feels better soon. She's supposed to go to that gala tomorrow."

"Thanks for coming over, Riley. I really needed another set of eyes on her." He stirred the pot. "Yeah, the gala. She insisted this morning she'd be there, but I'm not so sure."

Neither was Riley. Lucy hardly looked like someone who would be at a party with the who's who of the city in twenty-four hours. But her sister had a history of pulling off remarkable things in very little time when she put her mind to it.

CHAPTER 12

Jack

AT THE STATION, Winston entered the morgue to find Doctor Evans removing the dressing gown from Kate Block's body. Rather than cutting the gown off, he eased it from her in a respectful manner. Evans folded the clothing, then met Winston's eyes.

"Detective, you find me about to start. I know you're not usually comfortable observing."

"I'm not." Winston breathed deeply to steel himself, instantly regretting it when the lingering smell of the room reached his nostrils and throat. Through gritted teeth, he continued. "I can hardly expect a more suitable reaction from Miller if I can't control my own. Do you mind if I stay?"

"Not at all." Evans draped a sheet of cloth over the now-naked body. "I will begin at her head."

Despite the lack of gore, Winston battled queasiness as Evans moved his hands down the body, palpating as he went. Winston rocked from foot to foot, trying to overcome his reaction to the room's atmosphere. "Actually, Doctor, I will have to let Miller think what he will. You can find me at my desk when you finish."

Evans gave a low chuckle, and he shooed Winston from the room. "Until later, Detective."

As Winston left the morgue, Miller approached. "Sir, I've brought Mr. Block. His brother told me where to find him. The brother was here when I brought Block. They're both sitting in our interview room."

"Excellent. Did you tell him about his wife?" Winston motioned for Miller to follow him down the hallway, fighting the urge to gulp at the clearer air.

"I did. He's very upset."

"She was alive when he left for work this morning?"

"He said so."

Miller followed Winston into the interview room. As Miller had promised, two men occupied the room. One man sat calmly with his hands clasped on the table, his stare focused at the wall. Beside him, the one who appeared to be the older of the two was in clear distress. His hair stood on end where he'd raked his fingers through it. He turned, red-eyed, to watch them enter. This must be Clayton Block, and the other man his brother, Paul. That they were brothers there was no doubt. Their features were similar, and they shared the same thick, well-maintained moustaches, though one had fairer hair than the other.

"Gentlemen, my name is Detective Jack Winston. You have met Constable Thomas Miller. I am saddened by the reason that we meet today. Please accept our condolences." The policemen slid into the two empty chairs opposite the brothers. Winston spoke to the wild-haired man. "We met your wife, Kate, yesterday."

Both men looked at Winston now. Clayton Block's eyes were clouded with grief. Winston couldn't place the emotion in the brother's eyes. "You did? She didn't say. Where?" Clayton asked.

"In your apartment. We are investigating missing items from her former employer's home."

"Right. She didn't steal them." His voice had taken on a defensive tone.

"You're certain?"

"Kate told me everything. And she told me she didn't steal them." He paused. "She never lied."

Winston noted the man was already speaking of his wife in the past tense. For most, accepting someone's death took longer than the hour or so since Miller would have found the grieving man. Was his wife's death not a surprise? He held up his hand. Better if the husband thought the theft was insignificant to the police. "The theft isn't why we're speaking today." He leaned toward the table, and his chair creaked. "As you know, your wife's body was discovered today. We need information to discover the cause of her death. It is standard for any death that occurs outside a hospital." He pulled his notepad from his pocket. "Constable Miller brought you here because the medical examiner is determining the cause of death."

Face ashen, Clayton Block nodded. "I understand." Beside him, his brother lay a hand on his shoulder. "This is my brother Paul," said Clayton, as if suddenly reminded he'd forgotten the necessary formalities.

"Paul." Winston nodded at the man. He turned back to Clayton. "When did you last see your wife alive?"

"When I left this morning." The man blinked rapidly, perhaps the realization that was the last time he would see his wife just now dawning on him.

Winston had seen a similar reaction before when informing someone of a loved one's death. "When was that?"

"Early. I just started to work for the post office and needed to be early to sort letters for delivery." Block swept his hand toward the door. "I arrived there at seven."

"How long have you worked for the post office?"

"Just a few weeks." He wrung his hands. "I used to be a carpenter. It's good work. But I wanted to find something more reliable in case the building trade slows down around here." He paused and studied his hands. "And I wanted to marry Kate. Offer her stability." That status—married—still so new to him, was no longer his. "Most days I'm at the main branch, where he found me." Clayton Block jutted his chin toward Miller. "Sometimes I collect the mail from the train, or, if needed, I may go out to deliver letters or parcels."

"And when you left today, was that the time you typically leave for work?"

"This morning? Yes, I left at the usual time. Maybe just a little before." Block wiped his face with a calloused hand. "Kate was half-asleep." He looked away and flushed. "In the bed. She whispered for me to kiss her goodbye." He tugged at the collar of his shirt. "Who found her?"

Winston leaned forward. If Block last saw his wife in the bedroom, she must have moved herself to the couch. He nodded at Miller, who made a note.

"Was it you that found her?" Clayton rephrased his question. "Why were you at our apartment? Were you there to ask her more questions?" Block's tone had become defensive again.

"Her sister, Susie, came to the station this morning saying she had found Kate dead." Winston considered whether to share Susie's suspicion with Block. If nothing else, he could gauge the man's reaction to the idea, even though Evans had suggested it was a natural death. "Susie seemed convinced that Kate had been murdered."

"Murdered?" Colour seeped away from Block's face. "How did she die?" he whispered. While someone might be able to feign surprise with a gasp, no man could control how his face coloured. But was this the shock that his wife might have been murdered, or was it that Winston had mentioned murder in the first place?

"That's what our medical examiner, Doctor Evans, is determining." Horror flashed on Block's face. Winston imagined the man picturing his dead wife. "There was no evidence of violence, if that is your question. And perhaps I should clarify: Susie Pegg suggested Kate had been murdered, but I saw nothing at your apartment to indicate that was the case. Doctor Evans's investigation is a matter of routine."

Block nodded. "Thank you." The widower relaxed at Winston's reassurance. "When can I see her?"

"We will take you to her after Evans completes his examination."

"You're certain she's dead?"

Winston held the man's eyes for a moment, then answered, "Yes, Mr. Block. Doctor Evans has confirmed it. I'm sorry." He had seen this before—the bereaved clinging to the hope that the doctor had made a mistake. "Your wife had been ill recently?"

Block wrung his hands and tugged at his sleeve. "She had been feeling poorly, yes."

"Did she say anything to you about the missing items? The necklace or the game piece?"

"No. She enjoyed working with Mrs. Shuttleworth. When the lady died, Kate didn't know what she was going to do, but she stayed on at the house. She didn't think Mr. Shuttleworth would accuse her of theft and fire her. It made it difficult for her to find another job. Not that she needs one now." His voice caught, making the final words in his sentence sound like a croak.

"Can I get you a cup of tea or coffee?" Miller asked both men. "I should have asked when you arrived."

Paul shook his head and Clayton cleared his throat. "I'm not sure I can drink anything right now, thank you." He pressed his palms into the table and locked eyes with Winston. "If Susie thinks Kate was killed. . . Do you think Mr. Shuttleworth might have killed her? Because of the necklace?"

"Why do you ask that?"

"He was so quick to fire her. He must have been an angry man," said Clayton.

Winston recalled his conversation with Shuttleworth, who, like the man in front of him, had lost his wife. Such a loss could no doubt alter how a man reacted to others. Though he'd seen no sign of violence. Sadness, yes. Anger, no. "Did your wife say he was violent with her?"

"No, she never said that. But she said she'd heard him yell."

Beside him, Miller scratched something in his notepad. The sound echoed in the small room. Winston leaned forward. "Do you know what he'd been yelling about? At whom?"

Clayton shook his head. "She never said."

Paul shifted in his seat. "She told me once," he said.

Clayton spun around to face his brother. "Why'd she tell you?" Hurt replaced grief in his voice.

Paul swallowed. "I checked on her one afternoon, when you were still at work. Like you'd asked me to. She was crying. Said she missed working at the house. She missed Mrs. Shuttleworth. But not him." His sentences had come out in one breath. "She said she heard him yelling at his wife. Something about it being 'his game.' Then the wife was crying. The wife died shortly afterwards."

A tingle sparked in Winston's gut. "Did Mrs. Block tell you she thought Mr. Shuttleworth killed his wife?" Winston straightened himself in his chair, momentarily surprised by his own question. He wasn't aware of any speculation about Mrs. Shuttleworth's death, but with another young, healthy woman from her household recently dead, his unconscious had pieced this together; had something been overlooked? Could Shuttleworth have killed Kate?

Clayton Block pulled at his face. "She never told me anything like that. And if that Shuttleworth killed his wife, why would he kill mine?" He drew the words out, considering the possibility. "She wanted to go back and see if he would rehire her, see if he'd calmed down about the necklace." He wiped his face again. "She was going to try next week. Maybe she went yesterday. . ." His brows knit together as he tried to make sense of this. "But she died this morning. So how could he have killed her?"

Someone knocked at the door. With the sound, the tension in the room deflated. Miller opened the door to find the desk officer. They exchanged a few words in hushed tones. Afterwards, he resumed his position beside Winston and whispered, "Doctor Evans says he's done. Says we can bring him in." He gestured toward Block with a flick of his finger.

Winston thanked Miller and turned back to Clayton. "If you'd like, we can see Mrs. Block's body now. Doctor Evans has finished his examination."

"Please." Chairs scraped against the wooden floor as the men stood.

As they approached the morgue, Winston explained what they were about to see, keeping his voice soft. "The sight of your wife's body under the sheet may be disturbing, Mr. Block. It is just her body, mind you. Her spirit is. . ." Winston waved his hand toward the ceiling.

"I understand."

Winston pushed open the door to the morgue. Doctor Evans had covered Mrs. Block so that only her head was visible and had arranged her hair as neatly as the situation allowed. "Doctor Evans, this is Mr. Clayton Block and his brother Paul. I understand you are finished examining the body?"

Evans turned to Clayton, extending his hand. "Mr. Block, I'm sorry to meet you like this." He led the grieving man to the table on which his wife's body lay.

A cry escaped Clayton, low and deep. "Oh, Kate. My Kate. This isn't right." His shoulders heaved and he held his head in his hands. Paul had moved forward, ready to provide physical support if needed, but Clayton didn't collapse. After a few breaths, he looked back to Evans. "Can I touch her?" The question came out as a whisper.

"It will feel nothing like when she was alive. You may do better not to touch her so that it doesn't cloud your memory of her."

"But it won't hurt her? If I touched her, I mean?"

"No, it won't hurt her."

Block stretched his hand in front of his body, caressing his dead wife's cheek with a tenderness that mismatched his large physique. "I love you. I will always love you," he whispered. He leaned down and kissed her forehead. Turning suddenly, he walked from the room, his brother immediately behind.

Winston followed them, but Clayton raced through the station and out the doors before he could reach him. Paul left with a slight bow of his head, as if thanking Winston for the afternoon.

*

WINSTON LET BLOCK go. He would speak further with him after the man had had a chance to absorb the events of his distressing morning. He made his way back to the morgue. Inside, Doctor Evans had recovered the body and was cleaning his instruments in the sink the constabulary had installed in the room at his request. "Jack, is the husband okay? He was so distressed."

Winston looked at Evans. It was clear why the doctor had chosen a profession dedicated to helping others. Was he doing the man a disservice by having him work for the police, devoting his attention to the dead? "Yes, he was terribly upset, as I would expect any husband who had just viewed his deceased wife's body to be." Susie Pegg's assertion that her sister was murdered surfaced again in Winston's thoughts. "Did you find anything to explain what killed her?"

"What I found were signs that someone has killed her, Jack. I can't say whether it was him, though."

"A murder, then. Unless you think he was simply playing up his grief for us." Susie was right. Who would want Kate dead? Her husband? The man certainly seemed to be mourning his wife. But maybe he was displaying deep remorse for having caused her death. With his strong hands, he could have inflicted considerable damage. "These signs you've found, do they indicate she'd been subjected to violence, Doctor?" Winston asked.

"No bruises or broken bones. Although some bruises appear a few days after a person dies, so I'll check again in a day or two to confirm."

Winston's mind raced. Who else would want the woman dead? Her sister? Paul Block? He shook the questions from his mind, forcing his thoughts back to the doctor's words. "You said no broken bones. Was she strangled?" An image of Clayton Block's large hands hovering over Kate's face flashed across his mind.

Evans uncovered the body and gestured for Winston to approach. "In strangulation, we see the tiny blood vessels around the eyes break from the pressure. They'll show as red dots." He pointed to each of Kate Block's closed eyes, then, with a gentle touch, peeled open the lids.

Winston swallowed and leaned closer. "I don't see any."

"Exactly. There's no evidence that supports strangulation. In fact, I don't think she lost her life because of physical force."

Winston narrowed his eyes. "What makes you think someone killed her, then?"

Evans picked up the woman's hand. "Her fingers. They show signs of poison."

"Show me." Winston forced himself to lean in closer. His thoughts ran ahead to the implications of what Evans had just said. Poison complicated things. The murderer didn't need to be present when the victim died.

Evans pointed to her nail beds. Kate's fingers revealed her profession: calluses formed after long hours of cleaning. "They're dark. Darker than I'd expect."

"The discoloration is not caused by her being . . . dead?"

Evans shook his head. "No, this is unusual."

"Do you know the source? The poison, I mean?"

"That's a question I haven't an answer to. Further testing will be needed to determine that."

"But you don't think it was natural? Death due to illness, I mean."

"I'm not aware of anything other than poisoning that causes these same symptoms."

"Could it be accidental?" Winston asked.

"Until we know the source, it will be difficult to answer that, Jack."

When Winston had spoken with Susie Pegg, she had seemed quite healthy, in contrast to her sister. "Mrs. Block mentioned having felt ill recently. She thought it might be something in the apartment."

Evans shook his head. "If that was the case, all of the residents would be ill, as would her husband."

Kate had said that her brother-in-law felt no ill effects from living in the apartment, and the Block brothers both appeared healthy. "Perhaps not from the building, then." Winston frowned. "Still, should we speak to other residents, check if any share any similar physical symptoms?"

Evans pulled the cover to the body's shoulders. "If she was poisoned by something in the building, it will become apparent quickly. You may need to isolate all the residents."

Winston made a note. He would send Miller to speak to Kate's neighbours. If anyone else reported a similar illness, he'd move the residents and order the building closed while they searched for the source.

"I'd like to hold on to the body for a few days, Jack. Until I can identify the poison that killed her." Evans rested his hand on Kate's.

A shudder passed through Winston. He squeezed his eyes shut as Evans tugged the sheet over her head. Evans took purposeful strides across the morgue's tile floor and scanned a bookshelf in the corner of the room. He found the volume he was looking for and pulled it from the shelf. "I'll see what I can find, Jack." He waved the book and then set it on a writing desk.

Winston left the morgue as the doctor wheeled the body into the cooling vault. His head swam with unanswered questions.

CHAPTER 13

Riley

Dear Riley,

The maid I wrote of earlier, the one accused of stealing the necklace—Doctor Evans believes she was poisoned. Evans seems to think it was intentional, though I'd like to rule out accidental poisoning. I have not yet had time to consider suspects or motive. However, could you look up the name Kate Block and see if you uncover any information?

Warmly,

Jack

Jack's message sparked warmth from her toes to her fingertips. She loved helping him, and this was a task she could do. And with Nick meeting with Claire for most of the morning, she had some time to check the name while she worked on the exhibit research. She entered it into a browser window, though she didn't expect it would yield any useful results.

It was a welcome little break from her research for the exhibit. Claire had expressed confidence that Riley would flesh out the research, but she was finding it difficult to track down much information from her usual sources. Another warm wave passed through her as an idea took shape. What if she asked Jack for some information about the living conditions of maids and other domestic servants? Would it be wrong if it's for research purposes? She wrote a quick reply before she could persuade herself not to.

Dear Jack,

I will look up as much as I can. In fact, I have an excuse to search her, as the current exhibit I'm working on is about domestic servants in Vancouver in your time.

Riley paused. Until now, she had never asked Jack for help in her exhibits. Would he help if she asked? If he did, how would she explain where the information came from? She pushed the thought aside and continued her note.

Please don't feel like you need to do this, but I wonder if you could ask any of the domestic staff you speak with about their experiences, their working conditions, what their daily hours are. It is for an exhibit I am working on.

She flushed with the boldness of what she had written. How would he respond? How would she use the information if he did?

Riley worked for about an hour, finding Kate Block's marriage and death certificates. As Jack had suggested, the death certificate indicated poisoning as the cause of death. A pang of sadness hit her when she noticed how close together the dates of the two documents were. "Till death do us part" is never said with an expectation that death will follow so closely after such a happy occasion.

There were no additional marriage certificates for her husband, Clayton Block. Why was that? Riley considered the possibilities. He could have moved, he could have died, or he did not remarry. She imagined Clayton Block's heart so broken by the loss of his wife that he mourned her for the rest of his life. She found a death certificate for

Paul Block, dated a few years later. Clayton's brother? She made a note of it in case Jack asked about it. Otherwise, she would keep that information to herself.

Her additional searches for Kate revealed nothing more. Kate Block was just one of countless young women whose existence was all but forgotten. "I'll remember you," Riley said.

Next, Riley resumed her initial research on the Shuttleworths, Kate's employers. Since her earlier cursory search, this was the first real opportunity she'd had to dig deeper for information. She found Penelope Shuttleworth's death certificate. The document had two entries, the first one—*natural causes*—struck out and replaced with *poison, murder.*

Riley zoomed in on the certificate. Poison. Murder. Kate Block had also been poisoned. And murdered? In his note, Jack had pointed to poison as the conclusion Doctor Evans had reached. Her stomach clenched. Should she tell him about this revised cause of death? Nudge him toward an answer he would ultimately reach on his own? Wouldn't it be more helpful if she could back up this finding with more information? She took a calming breath. Research. She'd look up more about Mrs. Shuttleworth before deciding what to share.

She found a newspaper article that indicated that after initially declaring her death due to natural causes, further investigation suggested that Mrs. Shuttleworth died as a result of having been poisoned, and the poisoning was intentional. The murderer was identified as someone connected to the Shuttleworths: Bobbie Lyon. Riley noted the name. She scanned the article again. No indication whether Bobbie was male or female or how this person was connected to the Shuttleworths.

Was it fair to withhold this information from Jack? No, she reasoned. Particularly not if she was asking him for help with her own work. And surely he would still do his own investigation. It would just be guided by her suggestion.

Riley looked at the journal, open beside her. She'd experienced this uneasiness whenever she'd considered revealing information to Jack that might impact the course of historical events. So far they'd been careful, and still she'd managed to be a help to him.

> *Do you think it's possible that anyone else in the Shuttleworth household was poisoned? I'm asking because I've found some information to suggest this was the case. Specifically, a newspaper article from the time and the death certificate suggest that Mrs. Shuttleworth was also poisoned.*

She paused. Never before had she directed his investigation so actively.

> *The article refers to someone named Bobbie Lyon. Have you encountered this name in your investigation?*
>
> *R.*

Riley's heart thumped. Jack knew as much as she did now.

*

THE PING OF her phone roused Riley from her thoughts.

> Hi, dear. It's your mother. I'm thinking of you.

Riley cringed at her mother's message. It was sweet, but like sending a message to say the sky is blue. Aren't mothers always thinking of their children? And why did her mother insist on identifying herself in her texts?

Hey. I'm at work. Is it urgent?

Have you heard from your sister? She told me she hasn't been feeling well.

I saw her. She seems run down. A little rest and she'll be fine.

xx.

Within minutes, her phone pinged again. Riley sighed. She really needed to get back to work. She picked up her phone to put it on silent so she could claim she hadn't heard any subsequent messages. But this one was from Alex.

Heading to the hospital. Lucy is worse.

Riley's throat tightened. She sent an email to Nick to tell him she had to respond to a family emergency. She considered whether to tell her mother, then decided to wait. There was no sense worrying her unnecessarily. Instead, she dialled Johnny. "It's Lucy. Alex just sent me a text. She's going to the hospital."

She heard his intake of breath. "Why?"

"Alex didn't say. But he's worried. There wasn't much detail in his message," Riley said.

"Let's find out what's going on. I'm on my way."

Riley packed up her things and by the time she reached the museum doors, Johnny was waiting for her just inside the entrance. She hooked an arm through his and drew him outside.

Johnny flagged a cab while Riley confirmed which hospital Lucy had been taken to. During the ten-minute journey, she checked her phone at what felt like six-second intervals to see if Alex had sent any updates. When they arrived in the emergency room, they were told to wait, as Lucy had been admitted immediately when the ambulance arrived. With shaking fingers, Riley texted Alex to let him know where she was.

Johnny reached for her hand as she lay her head on his shoulder. "I'll do anything if it will mean Lucy is okay." Her words triggered the memory of the day her father had been rushed to hospital with a major heart attack. She'd made the same promise then, only it hadn't worked. Silently she promised she would tell her sister about the journal—even if she was never able to write in it again.

"I'm sure she'll be fine, Riley."

"Right. We just need to wait." She found an empty chair in the waiting room, its seat covered in leather-like upholstery for easy cleanup. She stretched her legs in front of her, trying to get comfortable. She shifted position and pulled her legs up. "But what if she's not fine? I can't lose her," Riley whispered, hugging her arms around her shins.

After an hour, Alex found Riley and Johnny. He held her in a long embrace, then dropped into the chair beside her. "The doctors don't know what it is, but they don't want to send her home either. They're looking for a bed for her so they can run some tests."

"Doesn't she need someone with her?" Riley tamped down her frustration. Wasn't Alex taking this seriously?

"She's sleeping. She won't realize I'm gone."

"What if she wakes up?" Johnny squeezed her hand, and she knew her voice was too high, too irritable.

Alex waited a couple of beats, then spoke. "They've given her something to make her sleep. I can't just sit there and watch her." He pinched the bridge of his nose. Fear had crumpled Riley's ordinarily calm and collected brother-in-law. "She needs to rest." He swallowed. "She went to the gala last night."

"What?" Riley was incredulous. Lucy had a history of making questionable decisions, but surely Alex could have convinced her to focus on her health. "Why did you let her go?"

"'Let' her go? Do you even know Lucy?" This time Alex's voice showed the strain. He sighed. "She had improved. I thought she was better."

"Maybe she just overdid it," offered Johnny.

Riley fought her immediate reaction to scream. How could Lucy have possibly been well enough to attend the gala? Alex shoved his phone in front of Riley with a social media account open. Lucy smiled back at her, hair shining, cheeks glowing. As she'd promised, she was wearing the necklace Jayne had given her, and it complemented her beautiful gown. The outfit suited Lucy perfectly. This was not the same person she had seen a few days ago.

"Okay. She looked much better. But clearly, she wasn't." Riley circled her finger in the air. "Or we wouldn't be here."

"You won't be able to see her until tomorrow, during visiting hours," Alex said.

"What time tomorrow?" Johnny asked.

"The nurse said after nine. Go home." Alex pushed himself from the chair, worry creasing his face. "They're running a bunch of tests, starting with blood work. But they won't have results before tomorrow."

Riley stood. "Are you going to stay here?"

"I'm going to sit here until they tell me where they're admitting her. Then I'll see if they have a family waiting area where I can stay."

"I'll stay with you," Riley said, dropping back into her chair.

Alex extended his hand to pull her back to her feet. "Go home. It doesn't do any good for us all to be here."

"She's the only sister I have, Alex. I can't leave." Riley turned to Johnny. "Thanks for bringing me here, but you should go." She reached in her bag for her phone. Riley dreaded having to tell her mother, but it was time.

Johnny looked between Alex and Riley. "I don't feel right leaving you, Riley. Listen, my place is close," Johnny said. "Why don't you both stay there tonight? Ask the hospital to call if anything changes, and we can be back here within minutes. Even if you don't get any sleep, you'll be more comfortable than in these chairs." He twisted at the waist to release his back as he spoke.

"I don't want to put you out, Johnny," said Alex.

"You won't. I insist." Johnny gripped Alex's shoulder.

Riley squeezed Johnny's hand and mouthed "thanks" to him, resisting the urge to kiss his cheek. She pushed her phone back into her bag. There was no use worrying her mother until she'd seen Lucy. If her sister's condition hadn't changed by tomorrow morning, she'd call her mother then. Johnny slipped his arm around her and guided her to the door, looking back to make sure Alex followed.

CHAPTER 14

Jack

WINSTON ARRANGED THE pages of notes spread out in front of him on his desk. Philpott's office window faced east, and the morning sun brightened the room. Winston was glad for the added light as he began his task.

He and Miller had spent several hours into the late afternoon of the previous day interviewing the residents of the apartment buildings that the Block brothers lived in. Nobody else was experiencing the same complaints that Kate Block had spoken of. Despite their protestations, Winston had inspected the fingernails of each of the residents. None had the same discoloration of the nail beds. Then they'd returned to Clayton's apartment to speak with him again. Without Kate Block's presence, her former living space had felt even starker.

The scene returned to Winston now. Clay, alone this time, had appeared withdrawn. The shock of his wife's death was still visible on his features. "Sure," he'd said, "she'd been tired. But she had worked hard for the Shuttleworths, and she didn't need to work any longer. Not with me providing for her. I was content to let her rest all day if that was what she needed. And she had just started to settle into our home."

Winston had recognized Block's answer as an opportunity to ask a question that would help Riley. When he'd received her request, Winston wasn't sure how he'd be able to help her without overstepping during an investigation. But it had proved easier than he expected. "Can you tell me about her typical day when she worked at the Shuttleworth home?" he had asked Block. And Block had detailed the long hours his wife had spoken of. Kate had often described Mrs. Shuttleworth as a kind woman. Winston scanned his notes. Her employer was perhaps kinder than most. Still, Kate often finished her days with aching muscles only to have to wake early the next morning to resume her duties.

Winston had asked Block about his wife's other interests. "Did she aspire to another position? Did she have creative pursuits?"

At this question, Winston recalled that Block had scoffed slightly. "She had no time for other interests. I'm sure once she'd settled here she would have found something to occupy her time. And she wanted children, of course. They would have kept her busy." His eyes had glistened. "And happy."

"Did you eat the same foods, drink the same water?" Miller had asked.

"Largely, yes. She sent me to work with a midday meal." Winston's notes recorded the man's puzzled facial expression at this line of questioning. "Why?" Block had asked.

Winston tested Block's reaction with his next statement. "The medical examiner. He thinks your wife was poisoned."

Block inhaled sharply. "Poisoned?" He'd pushed the word out forcefully. "Who? Who would poison her? Why?" Winston had found it interesting that Block immediately assumed it was deliberate, that she hadn't encountered the poison in some random way.

"It is my aim to find out, Mr. Block."

Winston's notes recorded Block's physical responses throughout the conversation. The man had pressed his palms into his cheeks as he absorbed the news, finally asking in a hushed tone, "But you are saying someone killed my wife? That Kate was murdered?"

Winston flipped over a page of notes and followed where the conversation had gone from there: Winston and Miller had ignored

Block's question and responded with their own, Miller first. "How long did you know her?"

"A few months. Long enough to know I wanted to marry her."

"How did you meet?" Winston this time.

Block had answered the questions without hesitation. "Before I worked at the post office, I was a carpenter. I did some repairs for the Shuttleworths."

"Mr. Block, sometimes poison is unintentional. Have you heard of any of your neighbours falling ill? Your brother? Perhaps a friend or acquaintance?"

Block answered that he was unaware of anyone else around them being ill, and of course their interviews with the building's other residents had already confirmed that nobody else had experienced similar symptoms.

Winston sat back in his chair and scanned the sea of notes before him. Who had targeted Kate Block? Why?

He turned to a fresh page in his notepad and began to draw up a list of names and reasons why they might want her dead, no matter how trivial. First on the list was Mr. Shuttleworth, who was convinced his former maid had stolen the items from his home. Riley's fresh information that Mrs. Shuttleworth had also been poisoned reinforced his position at the top of the list. The rationale for murder thinned as he worked down the list.

Her sister, Susie, for causing her to also lose her employment.

Her husband, Clay, though his motive was unclear.

Someone whom they hadn't yet identified, for their own unknown reasons.

Winston drew a line under the last idea. None of the reasons seemed particularly compelling. And none of the suspects matched the name that Riley had shared. Who was Bobbie Lyon? The name hadn't come up so far. He couldn't ask Block about the name, not in Miller's presence. It would be difficult to explain that question.

With a flash he was reminded of his embarrassment when he had first assumed Riley was male. Bobbie was also a name that could be used by a man or a woman. Why would this person poison Kate Block and Mrs. Shuttleworth? How would he convince Evans to consider whether Mrs. Shuttleworth had been poisoned? And another possible complication, if he did persuade Evans to take another look at her death: what if the doctor concluded that she hadn't been poisoned? Riley's information wasn't as immediately helpful as he'd hoped—yet. What was he missing?

✳

DOCTOR EVANS STOOD at the front of the station, chatting with the desk officer when Winston emerged from his uncle's office. "Evans. I wasn't expecting to see you today." Winston's stomach sank. Given his position with the police, the doctor's presence at the station usually signalled that a suspicious death had occurred. Or was Evans here for another reason? Winston shook Evans's outstretched hand.

"Jack. The Block woman." Evans wiped his hand across his mouth and chin. "Can we speak privately?"

The unexpected question sent Winston's stomach even deeper. What more could Evans have to share? He motioned toward Philpott's office and followed Evans inside. When the doctor had settled, Winston leaned back in his chair. "What is it?"

Evans licked his lips and swallowed. Winston bristled but kept his face impassive. Whatever Evans was about to say, he was buying time before saying it. The doctor began quietly. "I am surprised that you haven't brought this to me." He lowered his gaze and focused on the desk. "But I understand your mind has been elsewhere."

A tingle ran down Winston's spine. He recalled the night—an occasion when they were leaving the station at the same time—they had enjoyed a meal together at the Vancouver Gentlemen's Club. In a moment of vulnerability, Winston had shared with Evans that he'd learned about a bad decision his family had made, and how this had felt to him like a betrayal. He'd been careful not to reveal too many details, but Evans had likely pieced enough of the story together from the fragments Winston had shared.

"Something's changed in you, Jack. I see it in your face." He paused briefly, then continued. "And in how you treat Miller."

Winston started to push himself from his chair. How dare Evans presume he knew Winston well enough to say that he'd changed? "What does that have to do with anything?" Evans raised his hand to stop him getting up, and Winston paused, half out of the chair.

Evans placed his hands on Philpott's desk. He pulsed his hands slightly, as if drawing strength from the solid wood. "Did you wonder if the deaths of Mrs. Shuttleworth and Mrs. Block might be connected?"

Winston's mouth went dry. He sat in the chair, perched on its edge. "Connected? How?" he croaked. He hadn't even had a chance to approach Evans with Riley's information yet.

"Miller came to me with an idea, and his suggestion prompted me to review the Block woman's case last night. She had been employed by the Shuttleworth family. The lady of that household died just a few weeks ago. Two women who until recently had regular contact. That they died within weeks of each other. . . Surely that's worth looking into more deeply."

"Actually, I've come to the same thought, just a little slower than you, Doctor." As he spoke, Winston noted the defensive tone in his voice and felt heat rising up his neck. He recalled an exchange with Miller the evening before. Miller had tried to ask a question, and Winston had dismissed it without letting the constable speak. And it wasn't the first time he'd stifled him. The truth of the doctor's words stung. Winston collapsed into the chair's high back as all thoughts of his frustration with Evans evaporated.

Evans sat silently while Winston gathered his thoughts. If the cases were connected, as Riley had suggested, her information about Bobbie Lyon might also prove true. When his embarrassment abated, Winston pulled his notepad from his pocket. Best to let Evans explain his theory. "Mrs. Shuttleworth died of an illness."

"I thought the same at the time. Her husband told me she had been complaining of feeling unwell before she died. I didn't question him about it, and because I didn't suspect anything, I didn't get the police involved." Evans steepled his index fingers and brought them to his mouth. "You have to understand. . . Her death appeared perfectly natural." The doctor closed his eyes and dropped his voice. "She'd been ill." He ran a hand through his hair. "I checked my papers this morning. Her fingers. The room she was found in had a fire going. I assumed that the warmth of the room prolonged the time for her body to cool and accounted for why her nails appeared discoloured. She didn't come to the morgue, so I had no occasion to check them again." His hand passed through his hair again, pulling its strands to nearly standing. "I found the detail in my notes, but it wasn't significant enough to record in the official documents. But Miller's question stirred the memory for me: Mrs. Shuttleworth's nails looked the same."

"What are you telling me, Evans?" He bit back a criticism. Evans was still relatively new to his role as medical examiner. This conversation confirmed to Winston the importance of documenting everything, even if it seemed inconsequential.

The doctor swallowed, then leaned closer. "I think both women were poisoned."

Winston's hand went to his pocket. He felt for the stone, smooth where his thumb had rubbed it thousands of times. Its familiar shape settled him. "Do you think the method was the same? Mrs. Block was

Mrs. Shuttleworth's maid. Could it be related to her time at the house?" He needed to organize his thoughts. To give himself a moment to do so, he moved to the window.

"Yes, they could have been administered the same poison at the house," Evans said.

Winston spun around to face the doctor. "But a few weeks have passed since Mrs. Shuttleworth died. Why would Mrs. Block's death be so much later?"

"It depends on the intervals and the dosage of how the poison was administered."

Winston knew little about poisons and how they worked. In this, he was relying on Evans. "What should I look for?"

"Let me answer that after I've completed my research about what poison it might have been. And I will run the tests I spoke of yesterday while I still have access to Mrs. Block's body."

"Thank you," Winston replied. He sat again at the desk, glancing down at the notes he'd just been reviewing. If both women had been poisoned, the focus of their attention would need to shift from the Block residence to the Shuttleworth household. At last—some clear direction.

CHAPTER 15

Riley

IT WAS NO use—Riley wouldn't sleep tonight. She threw back the blanket and sat at the edge of the futon in Johnny's den. She flipped on the small lamp on the end table and pulled the journal from her bag.

Dear Riley,

I've just met with Doctor Evans, our medical examiner. He believes that Kate Block and her former employer, Penelope Shuttleworth, were both poisoned. This, along with the information you shared earlier, has me shifting my investigation back toward the Shuttleworth house. I have yet to come across anyone named Bobbie Lyon in connection with this case. With time, that may change, and I will stay alert to the possibility.

Thank you for what you've uncovered.

J.

Jack's case was growing more complex. Spending a few minutes thinking about it would help distract her from worrying about Lucy. His decision to shift focus to the Shuttleworth house made sense. If both Mrs. Shuttleworth and Kate Block had been poisoned, it must have happened while they were in the same household. She pulled out her laptop and called up the photo of Mrs. Shuttleworth. What was it that struck her last time she'd looked at the photo? She zoomed in. The necklace. Something about it looked so familiar. Riley's pulse quickened. She found her phone and opened Lucy's social media account to the photo that Alex had shown her, making the picture larger to get a closer look at her sister's jewellery.

Blinking, Riley looked away from the screen, then back again. The lighting and different angles made it difficult to be certain, but the necklaces looked nearly identical. Her mouth grew dry. How could that be? Maybe whoever had made Lucy's necklace had found the picture of Mrs. Shuttleworth and modelled Lucy's piece after it. Riley called up other images of jewellery from the late 1890s. The style was in line with the fashion of the time. It wasn't unreasonable to think a modern artist was creating similar pieces from these same images. She traced her finger along the lines of the necklace in Lucy's photo. But hadn't Jayne said it was from an antiques seller? Could it be possible?

Riley needed to figure out where Jayne had purchased the necklace. She flicked through her sister's friend's social media pictures. Standard influencer poses. If only Riley had half her confidence. Maybe then Claire would have offered her the position instead of Nick. She shook the thought away.

After scrolling through what felt like hundreds of photos, Riley found one caption that referred to a local craft market. No vendors were specifically called out, but this, at least, was a place to start searching since it was far too late to call Jayne. Riley settled on sending a message through the social media app, just in case Jayne was awake.

She loaded the craft market's website to search for a list of vendors and copied their names into a spreadsheet. She crossed a line through any that didn't sell jewellery, which left eight to search. Their websites favoured light, airy images, with the exception of a tattoo artist/jewellery designer who went with a darker theme. Riley searched their photos for similar pieces. She narrowed her list of vendors to three and sent each an email. By this time, she was finally tired enough to sleep.

When Riley stirred a few hours later, she got up and brushed the wrinkles from her shirt. She found Alex in an overstuffed chair in the main seating area of Johnny's apartment. He was passing Lucy's new necklace between his hands. The Slinky image reappeared in Riley's mind.

"Sorry, did I wake you?" Alex placed the necklace on the table.

Riley shook her head. Her fingers tingled. It was a truly beautiful necklace. She reached for it. Could it possibly be the one Jack was searching for? "Where did you get this?"

"From home. Lucy tried it on with different outfits before the gala. She seemed so happy wearing it, and I couldn't figure out what else to bring with me. I wasn't thinking straight." He pointed at the bag lying at his feet. "Look, I packed dresses for her. She's not going to want to wear a dress at the hospital."

Riley coiled the necklace into her hand. The sound of the pearls jostling against each other soothed her. "Knowing Lucy, that's exactly what she will want. Any word?"

Johnny entered the room holding two mugs. He handed one to Alex. "Sorry, Riley. I didn't realize you were up. Can I get you a cup of tea?" Drops of dark liquid sloshed from the mug onto the table. "I've made strong coffee, if you prefer."

"I can't drink anything right now. My stomach keeps flipping." She picked up her phone but set it down quickly. "Will the hospital call if she wakes up? Did you give them my number too, Alex?"

Alex opened his mouth to answer, but Riley fired off another question before he could. "What about my mom? What did she say when you told her?" If Alex had already spoken with her, Riley wouldn't have to.

Horror spread across Alex's face, and Riley's stomach sank. "I thought you would call her—" she started to say, but Alex cut her off.

"She's your sister. I just thought you'd tell Nancy. You know, because she's your mom. You've known her longer. . ." His voice trailed off.

"I know Lucy didn't take your name, but she's really your responsibility now." Riley's voice, high and loud, betrayed her frustration—though it was more with herself than with Alex. Johnny popped his head around the corner from the kitchen, his brow knit in concern. Riley ignored him. "Whatever. I'll call my mom." With her heart racing, Riley picked up her phone. She burned with guilt for speaking harshly with Alex and for delaying this call.

"Hi, Mom. It's me. Listen, I'm sure it's not a big deal, and maybe you've already heard it from Alex." Riley had turned away but could feel Alex's gaze drilling through her back. He'd recover from any anger her mother might direct at him, but it had felt good to lash out, if she was honest. Riley interrupted her mom's "Heard what?" response. "Anyway, Lucy is in hospital. She fell ill yesterday, and the doctors aren't entirely sure what's wrong."

"The hospital? Are you with her right now?"

"Actually, I'm not. Alex and I were just getting ready to return there. They said they'd call if anything changed."

Through the phone, Riley heard her mother's sharp intake of breath. She pictured her pursing her lips to let the breath go. "I'm surprised you're not there," she said in a flat voice. "I'll come over as quickly as I can. I'll say goodbye now so I can arrange a quick flight."

"It will be expensive, Mom." After a fiasco with a crypto scam, Riley had had several discussions with her mother about safe spending. Lucy in hospital qualified as an emergency, but for all Riley knew, Lucy was up and ordering hospital staff around.

"It will be fine, dear." Her mom's voice had softened.

"You can stay with me, if you'd like."

Her mother didn't answer. Riley expected the invitation to be declined. Nancy had spent as little time as possible in the apartment since Riley's father had died. "I'll think about it, Riley. Now please, as soon as you can, get to the hospital and let me know your sister is okay."

"I will, Mom. See you soon."

"I'll let you know when to expect me."

Riley ended the call. She turned and looked from Alex to Johnny. Alex and her mother got along, but he was probably right—it really had been her place to speak to her mother, and she should have done so earlier. She was about to admit this when Alex said, "The doctor would have called if anything had changed with Lucy. But you know how busy they can get." He grinned. "I bet she is awake, enjoying breakfast in bed right now, asking about the quality of the towels."

Riley's cheeks burned. Was Alex not taking this seriously? "How can you joke right now? Your wife—my sister—is in the hospital."

Alex leaned toward Riley. "If I joke, it means it's not serious. She's going to be fine." He brought the coffee to his lips. "She needs to be."

"We don't know that." Riley threw the necklace on the table. "We don't know how serious it is." She picked up her bag and stormed from the room.

"Riley, wait." Johnny followed her and pulled her into his bedroom. "Alex isn't being dismissive. It's his way of dealing with the situation. It's hard for him too."

"Why are you defending him?"

"I'm not. I'm supporting both of you. And he hasn't done anything wrong. He's worried about his wife. You're worried about your sister." Johnny wrapped his arms around her. "And I'm worried about you," he said as he pulled her to his chest.

After two breaths, she pushed herself away, avoiding looking into his eyes.

"Can we go to the hospital? Even if she's not awake yet, I want to see her."

Johnny kissed her forehead. "Of course. I'll tell Alex."

CHAPTER 16

Jack

A **PANG OF** guilt pinched Winston's stomach when he found Miller in the station's file room again. "You really can leave this until after we've finished the Shuttleworth case, Thomas." He tried to keep the embarrassment, which sounded more like frustration, from his voice.

"I was looking to see if we'd had any other crimes involving a knife like the one that was found in the other case you gave me."

A flush of pride warmed Winston's cheeks. Miller's innovation was commendable. "Tell me how you're doing that," he said.

Miller explained how he had started cataloguing the contents of the files, creating an index of the weapons they'd recovered and how they'd been used. "We can add to it as we get new cases. Then we can check here to see if they've been used before." He pointed to a document. It was similar to what Riley had suggested in response to his question about how to organize the room. That Miller had thought of it was remarkable, and he told him as much.

As Winston watched Miller check through the records, his conversation with Doctor Evans replayed in his mind. The doctor's observations about how Winston had been treating the young officer were right. He'd been tough on Miller. He'd tried to justify his behaviour by telling himself it was to help Miller improve his skills. But no—Evans's comments were legitimate: Winston had been unfairly taking his frustrations out on the constable. Admitting this to himself tightened the knot in his stomach. Perhaps the only way to loosen it was to acknowledge the truth to Miller.

"Join me in Chief Philpott's office, Thomas." Winston motioned for Miller to follow.

Winston swallowed against the dryness in his throat. "Please—take a seat." He smiled and indicated the chair in front of the desk. "Look, Thomas. You've shown some promise." His voice caught, and he swallowed again. "Your investigative skills are improving, and I. . ."

Miller stiffened in the chair across from the desk.

Winston began a third time. "I've noticed the work you've been doing. And I'm sorry if it has seemed that I haven't." Winston tensed his hands into fists. Would Miller understand what he was saying? He found it hard to be more explicit. He waited for Miller to respond, tensing and relaxing the muscles in his hands. Then he let the rest of his words tumble out. "I understand that you went to Doctor Evans with a theory that the deaths of Mrs. Shuttleworth and Mrs. Block are somehow connected. It's a fine theory. I only wish you had discussed it with me beforehand."

Miller flushed. "I tried, sir." He mumbled the words.

"I know. I wasn't listening. But I am now, Thomas." Winston met the constable's eyes and sensed the young man's relief. "Let's work through the facts as we know them." Winston moved toward the blackboard he'd wheeled from the main room of the station into the chief constable's office and erased a game of noughts and crosses. "Your idea sparked a memory in Doctor Evans. He reviewed his notes about the death of Penelope Shuttleworth, and he has confirmed he now believes Mrs. Shuttleworth and Kate Block were both poisoned."

"Murdered?" Miller asked.

"It would appear so, yes."

Silently, Miller pulled his notepad from his pocket and wrote dates on the blackboard. He pointed to the first one. "Kate Block was fired from the Shuttleworths two weeks after her mistress died, when objects of personal value were discovered missing. She hadn't been back at the house since then." Under the first date, he wrote *Kate last at the house*. "And her sister, Susie, is fine. She worked there until Kate was dismissed." He wrote *Susie last at the house* in the same column. "So we're looking for something or someone that Kate encountered between leaving the house and yesterday." He looked up at Winston. "Are you certain Susie is fine?"

"She was fine yesterday when she came here to tell me of her sister's death. When we saw Mrs. Block the day before she died, she'd seemed off, low energy. Confused, even."

"Could her confusion have been an effect of poison?" Miller wrote the symptoms in a separate column.

Winston shrugged. "Possibly." Suddenly the name Bobbie Lyon popped into his head. How would they find him . . . or her? And how could Winston follow this lead without making Miller question where he got the name from? He pushed the thought away. "We must identify who both women had encountered in the weeks leading to their deaths. Mrs. Block had suggested it was the apartment making her ill, which we now have enough evidence to discount, but I interpret her comments to mean she only became ill after leaving the Shuttleworth household. But that would not explain Mrs. Shuttleworth's death."

"Hadn't Mrs. Shuttleworth also been unwell before she died? Could it be something in both homes?"

Winston pinched the bridge of his nose. "Doubtful. While I don't think we can rule out an environmental source entirely at this stage, I think we'd do better to think about the acquaintances the women had in common." He brought his hand to his pocket and turned the stone over between his fingers. "Let's set aside the location for now. Doctor Evans feels the poisonings were intentional. He believes both women were killed."

"Sir, shall we list suspects?" Miller flipped to a fresh page in his notepad.

"If the same poison was used on Mrs. Shuttleworth and Mrs. Block, it would need to be administered by someone who had access to both of them." Winston paused as his idea continued to form. Was Kate Block using the name Bobbie Lyon? "Unless the first poison was administered by Kate." As soon as he said this, Winston realized it was wrong. Kate Block couldn't be Bobbie Lyon if Bobbie would be arrested. But Riley's note didn't say that was the case. Only that the murderer was Bobbie Lyon, who was associated with the Shuttleworths. His head spun with questions. He would need Riley to provide more information about Bobbie Lyon.

"Do you mean she could have poisoned Mrs. Shuttleworth, then someone else poisoned her?" Miller knit his brows as he tried to understand Winston's meaning. "Or are you suggesting that she poisoned herself?" he asked.

"I don't think that's what happened." Unless the poisoning was unintentional. Another thought formed. "Block had access to his wife, certainly. But did he have access to Mrs. Shuttleworth?"

Miller reviewed the notes he'd made during their conversation with Clay Block. "Sir, he performed work for the family. That's how he met Kate."

Winston recalled the conversation. Block had mentioned having done carpentry work at the Shuttleworth house. An association with the Shuttleworths, as Riley indicated. But why kill Mrs. Shuttleworth? Money? Love? "We'll need to look into his background. To rule him out."

Miller wrote *Clayton Block* on the page. "What about Mr. Shuttleworth?"

"He wouldn't be the first man to kill his wife. But why also kill his wife's maid? Especially as she no longer worked for them?"

"Was Kate a loose end? Had she seen or heard something she shouldn't have?" As he spoke, Miller added Shuttleworth's name to the list.

"We'll need to look more closely at him as well. If he is guilty, why did he call attention back to himself? Evans didn't consider Mrs. Shuttleworth's death suspicious until after Mrs. Block died."

"And I'm not sure he had any opportunity. Kate's sister didn't even know where she was. I doubt Shuttleworth would have known."

"True," Winston said. "He is a less likely suspect. But we cannot rule him out yet."

"What about Susie Pegg?" Miller wrote the name on his paper.

"She would have had opportunity. And she easily could have misled us about when she last saw her sister. Though we will need to uncover a reason for her to kill Mrs. Shuttleworth." Winston's voice rose. "I'm struggling to find a reason for any person so far to have killed both women, or for a reasonable way that one person would have had easy access to both of them." Winston began to pace the room. "There must be a connection."

"What if there isn't? What if it's two killers using the same poison?" Miller asked.

Winston paused to consider. "That seems unlikely," he said. "Let's return to identifying who knew both victims."

"Someone else who worked at the house? The cook?"

Winston spun around to face Miller. "Mrs. Plum could have slipped something into their food. But Kate Block's death came after she'd left the Shuttleworth house."

"For poison, the killer doesn't need to be present," Miller reminded Winston.

"Correct. And . . . we delivered scones from Mrs. Plum."

"We ate them. And we're not sick," Miller pointed out. "They were delicious. I would have noticed something was off, I am sure. And we gave some to her sister."

"I agree, it's far-fetched. It's also unlikely Mr. Shuttleworth has seen either sister since they ceased working for him. He wasn't even sure there were two of them."

"Meaning Susie Pegg and Clay Block are our most likely suspects."

Winston leaned against his desk. "Why would she kill her sister?" He reached for the stone in his pocket. He couldn't imagine harming either of his brothers.

"Money?"

"I understand killing your wealthy employer to get her money, but why your sister? You saw the conditions she was living in. Didn't appear to be many extra pennies in the Block household," Winston said.

"Why do people kill?"

"Money. Jealousy. To keep a secret." Winston listed the reasons on his fingers.

"Did Kate know something about Susie? Mrs. Shuttleworth could have known the same thing. Was Susie having an affair with Mr. Shuttleworth and Kate knew about it?" Miller asked.

"I don't think so. He couldn't distinguish the sisters from each other when I asked him about them. And neither sister spoke about him with anything resembling fondness. Seems unlikely he was intimate with either." Winston took a piece of chalk and wrote *Kate Block* and *Penelope Shuttleworth* at the top of the board. He added the names of Mr. Shuttleworth, Mrs. Plum, and Susie Pegg in a row below the names of the dead women. "Each of our suspects is connected to the two women." He drew a solid line between Susie's and Kate's names, and a dotted line between Kate and the other two suspects.

"Why dotted, sir?"

"Those connections were not as strong after Mrs. Block stopped working for the Shuttleworths."

Between Mrs. Shuttleworth and the three suspects he drew solid lines. "They were all in the household at the time. Any of them could have easily done it."

Miller picked up the chalk, turning it between his fingers. "Should we add Mr. Block's name?"

"Had he ever met Mrs. Shuttleworth?"

"Very possibly when he completed the carpentry work. He may have had more than one project at the house. She also may have met him through his role as a clerk at the post office. He may have delivered a package to the house," Miller said.

"Well thought, Thomas. But he wouldn't have been inside the house alone. And not likely in close proximity to Mrs. Shuttleworth."

"True. But he could have been in the kitchen, say, to get a glass of water. Or could he have poisoned something, then given it to Kate to give to her?"

Winston stepped toward Miller. "That brings us back to why he would have then gone on to kill his wife. His new wife." Winston threw his hands in the air. "We're talking in circles."

"What better way to make her feel secure than to marry her?"

"It's a theory. I'll add his name. For now." Winston added *Clayton Block* to the board in the row of suspects, drawing solid lines between him and Mrs. Shuttleworth and between him and Kate. "Susie Pegg and Clayton Block are the only ones with solid lines to both dead women." Winston surveyed the board. How might any of these names be connected to Bobbie Lyon?

"Now back to the why," Miller said. "How did Susie gain from Mrs. Shuttleworth's death?" He scratched a heading in his notepad. "Kate thought she was going to, didn't she?"

"That's right, Thomas. Which might be why she took the necklace and the game piece, because she wasn't recognized the way she'd hoped."

"And who benefits from Kate dying?"

"She wouldn't have left much." Winston stroked his moustache. "Whatever she had would go to her husband now that she was married. And if she took the game piece and the necklace, they might be worth something to him."

"And before she was married, where would they have gone?"

"To her father, or possibly her sister."

Miller stepped toward the board and tapped the sisters' names. "What if it was them? The sisters, I mean. Kate kills Mrs. Shuttleworth. Susie kills Kate. Uses the same poison to avoid suspicion, figuring we would assume it was the same killer."

"Another good idea, Thomas." Winston stepped back from the board. "So where does this leave us? Who do we look at first?"

"Let's start with the sister. She has solid lines connecting her to both victims and could have lied about not seeing Kate before she died." Miller drew a line underneath Susie Pegg's name. "I expect she will be at home."

"Let's find out," said Winston.

CHAPTER 17

Jack

Seeing dark curtains hanging in the windows of the Pegg house, Winston braced himself for a conversation with a family in mourning. Susie Pegg opened the door to Winston and Miller, her face set in a frown. "Do you have news about my sister?"

"Yes, Miss Pegg." Winston held his hat under his arm. "We'd like to ask you a few questions."

"Does this mean you're taking her death seriously?" The words came from her mouth sharply.

"We need to speak to you today." He paused. "I know this is difficult." Her assumption that the police wouldn't take her sister's death seriously rankled him. Winston had taken care to visit her after Doctor Evans' autopsy to let her know the direction the investigation was heading in. Was she lashing out now in anger and loss, or was she attempting to deflect questions?

"Fine." She held the door open to let the policemen inside. "Since you're here, can I fix you a cup of tea?" She took their overcoats and hung them beside the door, making room by shifting the family's coats off two pegs.

"That won't be necessary." Winston wanted to get to the questions quickly.

"What do you want to ask me?"

"Perhaps we could sit somewhere?" Seeing more of the Pegg family home might help answer what had driven Kate to leave and not tell her family where she was going.

Instead of the sitting room they had met in previously, Susie led them into the house's kitchen. "I know you said you don't want a cup of tea, but I think I would," she explained. Her tone had softened somewhat.

Winston and Miller chose the two seats facing the preparation area so they could see Susie as she worked. Miller pulled his notepad from his pocket. "When did you last see your sister before she died?" Winston asked.

"You know this, Detective. I hadn't seen her for two weeks. Not since we left the Shuttleworths'. Kate was angry with me about how I spoke of Clay." She closed her eyes. "I wouldn't have left it so long if I'd known she was going to die."

"Was it usual for the two of you to quarrel?"

Pain pinched her features. "Kate was stubborn. And quick to anger. We might be silent for a few days, but we lived here and worked together. Eventually we had to speak." Susie set slices of cake in front of the policemen. "We've received so much. Someone needs to eat it."

"Why didn't you look for her earlier?" Miller asked. He pulled his plate closer.

She dabbed at her eye with a handkerchief. "I thought she would come home eventually. She would see that Clay wasn't the right man for her."

Still raw after learning of his brother's death, Winston recognized her grief as genuine. Yet what would drive sisters so far apart, especially when they were supposed to be close? And was Susie grieving because she was the cause of her sister's death? Winston softened his voice. "Did you know of her marriage to Mr. Block?"

"Her what?" While preparing the tea, Susie had kept her gaze away from Winston and Miller. As if suddenly understanding what Winston had asked, she swung her head up to lock eyes with him. "They were married?"

Winston flushed at his oversight of not having shared this information with Susie immediately after Kate's death. "According to your sister, they were. I had suggested to her that she might tell you, but if you didn't see her after I spoke with her, she wouldn't have had the opportunity." Susie's reaction to this statement would be telling.

Still standing, Susie placed her palms on the table, as if drawing support from its wooden surface. "Why didn't she send word?" Her fingertips flattened. "Oh, Kate. What did you do?"

Winston leaned forward. "Why do you say he wasn't the right man for your sister?"

"She deserved more, Detective. You saw where they were living."

"She suggested it was temporary. Until Block saved some funds," Miller said.

Susie turned her attention to Miller, her cheeks reddening. "And what would he do with those funds? Drink them away. Lose them on cards." She wiped a tear. "Kate should have waited until he could provide her a proper home."

"Can you think of anyone who might have wished your sister harm?" Winston asked. "When you came to the station to tell me of Kate's death, you insisted that your sister had been murdered. The medical examiner agrees, and thinks your sister and Mrs. Shuttleworth may have died in a similar manner."

Her hand covered her mouth. "Mrs. Shuttleworth was also murdered?" Her face took on the pallor of grief as she worked through the possibilities. "Who would do such a thing? And why?" She collapsed into the chair across from them.

"We believe they were poisoned. And we're trying to figure out the answers to those questions."

Susie sat in silence with a stillness of someone fighting strong emotions. "Who would poison my sister? And Mrs. Shuttleworth? Why Kate?"

"Did you feel any jealousy about your sister taking on such a favoured role, working as Mrs. Shuttleworth's personal maid? It must have been easier than the tasks you had?" Winston asked.

Susie shook her head. "Physically, perhaps. But Mrs. Shuttleworth had high expectations of my sister. She was the kind of woman who made you feel important, and it worked on Kate. She kept her working late hours often so Kate could pamper her after an evening out. Hot bath, comb out her hair. The woman could have done it herself, of course, but she seemed to think she needed to use Kate in this way because it was expected for someone of her status." She closed her eyes and exhaled.

"How did Kate feel about it?" asked Miller.

"I don't think she minded. She enjoyed dressing and assisting Mrs. Shuttleworth. If she had to be up late to do it, Kate thought it meant Mrs. Shuttleworth needed her." Susie entwined her fingers on the tabletop. "Kate mentioned Mrs. Shuttleworth was planning to take her on an overseas trip." She leaned closer to Miller and Winston. "But Mr. Shuttleworth never mentioned it, and he makes all the decisions. I thought he would have said something. Trips need to be planned."

"Would Mr. Shuttleworth have confided his plans in you?" Winston asked.

She coloured and looked away at the suggestion. "Maybe you never worked in service, Detective, but the staff know what the family knows." Susie sat straighter and returned her gaze to Winston. "We often know it before the family. And Mrs. Shuttleworth wasn't going on a trip."

"And none of the staff knew about any travel?" Winston asked.

She sipped from her tea. "No, and his valet would have. A long journey needs time to organize, so the valet would be one of the first to know if it was happening."

Miller and Winston exchanged glances. Nobody had previously spoken of a valet. Winston's mind filled in the obvious thought: was this Bobbie Lyon? "And the valet would have told you?" he asked.

Susie smiled. "He fancied me. He tried to impress me by telling me things he should have kept in confidence." She twirled a lock of hair. "Between him and my sister, I knew everything happening in that house."

"Could the valet have also told your sister? Mistaken her for you?" Miller asked.

"Mr. Shuttleworth couldn't tell us apart, but everyone else could. And Tom—he's the valet—Tom definitely knew me from my sister."

"And how was that?"

"He told me things to get closer." She smoothed her hair.

"Was your sister jealous? Did she try to get close to this Tom?" Winston asked.

"Why would she do that? She had Clay. Even if he wasn't right for her, she didn't need anyone else." A note of jealousy had crept into Susie's voice. Perhaps this was the reason she hadn't sought out her sister in the preceding days.

"What is the valet's surname?" Miller's pencil was poised over his notepad. "Mr. Shuttleworth had said only Mrs. Plum remained from the staff."

"Cullen," said Susie. "Mrs. Plum might know where he lives. Somewhere in the West End, I think. He left when Mrs. Shuttleworth died. Said Mr. Shuttleworth was so changed, devastated by his wife's death, and he better find another boss."

"He didn't stay to support his employer?" Winston asked.

"Mr. Shuttleworth didn't want anyone with him. He refused Tom's usual attentions. Couldn't seem to stand the company of anyone. Tom was right to leave. The house became unbearably sad almost immediately."

"Do you know where he went?" Winston asked.

"He never said."

Miller pushed his empty plate toward the centre of the table. "Have you seen Tom Cullen since he left Mr. Shuttleworth's employment?"

Susie began to shake her head, then stopped. "Yes, actually. He was in the kitchen, speaking with Mrs. Plum."

"Do you remember when this was?"

"I was still working there. It must have been a few days before I stopped." Miller wrote the information down.

Winston leaned forward. How would Susie react to the name of Bobbie Lyon? "Do you know Bobbie Lyon?"

Susie thought for a moment. "I don't know who that is," she answered finally. "Is that who poisoned my sister?"

Winston shook his head. "It's a name that has come up."

Beside him, Miller shifted in his chair. "Is it?" he whispered so only Winston could hear. He'd need to think of a way to explain where the name had come from.

Winston gave Miller a stern look and started to push himself from his chair. "Where is your father, Miss Pegg? And your brother?"

She closed her eyes. "My father doesn't handle loss well, Detective. He's gone to the mill, where he can work without answering questions. It was the same when my mother died. And my brother, he went to his apprenticeship. It started today and he didn't want to miss it."

"Thank you for your time, Miss Pegg." As Winston slid into his coat, he held up a finger. "One more question. In what position did you find your sister's body? Was she under a blanket?"

Susie nodded her head. "But I don't think she wrapped herself up. It was too neat."

Who had tucked Kate under the blanket? Winston wrote the question in his notepad.

They left Susie Pegg sitting at the table, holding her head in her hands.

Miller followed Winston from the house. As soon as they were out of view, he shot his arm out and stopped Winston. "Who is Bobbie Lyon?" The words were clipped.

Winston swallowed. How could he explain himself? "You're right to be upset, Thomas. I. . ." Winston searched for the words. "I came across the name. I wondered if it meant anything to Miss Pegg."

"Came across it? Where? I haven't come across it. And I've been organizing the old files. I haven't seen you in the file room." Miller's voice rose as he spoke.

"I told you that you needn't continue working in there until after we finish this investigation. It's important work, but solving these murders is more pressing." Winston thought he'd already resolved this tension with Miller. Did the constable still feel like he was being taken advantage of? "Why don't you switch back to your own case for the balance of the day? It may be a welcome change. We'll start fresh tomorrow by speaking to Mrs. Plum to help us track down Tom Cullen. And perhaps, as Mr. Shuttleworth's valet, he will know something about this trip that only Mrs. Block seemed aware of. Then we will interview Mr. Block."

"And find out more about Bobbie Lyon," Miller muttered.

Winston let him go, hoping that an afternoon on his own case would soothe him.

*

WINSTON SPENT THE rest of the afternoon organizing the file room himself. The mindless task allowed him to think about the case. Perhaps Miller would see the gesture as penance to repair the rift that was growing between them. When he finished, he wrote another note to Riley.

Dear Riley,

Have you found any additional information about Bobbie Lyon? Were they ever arrested? Is this person male or female? I am struggling to figure out how to use this information without explaining where it came from.

With thanks,

Jack

With the question of Bobbie Lyon's relationship to the murdered women still unanswered, Winston slipped on his coat and left the station. He walked toward his home, following a route that took him by the home of Melodia Spectre. As he drew closer to her street, his palms grew clammy. How did this woman rattle him so? He breathed deeply to calm himself as he rounded the corner. A mix of disappointment and relief washed through him as he saw that the windows of her house were dark. He considered knocking on the door in case she was home but decided against it. If she was there, she clearly did not want company. And what would he tell her if she answered?

He walked past the house and turned around at the other end of the street. By the time he passed the house again, he'd decided to come back another time. Or maybe on another day, he'd stop at the little shop near the station where Melodia occasionally worked. As he crossed in front of the door, light seeped out between a gap in the curtains hanging in the front window.

His pulse quickened. Should he stop? No. He would go home, rest, and face the case in the morning. He turned his eyes to the ground and kept walking.

CHAPTER 18

Riley

GARBLED ANNOUNCEMENTS ON the hospital's intercom system and the sound of beeping monitors faded into the background as Riley reread Jack's message. To clear her head, she began pacing the hospital corridor. She paused outside her sister's room to look through the rectangular window. The curtain around Lucy's bed was drawn. Monitors for the patient nearest the door blocked Riley's view even further. She twisted the handle and nudged the door open with her foot, taking a quick glance over her shoulder. The staff were busy attending to other patients. Coast clear, Riley stepped into the room and quietly shut the door behind her. Rhythmic beeps sounded in the room. As she walked by the first bed, Riley made a point to avoid looking at the patient. Whoever they were, she didn't want to invade their privacy.

She tugged the curtain around Lucy's bed to make a space for her to fit through. All her imaginings had not prepared her for the sight of her sister connected to multiple sensors and machines. Riley felt a sudden coldness at her core. She pulled at the curtain behind her, and Lucy's eyes popped open. "Oh, sorry! I didn't mean to wake you," Riley said. A flood of relief eased the cold in the pit of her stomach. If Lucy was awake, this was a good thing.

"I'm just dozing. It's hard to sleep in here with all the noise and lights. I shouldn't even be here." She motioned as if she was going to remove the sensor from her finger.

Riley gently moved Lucy's hand away. "No, you shouldn't be here. But you are because you're sick."

"Alex overreacted. I'm tired. Or run down." Lucy tried to prop herself up on her elbows. "Actually, I probably just need a good detox routine."

"Luce, it's a little more than needing a detox routine, whatever that is. You look like your body is shutting down."

"Shutting down? More like firing up. This is what happens when you reawaken your body, Riley. It's completely normal."

Riley dug her nails into her palms. What was Lucy talking about? None of this was normal. "I'm going to suggest we listen to whatever the doctor says is normal. They wouldn't have you connected to these"—Riley pointed to the machines beside Lucy's bed—"if there wasn't a reason."

"They can run tests, but I won't take any of their medicine."

This was too much. "What are you talking about, Lucy? *Their medicine?* As if you don't believe in it."

"I believe we're told to believe in it. But I also believe that our bodies can heal themselves."

"Sure. If you get a cut, your body will heal. Good as new. But your heart racing, headaches, not being able to sleep. . . It's more than a cut. It's a big deal. And if your body needs help to recover, you need to accept it. No matter what that help is."

Lucy rolled over so her back was facing Riley. "I'm tired."

Riley stared at her sister's back and tried to calm her swirl of thoughts. Why was Lucy talking like she no longer believed in doctors or medicine? When had she started to think like this? How could Riley reason with her? Within minutes, Lucy's breathing was deep and regular. Good. Lucy needed rest, even if she wasn't listening to the doctors. Maybe with rest, Lucy would think more clearly.

The faux leather of the chair beside Lucy's bed crinkled as Riley settled into it. Lucy rolled onto her back, but her breathing remained steady. "Sorry," Riley whispered. "Did I disturb you?" She watched her sister's chest rise and fall. After another minute, Riley began to speak quietly, barely above a whisper. "Things are okay at the museum. Sort of. Claire, my boss, is taking some time away and has asked Nick—you remember Nick, we worked on the police exhibit together—Claire has asked Nick to be interim head. She didn't choose me because I'm inexperienced, which is fair. What's not fair is that Nick is hardly more experienced than I am. Johnny says I just need to show Claire how valuable I am, and this is my opportunity, as Nick won't have time to help me with the next exhibit."

The rise and fall of Lucy's chest was hypnotic. Riley even found the faint chatter from staff outside the room somehow soothing.

"The thing is, I'm nervous to do it alone. I need Nick's help. But I won't admit that to him." She shifted in the chair, leaning closer to her sister. "Here is something else I won't admit to anyone." Riley timed her breath with her sister's. "Lucy, I can communicate with a police detective from the late nineteenth century. I can see his entries in this journal I found. And he can see mine. We write back and forth, and I've helped him with a couple of cases. Pretty neat, eh? I have a time-bending journal, and I use it to solve crimes. I'm a superhero archivist girl!"

Someone entered the room and Riley froze. A head appeared from behind the curtain. A nurse, with a stern frown. "What was that?"

Riley brought her hand to her mouth. "Sorry. I got a little excited there, telling her a story."

"Be careful not to overstimulate her, please."

Riley nodded, cheeks flushing. She leaned toward her sister and whispered in her ear. "Never mind. Forget I said that last bit. Just get better, okay?"

The nurse checked his watch. "Visiting doesn't start for another hour. Sneak out before my supervisor sees you. She's strict about visitors, and you don't want her to prevent you from seeing your sister."

"Your supervisor would do that?"

"You don't want to risk it."

"Thanks." Riley squeezed Lucy's foot. "I'll see you later, Lucy." Riley waved to the nurse as she left the room. Maybe he could talk some sense into her sister.

✳

WHEN RILEY EMERGED from her sister's room, Alex was speaking with the doctor. She joined them. The doctor's face was kind, reflecting years of practice in dealing with concerned family members. But her eyes revealed fatigue with a heaviness in the lids and telltale shadows beneath them. In a burst of assertiveness, Riley introduced herself. "I'm her sister," she said, "so anything you say to her husband, you can say to me." The doctor looked at Alex, who nodded. "Please tell us what you've learned about Lucy."

The doctor led Riley and Alex to a corner, away from the ward's main desk. "We are running tests. You should take some comfort that Lucy's condition remains unchanged. But I have to ask whether she has been exposed to any toxins recently."

"Toxins? Like poison?" Riley's throat tightened as she thought of Jack's case. The image of the necklace popped into her head. It couldn't be that, could it? She dismissed the thought. "She has been eating really healthy, hasn't she, Alex? I would think that means she's had exposure to fewer toxins."

"We don't eat a lot of processed foods, though we eat at restaurants a couple of times a week." He drew his hand across his face. "I'm not as diligent as Lucy about washing produce. Could it be something we ate?"

"I'm not familiar with any food-borne illnesses that present like this. I was thinking poison, as your wife's sister suggests." The doctor nodded toward Riley.

His face growing pale, Alex formed an *O* with his mouth. "Who would poison Lucy?" He paused as if he was considering the possibilities. "A jealous social media influencer?" he blurted.

The doctor shot Riley a confused look. She was about to give her some context when Alex continued his stream of thought.

"Her number of followers has been growing steadily. She was thinking about quitting the boutique so she could curate lives full time." Alex had added air quotes around "curate lives." Riley couldn't suppress a giggle.

"Sorry." She covered her mouth. "It's such a Lucy thing to describe what she does as curation rather than admit she's just trying to sell stuff to people." She glanced at the doctor's face. Other than an arch of her eyebrows, it was hard to guess what she was thinking.

Riley refocused. Lucy was sick. Very sick. And the doctor didn't seem to know why. "Doctor, what kind of poison is it?" The doctor finally turned to face Riley, as if noticing her for the first time. "Could it be something she's touched recently? Like her clothing or her jewellery?" Was it possible for a necklace to poison someone? Maybe the idea wasn't so far-fetched.

"We are still running tests." The doctor checked her watch. "She's in good hands." She spoke the words deliberately, locking eyes with each of them before turning away.

Alex put his arm around Riley. "She'll be okay. The doctor would tell us if she knew more."

Riley remembered the conversation with her sister. "She just said something about not trusting doctors. That her body would heal itself." She searched Alex's features for his reaction. "How long has she been talking that way?"

Alex stiffened. "You know your sister. She picks up on an idea and runs with it for a while, then moves on to the next thing. I figured this would be the same."

"Still. Why aren't you sick? What has she eaten or touched that you haven't?"

Johnny appeared with coffee and muffins. "Come sit down you two. Let's get out of the hallway." He placed a takeout cup in Riley's hands, then handed one to Alex. "I know it's tough, but it sounds like we just need to wait."

"I don't think you understand, Johnny. Lucy is everything to me." Tears welled in Riley's eyes.

"I understand. She's your sister. And Alex, buddy, I get it. She's your wife. But the pair of you haunting this place is not going to help the doctors and nurses find answers any faster. The least you can do is give them space."

"I know you're right, but I feel so helpless." Riley sipped from her cup. "Thank you."

Johnny kissed her forehead and brushed a strand of hair behind her ear.

"Thanks, Johnny," said Alex.

They moved out of the flow of hallway traffic toward the waiting area. "It's no problem, Alex," Johnny answered. "Now, what was Riley asking? Why aren't you sick? It's a good question. You live in the same place, so let's assume whatever is affecting Lucy isn't environmental. At least not the environment you share."

"We can check to see if any of her colleagues are sick," Alex said.

"What about her friends?" Riley offered. "Lucy and I met with some of her friends the other night. I'll see if anyone else is sick."

"Great idea, Riley." Alex handed Lucy's phone to Riley. "Just in case you don't have their numbers."

"I've got most of them on social media, but this helps." Riley pulled out her phone, settled into a chair, and began texting and messaging Lucy's friends. When her phone started buzzing almost immediately, she mouthed "sorry" to a stern nurse and set it on silent. Within minutes, most of Lucy's friends had replied, offering well wishes and confirming they were healthy. Riley's heart sank when she saw the reply from Jayne, whom they'd seen the other night.

> I've had a rash. A reaction to new laundry soap, I think.

Riley showed the phone to Johnny. "What do you think?"

"Did your sister have a rash before she got sick?"

"She didn't say anything to me, but maybe Alex noticed something. Where did he go?"

"He's just gone to the washroom."

When Alex returned, his eyes were glistening. "Sorry." He shook his head as if to clear it.

"Alex, did you notice if Lucy had any rashes in the last couple of days?" Riley asked.

He rubbed his hands together. "Rashes? If she did, she didn't tell me. And a rash wouldn't send her here, would it?"

"What about redness? Anything like that?"

He started rubbing his neck. "You know, her neck looked red the other night. She said it was itchy but thought it was some scarf she'd been wearing. The fibres didn't agree with her skin, I think she said."

"What does that mean?" Riley fought an eye roll. "How do you put up with her?"

"She's not Influencer Lucy all the time."

"Influencer Lucy?"

"It's how I think of her when she's preparing for social media photos. You should see the lighting contraptions she sets up. I'm trying to get her to use the spare bedroom, but she said something about the light being better in the living room."

"Well, you do get so much light through that window," Riley said. She shook her head. "But that doesn't matter right now. What scarf did Lucy think the redness was from? Does she have a new one?"

"She was sent a dozen last week." Alex held up his palms. "I don't know what she does with all the stuff she gets. I mean, she needs to do something. It's cluttering up our place."

Riley blinked. "A dozen scarves? That's almost two a day. Who wears so many scarves?"

"Exactly." Alex threw his hands in the air with an exaggerated shrug. "What did Lucy's friends say?"

"One of them said she had a rash. Jayne. We saw her last weekend. She gave Lucy a beautiful—" Riley's hand flew to her mouth. "Oh no." Her heart sank. It must be the necklace.

"What's wrong?"

Riley leaned closer to Alex. "You said Lucy's neck was red?" Her foot began an involuntary bounce.

"Yes. Why?"

"Jayne gave Lucy the necklace you had this morning. Lucy wore it to the gala." She thought of the picture of Mrs. Shuttleworth wearing the same necklace, a picture taken shortly before her death.

"The pearl necklace?" Alex formed each word slowly, coaxing his mouth around the syllables.

"Yes."

"She wore it all day. Said it made her feel pretty while she otherwise felt lousy."

"Where is it now?"

"I just snuck into her room to put it around her neck. I thought she'd want to wake up beautiful. Do you think that's what's made Lucy sick?"

"I don't know. What if the necklace has something on it? Something she absorbed when it rubbed onto her skin?"

Alex stood, starting to pace. "Is that even possible? I need to get it off her. The doctors can run tests on it or something."

"Yes. Go." She squeezed Alex's arm.

Johnny put down his phone. A frown creased his brow. "Riley, I have to go to work for a couple of hours."

"You do?" The ache of disappointment that swept through her surprised her.

"I thought I'd be able to put off this meeting, but I can't."

She slumped in her chair. "I understand."

Johnny gave her a side hug, then got up from his chair. Despite medical staff moving around her, the sight of his back moving down the hall left her feeling so alone. What did that mean? It was too much to analyze her feelings for Johnny now. She pulled her bag onto her lap, her breath calming as she felt the journal inside.

CHAPTER 19

Riley

As Riley walked down the museum's hallway toward the archive, she drew strength from the familiarity of her surroundings. Alex had given the necklace to Lucy's nurse for testing, then insisted that Riley go to work. The distraction would help time pass while the doctors continued tests. Alex assured her he would call if anything changed.

She pushed open the archive door, bracing to see Nick. Then she remembered he was spending the day with Claire as she transitioned responsibilities to him. Perfect. This space had quickly become one of her favourites in the museum, and she liked it best when she was alone.

She gave herself two hours to track down more information about the necklace. Before she opened her laptop, she placed her hand on the journal, willing Jack to help her find an answer. She shook her head. Wasting her time on fanciful thinking wasn't going to help Lucy.

As her laptop powered on, she checked her phone. A message from Jayne. She'd promised to send details of the craft-show vendor who had sold her the necklace. Riley thanked her, noting that the name matched one on her short list of three from the night before. She decided to call the woman directly, see if she might be able to persuade her to share some details in light of Lucy's hospitalization: Where had she found the necklace? Had she experienced any symptoms herself? Riley dialled the number and waited for the call to connect. A guarded voice answered.

"Hello." Riley's face grew warm. "My name is Riley Finch. My sister's friend bought a necklace from you, and now my sister is sick. I need to understand where you got the necklace so I can figure out—"

"It wasn't my necklace. I didn't do anything to it." The woman cut Riley off with a defensive tone.

Riley forced herself to reply calmly. "Oh no. I don't mean to imply—"

"It sure sounds like you're implying I've made your sister sick. Stop hassling me."

Riley's hands grew clammy. This woman had completely misunderstood her. "Wait." Riley held her hand up even though the woman couldn't see her. "Please. Don't hang up. I don't think you did anything to the necklace." Her voice started to waver. "My sister, Lucy. She's in the hospital, and if I know more about what she's touched in the last few days, I might be able to help her. I'm starting with you because she only received the necklace just before she fell ill." She lowered her hand and closed her eyes. "Please."

Riley counted to ten. When the vendor didn't say anything, she continued. "I just wonder if it wasn't something Lucy's touched that she is reacting to. She posted a picture of herself on social media. Look up lucydoes on PictureMe." She spelled her sister's profile handle and waited, hoping the woman would follow her instruction. Riley scrolled through the photos, certain the vendor was doing the same thing.

"I see her. Pretty. And she looks lovely in the necklace," the vendor said. "She has a lot of followers."

With that sentence, Riley sensed the woman's attitude soften. She considered her approach. Would the woman respond better if Riley hinted that Lucy might promote her business to those followers? How would Lucy react at Riley offering her services for free? She'd deal with her sister later, once she was recovered. Surely she'd see that it was the only way Riley could get the information she needed.

"She does. And brands have started approaching her for collaborations. I can't promise she'll do it, but I could ask her to post about your business." Riley counted to three. "If she survives." She wasn't used to being so assertive, but her sister's life counted more than being polite. Lucy was being offered jaw-dropping amounts to promote brands to her followers. If nothing else persuaded this woman to share what she knew, the promise of free publicity was all Riley could offer. She counted to three again, willing the emotion from her voice. "Will you tell me where you got the necklace?"

"She'll promote my brand if she lives?"

Riley fought the urge to yell into the phone. How insensitive! The woman couldn't have put it more coldly. She held her tongue. Clearly, money talks. "I'll ask her," she said. Riley's flare-up of anger shifted to excitement. She should try assertiveness more often.

"Fine. My brother found it. He was doing demolition in a house as part of a renovation. The necklace was there when he knocked out a wall."

Progress. If Riley could find the house, she could direct Jack to it. Her mind raced. Maybe he could prevent Lucy from ever getting the necklace. "Where is the house? Is he still working at it?"

"It's in Mount Pleasant, on Manitoba Street, near Fourteenth Avenue. It's one of those buildings where they keep the exterior frame but gut the inside." Riley knew the renovation method the woman described. She appreciated the nod to preserving a building's heritage. "I assume he's still working on that job. It sounded like it was going to be a big one," the vendor said.

"Thank you. I really appreciate it."

"You sounded desperate."

So did you. "I am. What's your brother's name?"

"Ryan. Ryan Griffin. I hope your sister is okay."

"Thank you again." Riley ended the call and repacked her bag, hoping she'd find a taxi on the street.

✳

THREE TAXIS WAITED outside the museum, and Riley whispered thanks to the powers that be. It was handy that she worked in a relatively popular tourist area of the city. She hopped in the first one and gave the intersection where the jewellery vendor said her brother was still working on the house renovation. Within minutes she was at the corner, paying the driver.

Two houses were under construction: one with insulation sheeting flapping and the other only a wooden frame. Construction noises floated from the house with insulation, so Riley approached it first. She balanced on plywood boards that covered the muddy pathway, following them to steps fashioned from cinder blocks.

"Hello?" she called into the doorless house as she climbed the steps. "Can I come in?"

"Who are you looking for?" a voice asked from behind her. "You really shouldn't be here unless you're wearing boots. Are those steel-toed?"

Riley pivoted to find herself eye to eye with a hammer-wielding man with a pencil tucked behind his ear. "Sorry, they're not," she stammered and pointed at her running shoes.

"What are you doing here?"

She squared her shoulders, remembering the image of Lucy in her hospital bed. "I'm looking for someone named Ryan Griffin. His sister told me he was working on a house around here, and I have a couple of questions for him. Do you know him?"

The man in front of her thought for a moment. "No. I can ask if there's a Ryan working on this job. I've only been here a couple of days. Do you know what trade he is?"

Riley shrugged. "He was doing something with walls?" She mimed sliding her hands against an invisible wall.

"Demo?"

"You want me to demonstrate?" Riley clasped her hands together and started to swing as if she were hitting a wall with a bat. A grin spread across the man's face.

"No. I mean, was he demolishing?"

Riley kept her face neutral. She had more important things to do than wonder how big of a fool she'd just made of herself. "I don't know. Look, I'm kind of in a rush. Can I just go ask the others?"

"Better not." He tapped his toe against the cinder block she was standing on, making her wobble. "I'll ask for you. Wait here."

He stepped up to her level, which Riley assumed would be one step below porch level once the renovations were complete. She pulled out her phone to see if the city archives had a picture of the house before it had been gutted. Did builders work with historians to ensure that they were preserving a house's original architectural style? She was mid-search when the man returned, followed by another, shorter man. Tools clinked together on their work belts as they approached.

"You're looking for me?" he asked, eyes appraising Riley, then glancing over her shoulder. "I don't know you."

Riley got straight to the point. "I've spoken with your sister, and she told me you found a necklace. She sold it to my sister's friend, and I think—" Riley waved her hands. "It doesn't matter. I need to know where you found the necklace and anything you can tell me about it."

Ryan looked back at the other man, who shrugged. "I guess I can take a short break." He motioned for Riley to step onto a plywood bridge, then followed her. "Come on this side of the fence."

They stood beside a sign that read Authorized Personnel Only. Riley cringed and pointed at the sign. "I didn't notice this sign when I got here," she said. "I really needed to speak to you." Her voice was doing that thing when she was nervous, getting higher and louder.

"What sign?" He looked where she pointed. "Oh, that's up for insurance. You won't get a fine or anything. You're asking about that necklace?"

"Yes. Anything you can tell me. Where was it in the house? Did you find anything else near it?"

"I found it a couple of weeks ago on a different job."

Riley glanced briefly over her shoulder. Not this location. She nodded at Ryan, signalling her encouragement for him to continue.

"We were cleaning out the place. Must have been original walls. I found newspapers from a hundred years ago stuffed inside once I opened them up." He wiped his hand across his chin, leaving a trail of dust. "Anyway, I keep an eye out for things. You never know what people stick into their walls, and sometimes my sister can sell them."

"That's interesting. And the necklace?"

"The necklace was in one of the walls on the ground floor. I don't know what the room was for. It wasn't a bathroom or anything like that, though, because there was no plumbing nearby. Anyway, I found it after I knocked a hole in the wall."

Riley nodded again.

"First I found newspapers." He rubbed his face again, smearing the dust. "I found the necklace wrapped in one." He cocked his head. "That was a first for me."

"Do you remember the address? Where you found the necklace, I mean."

"Sure." He pulled out his phone. "I have it here somewhere."

Riley noted the address as he read it out. "What did you do with the necklace after you found it?" she asked.

"I put it in my pocket for my sister and kept on with the demo. I thought there might be something else. Maybe more jewellery." Ryan shook his head. "But there wasn't anything else worth keeping." He ran his fingers through his hair.

Riley bit her lip. What about Jack's missing game piece? "Did you check in the newspapers? Was there a little wooden game piece wrapped inside one?"

"I don't think so." He shifted his weight from one foot to the other. "Actually, I don't know. I don't look at everything carefully. Just whatever catches my eye. It's a pretty necklace." Ryan leaned a little closer and said, "You said your sister bought it from mine. How much did she pay? My sister told me it was only worth a few bucks, so she didn't give me anything for it. Was she telling me the truth?" Ryan flushed. He'd revealed something of his relationship with his sister and looked a bit uncomfortable.

"My sister's friend bought it, but she didn't say how much she spent." There was no sense causing a rift between the siblings, but Ryan was helping her. "You might want to negotiate a better deal with your sister if she sells a lot of stuff you find, especially if she's not paying anything to you for finding it."

"Yeah, maybe. I found an old toy once, metal. A little monkey with cymbals. She didn't want it, because it was broken. I find lots of old newspapers, but those aren't worth anything." He narrowed his eyes. "Are they?"

Only for the history they represent. But he wasn't going to care about that. "Doubtful. But you should give them a read. You might uncover an interesting tidbit about the city."

Ryan shifted his weight again. She doubted he would find reading yellowed newspaper pages interesting. "Do you have any more questions? I should get back to work."

"You've been really helpful, Ryan. One more thing. Did you get a rash or anything like that after you touched the necklace? From where you touched it?"

He narrowed his eyes. "Rash? No. I slipped it into my tool pouch." He pointed to a zippered pouch on his work belt, tools dangling from the band beside it. A chain with an attached carabiner looped from the belt and disappeared into Ryan's pocket. Riley assumed his keys were on the other end of the chain. "I didn't get any rashes or anything. Is there something wrong with the necklace?"

"I'm trying to find out. Thanks again for your time." She turned to the house and waved her hand in a broad arc. "I'm sure this place will look great when you're done."

Ryan said goodbye and left Riley standing at the fence, deep in thought about all the what-ifs. What would happen if she told Jack where to find the necklace? Would Lucy still get sick? Would something worse happen?

She started walking down the hill toward a street where she could flag a taxi to take her back to the museum. Many of the structures that Jack knew in this area had now been replaced with light-industrial buildings. On the next corner was a small green space with a bench. She stopped to write a note to Jack.

CHAPTER 20

Jack

WINSTON AND MILLER approached the Shuttleworth house in silence. The words of Riley's most recent message circled in Winston's head.

Dear Jack,

My sister has been admitted to hospital because of an unknown illness. Her doctors think she may have been exposed to a poison. Here's the strange part: Lucy's friend gave her a necklace very like the one you described as having been stolen from the Shuttleworth house. I've compared this necklace with photographs of Penelope Shuttleworth wearing what I believe is the one that was stolen. Lucy was wearing it the day she fell ill. Do you think it's possible that whatever poison killed the women in your investigation is killing Lucy? If so, I need your help to discover what it is so I can save my sister. I'm sorry to dash this off in such a short message, but I must get back to my sister.

I'm so worried.

Riley

PS: The necklace was found within the walls of a house that was built in your time—a house located in Mount Pleasant.

PPS: I have been unable to look for any additional information about Bobbie Lyon.

The situation mystified Winston. Could what Riley suggested possibly be true? Could Lucy have been wearing Mrs. Shuttleworth's necklace? And is it possible that the necklace is what made her sick—and killed Mrs. Shuttleworth and Kate Block?

Winston drew a deep breath of cool morning air and recalled the scene when they'd arrived at the Block apartment to examine Kate's body. She hadn't been wearing the necklace. And with the focus so suddenly shifted from a burglary to a murder investigation, he hadn't searched the apartment for the jewellery. He would need to speak with both Susie Pegg and Clay Block. Perhaps one of them now has it in their possession. If he retrieved it, Lucy wouldn't be able to wear it. How would that change things?

Winston shifted his satchel to his other hand and focused on the task at hand. He couldn't search for the Mount Pleasant house now, although he had an idea of where it might be. Several homes were under construction in the area. First, he and Miller were going to speak to Mrs. Plum.

"Thomas." Winston put out a hand, signalling for Miller to stop. "Before we call at the house, I'd like to say something." He had been rehearsing his apology all morning.

Miller's eyes widened with surprise. "There's no need."

"There is. I hope you'll agree that we are a good investigative pair. We complement each other."

Miller nodded, his face impassive.

"That's why I hope you'll believe me that I didn't intentionally keep anything about the investigation from you. I read a reference to Bobbie Lyon in relation to Shuttleworth. I thought it might have had some meaning to Susie Pegg, which is why I asked her."

Miller's expression dissolved into disbelief. "I haven't seen the name on anything. We've had hardly any papers to sort through."

"Which is why I'm frustrated that I cannot seem to pinpoint the source, Thomas. As you said yesterday, it wasn't in the file room." Winston had left the journal in his rooms at Mrs. Bradley's house, meaning his statement was partially truthful. "I spent some time in the file room yesterday. I'd like to make it part of our regular routine to tidy up in there, keep the records updated. We can share that responsibility, if you'd like. Or, if you'd prefer, it can be solely yours."

Miller pursed his lips. "You trust me with that?"

"I do. And I think you'll manage it well. I am certain the work you do in there will be invaluable. But I still want you to investigate with me. Your instincts are good."

Standing taller, Miller responded with a slight smile. "I will think about it while we finish this case." He swallowed without betraying his thoughts. "No more secret sources of information."

A more enthusiastic response would have eased Winston's discomfort. Perhaps, in time, Miller would agree. At least he hadn't refused completely. "Let's speak to Mrs. Plum."

*

"OH, HELLO AGAIN. What are you doing here?" Mrs. Plum said as she ushered Winston and Miller into the kitchen. "Not that I'm unhappy to see you again, of course." Polly, the maid they'd met earlier, was busy chopping vegetables.

"We were hoping you could answer some questions. About the Pegg sisters, specifically."

Mrs. Plum looked toward Polly and patted a strand of hair into the loose bun pinned at the nape of her neck. "You have questions? For me?"

"And some sad news, I'm afraid." Winston looked past her toward Polly.

"I haven't much time, Detective. But I'll spare you what I can, seeing as your face is so glum." She turned back toward the maid. "Polly, leave that for now. Go start on cleaning the library." Polly set down the knife and left. Mrs. Plum returned her attention to the policemen. "No need for Polly to be present for your news. I'll tell her whatever it is later."

A welcome blast of warmth from the oven hit Winston as they passed it on the way to the kitchen table. Mrs. Plum moved aside a bundle of herbs so she could sit, and clasped her hands in front of her. Miller and Winston chose chairs opposite her. "What is it you have come to share? It's best if we start with the sad news, I should think."

Winston inhaled, drawing the breath slowly as he pulled his notepad from his jacket. "Mrs. Plum, I'm not happy to inform you of this unpleasant news, but Kate Pegg, now Kate Block, is dead."

Eyes wide, she shook her head. "Kate?" She leaned back as she let out a groan. "What happened?"

"It's not clear yet. The medical examiner is looking at her body today."

She blew her nose into a handkerchief. "Did you say she was Kate Block now? When did she marry that carpenter?" Mrs. Plum seemed to have forgotten the news of the former maid's death. "That is such wonderful news. I'll have to send her a—" She caught herself too late. "Oh my." She twisted the handkerchief in her fingers.

Winston waited silently as she recovered herself. She met his eyes and said, "I haven't seen her since she left. I told you that when you asked the other day." She leaned forward. "Did you speak to her? Get the answers you were hoping for?"

"We did, thank you."

"And her husband. He must be upset. Unless. . ." She leaned forward, as if to share a confidence. "Unless he did it?"

"Why would you suggest that?" Miller asked.

"He. . ." Her lips moved soundlessly as she searched for a word. "He'd done some work here at the house. That's how they met. I didn't speak to him much then. It was only after she'd taken a fancy to him. I sat him down at this table and we had a good talk." She wrung her hands. "Those girls, not having their mother around. They needed someone looking out for them."

Winston made a notation in his notepad. The facts were consistent with what they'd already learned. "When was this, Mrs. Plum? And why would you suggest he killed his wife?"

"Not long ago. Before Mrs. Shuttleworth. . . " Her eyes glistened and she dropped her gaze. "It was a passing thought. Nothing serious."

While she composed herself, Winston made a note. Right around the time Block joined the post office. Perhaps something Mrs. Plum had said had persuaded him to pursue different work. "Can you tell us about Mr. Shuttleworth's valet, Tom?"

Mrs. Plum's features pinched when she heard the name. "Tom? He left when Mrs. Shuttleworth died."

"Why didn't you mention him when we spoke last? I asked about other staff," Winston said.

"He wasn't staff when you asked. Not anymore, at least."

"Neither were the Pegg girls, and we spoke about them," said Miller.

She wagged her finger at Winston. "You asked specifically about them. Had you asked about Tom, I would have spoken of him."

Winston drew a breath to tamp down his frustration. "Everyone in the house when Mrs. Shuttleworth grew ill and died is important, Mrs. Plum. Should we know about any other staff? Or former staff members?"

"It's Polly and me here every day. Charlie a few days each week. Mr. Shuttleworth fired everyone else. Or they left."

"And what about Tom? Did Mr. Shuttleworth fire him?" Winston asked.

"Tom is a nice boy, but a little too full of himself. He chased after those Pegg girls, Susie mostly, and Mrs. Shuttleworth caught him cornering Polly. The next day, Mr. Shuttleworth fired him, reluctantly. But it was unfair. It was only another day or so before Mrs. Shuttleworth died. He's managed without a valet because he hardly leaves the house now that she's gone."

Why would Susie have told Winston that Cullen left voluntarily after Mrs. Shuttleworth died? Winston wrote the question down.

"His actions didn't warrant being fired?"

"Not at all. He flirted a bit with the girls, made them laugh, sure, but who can blame a young man working with pretty young women? I don't think they meant to turn his head, but I'm sure even you and your young constable have admired a pretty face or two. And to work somewhere with not one but two attractive, if foolish, girls. . . It's quite tempting, don't you agree, Detective?"

"Are you saying Tom and the Pegg sisters behaved inappropriately?" Miller asked.

"Not that I ever saw." She set her shoulders back. "He might have fancied Susie, though. Kate was always speaking of her Clay, so Tom wouldn't have wasted much time trying anything with her." She leaned back. "I warned him to be careful. It's better not to have romantic feelings for someone you work with."

Winston set his notepad down. "I understand that you were close with him."

"Not like how you're suggesting, Detective. We are related." She looked at her fingers, splayed wide on the table.

"Then you should be able to tell us where we can find him, Mrs. Plum. Cullen is his surname, correct?" Winston asked. "His mother is your sister?"

"She is my cousin, more accurately." She balled her hands. "When Mr. Shuttleworth took Tom on, I told him to use the name Thomas, but he said he had always been Tom and would stay that way no matter where he worked."

"Where will we find him?" Miller asked.

"My cousin and her family live in a small house near English Bay. I'll write the address for you. Tom's got himself a new job, working in a shipyard. He's always been handy, and there's so much construction going on. The pay is better, too."

"But the work is harder, I imagine? He didn't want to find another position as a valet?" Winston asked.

"I think he found the work here to be boring. We're not all suited for service. This way, he is around other men his age and doesn't have to worry about shoe polish and ironing." She unclenched her hands. "I'm sorry to hear about Kate. She was a lovely girl. Is Susie okay?"

"She is grieving," Winston said.

"Oh, the poor dear." Mrs. Plum stood. Winston and Miller scraped their chairs along the floor as they rose a beat after her. "I'll send some food for her. Would you bring it? And maybe something for Mr. Block? He must be so upset to lose his wife so soon after their wedding."

"That is very kind of you, Mrs. Plum," Winston said. "Are you sending more of those scones from the other day?"

"I made some today. Would you like some for yourself, Detective, or you, Constable?" She pointed to a cooling rack.

"We will take one each if there are extras," Winston said.

"I insist." She started preparing the packages.

Miller tilted his head at Winston, his eyes narrow. "Sir?"

"Do you know of any tensions in the Shuttleworths' relationship?" Winston asked.

Mrs. Plum set her hands on the large work table. "I couldn't say for certain as I rarely saw them together, being in the kitchen. Mrs. Shuttleworth was always kind, and she certainly never said a harsh word about her husband to me."

"Did you hear anything from any of the other staff who might have seen them together?" Winston asked.

"I discouraged gossip, Detective. It isn't good for anyone."

"It rarely is. Still, stories have a way of circulating, don't they?" Winston asked. "Did you hear any about the Shuttleworths?"

"Nothing I believed." She resumed preparing the packages.

"I appreciate your sharing what you know with me." Winston waited a beat and asked, "On that note, do you know who Bobbie Lyon is?"

One of the packages dropped from Mrs. Plum's hand. "Oh, dear me," she said and stooped to collect it. "My fingers. I fear there's a little arthritis creeping in." Miller bent to help her. "What was that name again? Robbie? Bobbie? I don't know anyone by that name." She handed the packages to Miller, who passed them to Winston to put in his satchel.

"Thank you for these." Winston gestured with a package of the scones. "I'll see that they are delivered."

"Please pass along my condolences. Kate was a sweet, sweet girl." Her cheeks flushed. "I know I called her silly, but it was only in the most affectionate way."

"I understand, Mrs. Plum," Winston said.

Once they were outside the house, Miller grabbed Winston's arm. "Are you really going to give those to Mr. Block and Susie Pegg? When we're not sure what kind of poison killed Kate?"

Winston thought of Riley's note and her theory that the necklace might be the source of the poison. "Thomas, you ate cake at Susie's house, and we've eaten Mrs. Plum's scones without harm. But you're right. Until we know what poisoned Kate Block, we should be cautious."

"Do you suspect her, sir? Mrs. Plum, I mean."

"I'm not sure. To speak to her, she doesn't seem to have an unkind word for anyone, and I cannot see what Kate could have done to deserve her fate. As for Mrs. Shuttleworth, I am similarly perplexed. Mrs. Plum seems to have cared for her, and I struggle to imagine her killing anyone."

"What next? Who do we speak to?"

"If we figure out the source of the poison, we may be able to identify the poisoner."

"Sir, is it possible the poisoning was unintentional?"

"If they'd accidentally been exposed to a poison, surely we would see others who were sick or dying," Winston said.

"How do we go about figuring out the source of the poison?" Miller splayed his hands, in a gesture of exasperation.

"Evans will identify the poison, Thomas, and his findings will suggest potential sources. He's working on that now, but I expect it will take some time." Winston lightly clasped Miller's shoulder and said, "While he performs that work, let us continue to interview those we've listed as suspects."

The necklace still loomed in Winston's thoughts. If Evans concluded that the poison was somehow absorbed by skin contact, Winston would insist that Riley share the exact location of where the necklace was found. He squared his shoulders and set his mind on next steps. "While we are in this neighbourhood, Thomas, let's speak to Mr. Block and Susie again. Then we will find Tom Cullen."

Riley

RILEY LOOKED UP at the sound of a key in her lock. Mom. Staying for the first time in Riley's apartment. Or rather staying for the first time since Riley's father had died. This apartment—the one her parents had bought to retire in—now held painful memories for her mother. Riley poked her head into the spare bedroom on her way to the front door. The lavender she'd placed beside the bed had filled the room with an inviting scent. She breathed deeply as if doing so would help calm her mother's nerves.

Riley and her mother greeted each other with tearful hugs. "Visiting hours at the hospital are over for the day, Mom," Riley said, after her mother had set down her bags. "We'll go first thing tomorrow. Besides, the doctors want her to rest while they try to figure out what's making her sick."

"I can't believe they haven't found an answer yet." Her mother's forehead was creased with worry. "What have they been doing all this time?"

"Running tests. They wait for the results on one round of tests before performing others. It's a process of elimination. Our health care might be free, but it's not fast." Riley tried to keep the tone light, even though she shared her mother's concern.

"I just worry so much about you girls." Her mother held Riley's eyes. "I was going to wait to tell you this . . . but I've decided to move back to Vancouver. After Educoin and Peter, now Lucy. . ." She placed her hands around Riley's. "How would you feel about me living here?"

Riley's mouth grew dry at the unexpected news. "Here? With me?" Riley had only just gotten used to being in the space alone after Lucy had moved out. "Permanently?" Riley's voice squeaked on the last question. Who in their twenties wants to live with their mother?

"Let's call it an open-ended, temporary arrangement. No fixed end date, with periodic reviews."

"Will you work? Can you get another job with the school district?"

"I'll finish out this year in Victoria. That will give us time to sort out the details. I'm only working part time at the moment. I'll ask here about getting my old job back."

Riley knew her mother's unspoken words were that she was hoping Lucy would become pregnant and require a child care provider sooner rather than later. Lucy needed to recover first, but having their mother around would surely help with that. Riley could almost smell her mother's chicken soup already.

"The last few months have really shown me how much I want to be near my daughters. If you'll have me, of course." She let Riley's hands drop.

Riley cupped her mother's hands in hers. "Of course, Mom. It will be a change, but it will be nice." She gave her a wink. "I just don't want to give up my room, okay?"

*

RILEY'S PHONE BUZZED with a message from Johnny.

> How are you doing?

> Good. My mom is emoving to Vancouver. She's going to live with me.

As soon as she sent her reply, Riley realized this was a conversation that would be better live. Nothing had the potential to derail a new relationship than a new, older "roommate." She tapped the dial button.

"Sorry. I should have waited until we were speaking to spring that on you," Riley said after Johnny answered.

"Spring what? That your mother cares, that she misses you and wants to live with you? It's sweet."

"You think so?" Her pulse quickened, an automatic response that flustered her. She didn't have time to sort out her feelings right now.

"Definitely. I like your mom. I like your sister. And at the risk of sounding like a corny poet, I l—"

"You'll regret sounding corny," Riley said, cutting him off. Was he going to say "like" or "love"? How did she feel? Like. Definitely like. How did she feel about Jack? Also like, but a different like. "This isn't the right time to have that conversation."

"Oh." The hurt in Johnny's voice resonated through the phone.

"Listen, with my sister, and my mom, it's just not the right time." She pictured his eyes pinching. Her heart burst. Had she said something irreparable? "But I like you too. I have to go. Will you come to the hospital tomorrow?"

"Of course. Good night."

"Good night." She hung up the phone and slumped against the wall. Had she just ruined things with Johnny? She thought of calling him back, but that might only cause more damage.

✳

RILEY COLLAPSED IN the waiting room chair, exhausted. For the second night in a row she'd had little sleep, this time the result of her mother's news and her conversation with Johnny. Technically, the apartment was her mother's and she had every right to live in it. Riley's housing situation was always supposed to be temporary. Living with her mother might work for a short time, but eventually she'd need her own space. Sharing the apartment with Lucy had worked well because her sister was often out, leaving Riley with plenty of quiet time alone.

She leaned back in the chair and closed her eyes while she tried to consider her options. Seconds later, she had a vague awareness that she'd snorted. A hand on her leg roused her from her restless nap. "What happened? Lucy?" A jolt of panic surged through her. She flapped her arms involuntarily as if catching her balance. Only then did she realize that Johnny was sitting beside her. She felt her colour rise.

He leaned in and kissed her forehead. "I just got here. The nurse didn't have an update when I asked."

"My mom is with her now. Alex said he'd be here in about an hour."

Johnny pulled Riley close. "She'll be okay. They just need to monitor her. I'm sure it looks worse than it is."

"Please don't say that. You don't know." She pushed away from him. She should say something about the night before. But the words wouldn't come. Instead, she hung her head in her hands and massaged her temples.

When she found the words, they weren't an apology. Instead, she decided to tell Johnny about the necklace. "Something about this reminds me of a case I read about. One your great-grandfather worked on, in fact."

"Really?" Johnny leaned in.

"Two women died after wearing a necklace. They were poisoned." Jack might not have identified the necklace as the source yet, but he'd said they were poisoned, and the newspaper article she'd found had confirmed this.

"Do you know what poison?"

"I don't. I read about the case in an article." She gripped the chair's armrest, realizing her oversight—she hadn't looked deeper to see if the poison had been identified. Her sister's illness was distracting her. Not a great reflection of her research abilities. "I could check at the archive to see if the case file has any information." She released the armrests. "But I don't want to leave here."

"What are you thinking? That the toxin Lucy's been in contact with might be the same ones that caused these women's deaths?" Johnny asked.

"I don't know, honestly. It's just an idea, but the necklace Jayne gave Lucy looks very similar to the one in that case. Lucy's necklace was found in the wall of a house. I haven't checked yet, but it was in Mount Pleasant. Likely built around the same time as the necklace in your great-grandfather's case disappeared."

Johnny bit his lip as he considered what Riley had said. "You're telling me it's the same necklace?"

Riley nodded. "I think so. What I don't know is if the poison could be the same."

Johnny rubbed his palms on his lap a few times, then pressed his fingers into his temples. "Is this even possible? Is there a poison that is so strong, it could still kill someone one hundred years later?" He dropped his fingers and pulled out his phone. "Do poisons have a half- life?"

"Like radiation?" A twinge of excitement pulsed through Riley. It looked like Johnny was coming around to the idea. Would this conversation eventually lead to her telling him about Jack? She pushed the thought away to focus on Lucy. "I don't know, but I could ask Jules if he ever encountered anything like this when he worked as a coroner's assistant." She pulled out her own phone and began composing a message. He'd be at work, but off soon and might be able to speak.

When she finished, she tucked her phone away. "Alex gave the necklace to her doctors. They said they'd run tests. So maybe it isn't as far-fetched as we think."

"Let's hope they find answers." Where his voice could easily have dripped with sarcasm at the idea, he seemed to be open-minded. Maybe he'd react the same way to learning about the journal. Warmth spread across Riley's chest at the thought.

∗

RILEY GATHERED HER things, preparing to head to the museum. As she reached for her phone, it rang. A nurse passed by and pointed to the No Phones sign above Riley's head. She mouthed an apology and flooded with heat at being caught breaking the rules again. She silenced her ringer and answered Jules's call on her way to the elevators.

After she updated him on Lucy's condition, a beat of silence passed. "You think she's been poisoned? By an old necklace?" he asked.

"Maybe. I don't know if it's possible. Her symptoms came on quickly, so whatever it was, I assume it was strong."

"There isn't much that would linger after all this time and remain so toxic just through skin contact. If so, anyone who had handled it would be sick, or at least unwell."

"Yeah, I guess that makes sense." She remembered that Ryan had said he'd slipped the necklace into his pouch. He wore work gloves. But he would likely have removed them when he retrieved it after finishing work. He hadn't mentioned feeling ill. The vendor had been surprised that the necklace could potentially cause someone to fall ill as well. And although she'd had a rash, Jayne didn't seem to have any symptoms similar to Lucy's. Maybe it wasn't the necklace. So what was it?

"What about something your sister is eating?" Jules asked.

"Alex said she's been doing this thing called careful eating." Riley sat on a bench in front of the hospital.

"I haven't heard of that. What does it mean?" Jules asked.

"I don't really know." She remembered the bottles on her sister's bathroom counter. "She might be taking some supplements or vitamins too. Alex said people send her things all the time."

"Maybe you should check those out, Riley. Supplements are notoriously unregulated. Anything could be in them."

Riley thanked Jules for the idea and made a mental note to get the details on Lucy's supplements. A taxi drove slowly through the semicircular drive of the hospital's main entrance. The driver leaned across the passenger seat, his face a question mark. Riley smiled and shook her head.

"How are you otherwise, Riley? Have you figured out when you're planning to visit?"

"Honestly, I haven't had time, Jules. I've been so distracted."

"But you'll set a date to come? When Lucy's better?"

"I promise. As soon as she's better, I'll send you a list of possible dates."

Riley ended the call with Jules and stood, arching her back into a stretch. A brisk walk to the museum was just what she needed to clear her crowded head.

CHAPTER 22

Jack

WINSTON KNOCKED A second time on Clay Block's door. Still no answer. He gripped the handle and tried the door.

"Sir, are you going to break in?" asked Miller.

"We'll need to find the landlord and ask him to let us in," Winston said as he twisted the door handle again. "Block may be sleeping. Even if he isn't at home, we can search for the necklace. If Mrs. Block had it in her possession when she died, it must be inside."

"Shall I go look for him and you wait here, in case Mr. Block returns home?" Miller asked.

"Good thinking, Thomas."

A few minutes later, Miller appeared on the stairs, followed by Mr. Chance. The landlord's face was red, though whether from exertion or anger, Winston couldn't tell. Chance fiddled with the keys and stepped away from the door to wipe his brow. Winston tapped him on the shoulder. "Are you nervous, sir?"

A sheen of sweat glistened on the landlord's forehead. "I'm not nervous," Chance grunted. "I've just never had to open a tenant's apartment twice with the police at my back. What am I going to find inside this time?" The keys jangled. "Not another dead body, I hope. I'll never be able to rent the apartment again. Bad for business, all this." His whine grated on Winston's nerves and he had to restrain himself from turning the man back to the task at hand.

"Once you unlock this, Constable Miller and I will take over. There's no need for you to enter."

After freeing the lock, Chance pushed on the door between the handle and the frame, and it opened. "It's my apartment building. I'll enter if I like, Detective."

"Not until I say." Winston kept his tone steady, despite his dwindling patience.

Chance backed away, arms raised. "I don't want any more trouble." He remained at the doorway while Miller followed Winston inside.

The air was stale. "Has Mr. Block died?" called the landlord.

"He's not here," Winston called back to Chance. "We will continue our search. Thank you for your assistance." Retreating footsteps confirmed the landlord had understood the implication.

"As we are here, Thomas, we might as well search for any evidence that might suggest Block killed his wife—or Mrs. Shuttleworth, for that matter," Winston said. "I will start in the bedroom. See what you can uncover in here. There may be something to lead us to Block."

Miller agreed, and each man began searching his assigned room. Inside a small chest of drawers in the bedroom, Winston found folded pieces of paper instead of any clothing. He unfolded them and called out to Miller.

"What have you found, sir?" Miller asked as he entered the bedroom.

"No sign of the necklace." Winston held up the papers. "But these appear to be instructions for a game. Given that Shuttleworth is a game inventor, finding these here may prove significant." He tucked them into his satchel to review more closely later.

Searching the remainder of the room revealed little. In addition to the dresser being empty of any women's clothing, the linens had been removed from the bed. An armoire contained a suit, a single pair of stained work jeans, patched at the knees, and well-used work boots. "Do you think he's gone, sir?" Miller asked.

"It would appear he has packed away his wife's belongings or perhaps given them away." Winston swept an arm toward the open armoire. "He is a modest man and may not have many clothes of his own."

Miller peered under the bed. "Still, it seems odd, doesn't it?"

"It does, Thomas." Even if the items of clothing had revealed nothing, Winston couldn't help thinking that he'd missed an opportunity to check them for clues. He made a mental note for future searches: he would be sure to search the premises at the earliest opportunity before any suspect could remove incriminating items.

"Why take her dresses? Did he donate them to someone? Give them away?" Miller asked.

"Perhaps he's returned them to her sister. We'll ask when we see her." Winston circled the room methodically, unwilling to let another clue escape his attention. Once he was satisfied there was nothing left to find in the bedroom, Winston motioned for Miller to return to the kitchen. "What did you find in the kitchen?"

"Nothing of interest, sir." Miller stood by the stove, his hand hovering above its surface. "This hasn't been on recently."

"When did we last see Block?" Winston asked.

"Two days ago, when we interviewed him in this apartment, after he'd already seen his wife's body at the station," Miller said. "Do you think he has fled? Does that mean he killed her?"

Winston felt for the stone in his pocket. The scene was unusual—this nearly bare apartment—but he didn't get the impression Block could afford to abandon even these few small possessions that remained. "What was his motive, Miller? And for killing Mrs. Shuttleworth?"

"The necklace, sir. What if Mrs. Block did steal it? Block discovered it, then killed her because she stole it? And now he's run off, planning to sell it?"

"Would he really react with the urge to kill her if he learned she'd stolen it?" Winston scratched his temple. "And poisoning seems an odd method to choose to kill her if he was angry," he said. "Surely he'd take whatever was to hand as a weapon in the heat of the moment. And how is he implicated in Mrs. Shuttleworth's death? The necklace only disappeared after she died."

"It was only reported stolen after her death," Miller offered.

"An interesting idea, Thomas. Perhaps he has run off with the necklace, expecting he can sell it. Even so he's unlikely to be the poisoner." Riley's worry about the necklace flashed in Winston's thoughts. If Block had the necklace, might he be in danger—unaware of the possible toxic properties of the prize he held? "Until we know the poison and its source, it's all speculation."

Miller nodded. He pursed his lips, as if considering his next question.

Winston decided to invite Miller into his thoughts in case the poison turned out to be connected to the necklace, as Riley feared. "If the poison wasn't ingested, let's say, but absorbed by skin contact, even something like the necklace itself could transfer the toxin."

Miller's hand flew to his throat as if he might be wearing the offending jewellery. "So who poisoned the necklace? Shuttleworth? Is he responsible for the deaths of his wife and Kate Block?"

"If the necklace is the weapon, it would be unlikely that the poisoner is the thief. Do we agree, Thomas? They'd be knowingly exposing themselves to the poison. We need to find Block so we can find the necklace," Winston said.

"Yes." Miller nodded.

"We also have other leads to follow." Winston counted the names on his fingers. "Susie, Cullen, Shuttleworth. Thomas, would you go to Block's workplace? If he isn't there, ask if they were expecting him. Find out if they know where he's gone. I'll speak to Block's brother and Susie Pegg. Then let's meet back at the station to decide what is truly the most urgent lead."

✳

WHEN SUSIE PEGG answered Winston's knock, she didn't immediately swing the door open to welcome him into the house. "I've come to ask you some more questions, Miss Pegg. It's important that you're honest with me." Immediately, Winston regretted the abruptness of his statement. The woman's red eyes and sallow features signalled someone who was grieving. He had retreated in his own grief; he was unsurprised that Susie was doing the same. She took a step back to let him in, then walked toward the kitchen. Winston followed, thinking about how to acknowledge the woman's pain.

"I have more baking from Mrs. Plum. She was saddened to hear of your sister," Winston said. He gave her the package.

"Thank you. She's a kind woman." Susie positioned herself in front of the stove, where a kettle was close to boiling. She held her chin high and said, "You have asked me to be honest. I have been. Why would I change now?" Her words were clipped. Grief had turned to resentment and frustration.

"I need to understand more about your sister." He sat in the chair she pointed to. "Are you certain she didn't take Mrs. Shuttleworth's necklace?"

Susie slammed her hands on the kitchen table, knocking over an empty teacup. "Why are you asking about a piece of jewellery when my sister is dead? Does it matter if she took it? It's gone. She's dead."

Winston knelt in front of his chair to collect the broken porcelain. "Miss Pegg, the necklace and your sister's death may be connected. We want to understand if they are." He handed the pieces to her. She curled her fingers around the shards. Winston imagined the Pegg sisters sitting at this table, sharing news about their day over cups of tea. The woman's heart was broken now—in pieces, like the cup. Winston pushed the thought away to regain focus.

"Connected?" Susie deposited the shattered cup into a bin and sat in the chair opposite Winston, staring vacantly over his shoulder. "Kate and I spent so much time in here." She pointed toward a small window with light streaming through. "I couldn't bring myself to darken the kitchen yesterday. We don't get much light back here, and what little gets in comes through that window. It just didn't seem right to block it." She dragged her fingernail along one of the grooves in the table, the marks of countless meals shared here. "My father didn't even say anything. I'm not sure he understands that she's gone."

"Grief affects us all differently, Miss Pegg."

Susie got up to remove the boiling kettle, then returned to her seat. "Truth be told, I don't want another cup of tea, Detective. But I'll fix you one if you'd like."

"No, thank you." Winston waited until she nodded before continuing. He pulled his notepad from his satchel, then clasped his hands in front of him. "When I spoke to you last, I told you that the medical examiner thinks your sister might have been poisoned. And we think the same is true of Mrs. Shuttleworth. Doctor Evans noticed similarities between them."

Susie's attention was fixed on Winston's words now. She tilted her head and leaned in.

"We are trying to understand how they were poisoned, which is why I'm asking about the necklace. Did your sister take it? Mrs. Shuttleworth wore it before she died. If your sister stole it and she was wearing it, that would explain how they were in contact with the same poison."

Susie blanched. "You know this?"

"It's an idea I'm exploring right now. I've sent Constable Miller to find your sister's husband."

At this, her shoulders stiffened. "Do you think he killed them?"

Winston shook his head once. "We want to speak to him. He's taken your sister's belongings. And the bed linens were gone."

"I took the bed linens, Detective. Kate actually took them from here when she left. She must have snuck in when I was working. I brought them home earlier today. My employers have given me another day to grieve, which I am ever so thankful for. I went to Clay's apartment this morning. I didn't see him, but I assumed he was at work."

Winston frowned. "How did you get in? When we arrived, the door was locked."

"It was unlocked when I arrived. I left it the same way," Susie said.

Winston wrote this in his notepad. Block must have been home and locked the door after Susie had been there. "Did you notice that her clothing had been removed?"

"I took her clothing as well, though there wasn't much." Susie's cheeks reddened as she spoke. "I didn't spend much time there at all."

"Why did you take the bed linens and her clothing?"

"As I said, Detective, my sister took them from here. I couldn't bear for them to remain there. I've sent them to be washed."

And with them any opportunity to examine them first. Although, what Winston thought he might glean from them he wasn't sure. Perhaps they should have collected them along with the body. He admonished himself and jotted a note to that effect.

"My father, despite his absence, is a caring man," Susie continued. "Since my mother died and Kate and I started working, he leaves me a few coins each week. I use them to send out laundry. I can't bring myself to do it once I return from cleaning up after others. Our washerwoman will be back tomorrow with them, pressed and smelling fresh, I hope."

"Did you take anything else?"

"Are you asking whether I took the necklace while I was there? I didn't even see it."

Good. She had brought the conversation back to the jewellery. "Do you have any idea where it might be?"

"I do not."

She held his gaze. Her features, though heavy with grief, betrayed nothing to suggest she was lying. "What about Clay Block?"

"I would have liked to see him. Though I'm unsure whether I will cry with him or shout at him when he next crosses my path. He was my sister's companion, not mine. But she loved him, and we have that in common."

"If you do see Mr. Block, please inform him that I would like to speak to him," Winston said. He looked out the kitchen window to the backyard of the house. Diagonal to their garden, a new house was being constructed. Even as the city awakened from winter, the building continued. "Miss Pegg, if your sister couldn't read, why would she have documents in her home?"

Susie frowned. "What do you mean?"

He reached into his satchel and pulled out the pages he'd taken from Kate Block's dresser. "I found this at her apartment. Could your sister have written these words?"

"No. Neither of us read. Mrs. Shuttleworth had started teaching Kate. But she couldn't have written that." Susie pushed the pages back to Winston.

"Do you recognize the writing?"

Susie shook her head. "It all looks the same to me, Detective Winston."

He returned the document to his satchel. "Thank you for your time, Miss Pegg." Winston donned his hat and exited the house.

CHAPTER 23

Jack

A FINE DRIZZLE had started to fall by the time Winston returned to the station. He shed his damp coat as Miller described his attempts to find Clay Block. "The main post office branch confirmed that he is a clerk and frequently works at the rail station receiving the letters that come by mail." Miller pulled his watch from his pocket as Winston looked longingly at the cup of tea in front of his constable. "If we leave now, we should be able to find Block before he leaves the station."

Winston set aside thoughts of the tea. "You're assuming that he decided to work today, Thomas. I spoke with Paul Block before I saw Miss Pegg. He hasn't seen his brother. Which suggests to me that he may have run off, especially if he thinks we suspect he's killed his wife."

"Do we think he killed his wife, sir?"

"We haven't eliminated him. But we haven't found any reason for him to have killed Mrs. Shuttleworth, and I think that's the key—finding someone who benefited both from her death and from the death of Kate Block." Winston dragged his hand through his hair.

"That does seem the most logical, that there is one killer, sir." Miller paced as he spoke. "There must be a detail we haven't uncovered yet that explains who gains from their deaths."

"Clayton Block doesn't seem to fit that description. But I'm also not sure he has told us everything he knows about his wife's death. We can't rule him out until we find him." Miller shifted his weight. "Is there more, Thomas?"

"Not really, sir. Doctor Evans left a letter for you with the desk sergeant. Shall I get it for you?"

"If you wouldn't mind. Afterwards, we can look for Block."

Miller reappeared within moments, handing the letter to Winston. He read it and returned the single page to Miller. "Read this. Evans is still unable to identify the poison, but he's certain it's something the women ingested, based on the internal damage to Mrs. Block."

"Does that help, sir?"

"It means we can rule out the necklace." At the first available opportunity, he would write to Riley and ease her worries about her sister's necklace. "Evans says the damage was severe, and he saw signs of both acute and chronic poisoning."

"What does that mean?" Miller asked.

"With chronic poisoning, the doses are repeated. Acute could be just one, higher dose. Evans can only say what he's observed in the body of Mrs. Block. Let's assume the same is true for Mrs. Shuttleworth."

"It must be someone at the Shuttleworth house," Miller insisted. "Mr. Block wouldn't have been able to administer poison repeatedly to Penelope Shuttleworth, would he?"

"Perhaps if Kate assisted him, though I must admit that doesn't seem likely."

"If he isn't behind the poison, why can't we find him?" Miller moved toward the door. "Shall we see if we can track him down at the rail station?"

"Yes, let's. We will move on to Shuttleworth when we've learned all we can about Block. This weather is sure to drive many from lingering outside. His brother knew little to suggest where else we might look if Clayton has already finished work."

The policemen hailed a cab to take them to the rail station, where the post would be collected by Block. As they rode, Winston watched the passing scene, the rain sending rivulets of muddy water down the city streets. He'd been thinking of the railway, how the young city had become so dependent on the benefits it had brought in the short decade and a bit since its completion.

Winston recalled his own recent return trip to Toronto for George's wedding. Despite being the younger son, Winston's brother was set to assume his father's position as the head of the railway. Winston had been pleased to see George thriving in the role—doubly pleased because it meant that he could remain a police officer in Vancouver.

A cab passed in the other direction, the driver with his cap pulled low around his ears. Winston pulled his coat tighter against the cold. He let his thoughts drift back to the wedding. He'd been reluctant to attend his brother's celebration so soon after learning the truth of their older brother's death—that Ellis was not still missing but had died by suicide. The memory of his parents' betrayal cut him to the quick again, and he felt the bile rise in his throat. But George had nothing to do with that deceit.

Winston had purposely avoided being alone with either of his parents. He'd had no interest in hearing them try to explain away their lies. It had taken all of his patience to see them without demanding an explanation. At one point, he'd had to speak very directly, flatly declining their request to meet privately. His mother's anguished face returned to him now. He'd struggled to keep his voice even and offered no explanation, steeling himself against her pleading expression. Winston shut his eyes at the memory.

George, despite his pending nuptials, had sensed Winston's discomfort and pulled him aside one afternoon. "Is it something in Vancouver that is troubling you, brother?" he'd asked. Winston had wrestled with his answer. He could not bring himself to sour George's happy event and dismissed his concern with a half answer. "Life is good there, George. But I've recently had a case that has left me . . . unsettled. It has shaken my trust in ways I never imagined."

That moment was as close as Winston had gotten to revealing the truth, and now he wondered if it had been the right decision. Was Winston now contributing to the deception by withholding what he knew from George? Surely their parents should hold the burden of revealing the truth. He'd remained silent, and that decision continued to weigh on him.

The cab turned onto the streets of the city's northern shore, and the newly constructed Pacific National Railway station came into view. When the original station became too small within years of its opening, work had quickly begun on a grander welcome for travellers. Winston admired again the lines of the new building as the cab pulled to a stop. Beside him, Miller roused and stepped out. Winston followed and paid the driver.

The detectives entered the station and were directed to the mail car. On their way, the train hissed beside them as the engine released a burst of steam. It was nearing departure for the return eastward journey. The platform filled with passengers preparing to board. Many clutched satchels and suitcases. The people around them exchanged goodbyes, and the travellers jostled through the throng with excitement. When they got to the mail car, Miller said, "The mail has already been collected, sir."

"I can see that, Thomas," Winston replied, frustration seeping into his voice. "Sorry. That was harsher than it needed to be." The dead ends in this case were becoming very frustrating. "Where would Block go with the mail once he'd collected it?"

"Back to the post office to sort it, wouldn't he?" Miller asked. They'd just set off when Winston spotted Block further down the platform.

"Thomas, that's him." Block was dressed for travel, with a single suitcase under his arm.

The train's whistle sounded, and the crowd of passengers pushed toward the train. Winston searched the crowd to find a train official.

He needed the train to wait so he could retrieve Block. He raced toward the engine with Miller at his heels.

"I'll speak to the conductor." At the engine, Winston waved to the conductor, pointing at his badge.

"We're scheduled to leave shortly, sir." The conductor pointed back at the train after Winston explained who he was looking for. "We cannot leave late without permission."

"From whom do you need permission?"

"Someone other than me. It's not a decision I can make."

Winston closed his eyes for a breath. "I have the authority of George Montague."

Beside Winston, Miller stiffened. Winston kept his gaze focused on the conductor, whose eyes grew wide at the name of someone so senior with the railway. "You do?" His brow furrowed as he weighed whether to accept Winston's declaration. "If you say so."

"I do. And it shouldn't be a lengthy delay. We will remove the passenger as soon as we find him, at which point you will be able to leave."

"Can I continue to have the fire put on?" the conductor asked. Winston smiled inwardly at the man's commitment to meeting the train's schedule. He would let George know.

Winston gave a single nod. "I will join the search to avoid delaying you further. Send anyone who asks why you aren't leaving on time to look for me." He spun on his heel and left the conductor clambering back onto the train.

Winston and Miller searched through three cars before they found Block. He crumpled into his seat when he saw the policemen but rose without complaint. Miller descended the stairs with his hand on Clayton Block's elbow. Winston followed behind them.

"Mr. Block. We need to ask you a few questions. This train needs to leave. You'll come with us to the station, and if your answers are satisfactory, we will secure your passage on the next one," Winston said in a subdued voice, conscious to avoid calling undue attention to the man.

Block kicked at a stone. "If you must."

"Why are you leaving before your wife's body is buried? Don't you want to hold a service for her?" Miller asked.

"We were only married a few days. I will let her sister look after that."

Winston and Miller exchanged glances. "Her sister said she hasn't seen you. And it's unusual for a grieving husband to leave so quickly," Winston said.

Block's shoulders slumped as he walked beside Miller. Winston stepped away to find the conductor, who was relieved the train could now depart only five minutes late.

*

AT THE POLICE station, Winston and Miller escorted Block into the interview room. "Take a seat, Mr. Block. We would like to ask you a few more questions about the morning your wife died," said Winston.

Block stiffened in the chair. "What do you want to know?"

"Would you mind describing the events of that morning before you left for work? You said your wife was awake. What did you discuss? Did she prepare your breakfast? Send you off with lunch? What was her mood?" Winston knew he'd asked too many questions. "Start with what you discussed."

Tears welled in Block's eyes, and he wiped them away roughly. "You already know, don't you?"

"Know what, Mr. Block?" Miller asked.

"Kate was dead when I woke that morning. I didn't move her."

Winston stiffened. Was this why Block was running? He'd lied about speaking to his wife before she died? "Had she spent the entire night there? Or had she moved from the bed at some point?"

"I fell asleep before her that night. Her stomach had been bothering her, so I wasn't surprised she hadn't come to the bed. She was worried about disturbing me. When I woke and she wasn't lying beside me, I looked for her. She was lying there, beautiful as ever." Block inhaled with a loud snuffling.

"Was she dressed as we found her?" Winston asked.

"I didn't change her clothes, if that's what you're asking. But Susie found her after I did, didn't she?"

"It sounds like you discovered her, then left her. Dead," Miller said. The constable's mouth was a firm line, leaving no doubt about his contempt for the man's actions.

Colour drained from Block's face. "There was nothing I could do."

"How did Susie get into the apartment?" Winston asked.

Block shrugged. "It would have been easy enough. Anyone can walk into the building, and our apartment door never locked particularly well. It sticks, so we often leave it unlocked, especially if we're home. Susie—or anyone—could have walked right in with a nudge." Winston recalled the solid shove Chance had given the door to open it earlier. Block stared at the table. "Is that what happened? Someone walked in and killed Kate while I was sleeping in the next room?"

"Are you that heavy a sleeper? Do you think you would not have heard?" Winston waved the idea away and refocused. "More important, I don't understand why you left your dead wife on your sofa and went to work as if nothing happened."

Colour rose up Block's cheeks. "I need to work." He pushed air through his pursed lips. "And I didn't know what else to do when I found her."

"Did you leave her exactly as you found her?" Winston asked.

Block slumped against the chair, head down. "She was wearing that necklace."

"Can you repeat that, Mr. Block?" Winston stared at the man in front of him.

"I removed the necklace she was wearing." Block swallowed, rubbing his temples. "The one you asked me about before."

Winston leaned forward. "Did she steal it? Why did you remove it?"

"I knew you'd think she stole it. But I also know she didn't."

"How did she get it if she didn't take it from Mrs. Shuttleworth's house?" Miller's pencil was poised above his notepad.

"She told me that Mrs. Shuttleworth asked her to keep it safe." Block pressed the heels of his hands into his eyes. "She showed it to me when she brought it home. When I found her dead, and she was wearing it. . ." Block swallowed. "That scared me."

"What did you do with it?" Winston asked the question gently. Why did Mrs. Shuttleworth want the necklace kept safe? Was she going to sell it? Use the money for something? Winston jotted the questions in his notepad.

"I took it off her. Stuffed it into my pocket." Block pinched the bridge of his nose with his thumb and finger. "I tucked her in, then left for work."

"Where is the necklace now?" The question came out gently again. Softness might coax Block to reveal more. Though Winston now knew it wasn't the source of poison, he wanted to return the necklace to Shuttleworth.

"I don't know."

"I find that hard to believe." Winston's tone was sharp. He forced his hands to relax from their clenched state.

"I was shocked to see her wearing that necklace. I asked Paul to keep it for me. You found me." He pointed first to Miller, then to

Winston. "Then you interviewed me. Paul met me here with the necklace. Then you spoke to me again."

Block heaved a sigh. "After that, I took the necklace with me, got drunk. I went for a walk and when I came back home, I no longer had the thing. I don't know what's happened to it." He hung his head. "I know I should have given it to you. Or said something. But I didn't want you to think that Kate had stolen it. She didn't."

"Do you remember anything? Who you saw? How you returned home afterwards?" Miller asked.

"Nothing. Absolutely nothing." He raked his hand through his hair. "I loved Kate. What am I going to do now?"

Winston gave the man a moment to compose himself, then continued. "Mr. Block, in the days before your wife died, did you notice anything unusual? Was she well? Had she been given anything else to keep safe?"

"She didn't mention anything else." Block ran his hand over his chin. "She complained of being tired, was off her food a bit. I thought it was her adjusting to being a wife, missing her work. She was sensitive, my Kate." Block's eyes glistened as he spoke. "I knew she would find a new position, and honestly, it wouldn't have bothered me if she'd stopped working entirely and was just my wife. Being a maid is exhausting. She'd have to stop when she became a mother anyway."

"Was your wife with child?" Miller asked.

Block reddened and shifted his gaze to a spot on the table. "Not that we knew." He locked eyes with Winston. "But we wanted to start a family whenever we were blessed with that good fortune."

"Mr. Block, why were you boarding a train? Where were you going?" Winston asked.

"With Kate gone, there is nothing left for me. I'd rather return to Ontario. Most of my family is there—" Block held up his hands. "I can build anywhere. This city holds too many memories for me now."

"But your brother, Paul, is here. Your former roommate?" Miller said.

"He is. We have other brothers in Ontario. This place isn't for me. It's too wild, too rough."

"Be that as it may, Mr. Block, I must insist that you delay your travel until we have concluded our investigation," Winston said.

Block's features twisted in pain and loss. "Find out who did this to Kate. Find out why."

"I intend to, Mr. Block. I intend to." Winston stood and motioned for Miller to do the same. Together they escorted Block to the station's door. "Thomas," Winston said as the door closed behind Block, "follow up with the man's colleagues tomorrow and verify what he's just told us."

✳

AFTER HIS EVENING meal, Winston sat at his desk in his rooms. At last he could share Evans's findings with Riley.

Dear Riley,

I have some news. I can confirm that Doctor Evans believes the poison that killed Mrs. Block was ingested, not administered via the necklace. Even if your sister's necklace is the missing one, it is unlikely that it is the source of her illness. I trust that this news brings you some relief, even if it doesn't help identify what is ailing your sister.

Warmly,

Jack

When he returned the journal to his satchel, his hand brushed the envelope Mrs. Bradley had handed him before his dinner—another letter from his mother. He poured himself a glass of whisky, then another, details of the day swirling in his head as the liquid warmed his throat. What sort of family lies about death the way his family did?

Lies.

What sort of lie is worth killing another person for? Someone was lying in the case of the two poisoned women. Who? What was he missing? Where were the lies? He ran through each of the people related to the case.

Edward Shuttleworth. Made wealthy through his popular game. Husband of first dead woman and former employer of second.

Clay Block. Mail clerk and former carpenter. Husband of second dead woman and briefly employed at the house of first one. Found attempting to leave the city in haste.

Susie Pegg. Sister of second dead woman and former maid in household of first one.

Mrs. Plum. Cook in household of first dead woman and former colleague of second.

Lies. And those, Jack knew, were the key to the murders. Were they all lying? No. One of these people killed these women. He needed to find the liar.

He looked back at his satchel.

Lies.

He looked at the stack of unopened letters from his mother.

Lies.

He looked at the fire burning in the fireplace.

Lies.

He finished his drink and pulled the letter from the bag.

Lies.

CHAPTER 24

Riley

THE JOURNAL SHOOK in Riley's hands as she read Jack's message. The poison was ingested. Likely through food. The confirmation she'd been waiting for—the necklace wasn't the source. She set the journal down beside the necklace, still wrapped in protective plastic after the hospital had run its tests. With more force than necessary, Riley tore the plastic open, letting the strand fall into her lap. She clasped it around her neck as Johnny walked into the hospital waiting room.

"What are you doing, Riley? I thought that thing is responsible for why your sister is here."

Riley shook her head as she slid the journal into her bag. "The hospital just returned it to me. Their tests showed nothing on its surface." She gestured at the necklace. "It's got nothing to do with why Lucy is sick."

"What about her friend, the one who gave it to her? Didn't she get a rash?"

"The rash could have been from anything. The necklace sat inside the frame of a house for a hundred years. It must have been dusty and covered in who knows what, any of which could irritate skin." Riley leaned toward Johnny to whisper in his ear. "Especially all-natural, organic, artisanal skin like Jayne has." She pulled away, covering her mouth. "I'm awful. She's lovely, but a little over the top, you know?"

Johnny grinned back at her. It must be a relief for him to see a little of her spark return. He leaned in and asked, "Have the doctors said anything new? What is it that's making Lucy so ill?"

"They took more blood just a little while ago. It's still a process of elimination. But they're thinking it must be something she ate or drank." Riley checked the time. "Johnny, Alex will come out here for a break soon. Can you tell him that I've gone over to their place?"

Johnny nodded and waved her from the waiting area. "Go! I got you covered."

Jack

THE CRISP NIGHT air sharpened Winston's senses. Mrs. Bradley had frowned when he left, but she'd agreed to leave the house unlocked and sent him off with a sharp reminder. "Your wanders are getting later and later, Detective Winston. I don't care to have drunkards or trouble in my home."

An extra coin would restore her tolerance of his "late-night wanders," as she'd called them. Walking without a destination in mind had helped him get to know the city. And walking at different times of day let him see the different sorts of people who inhabited it. Tonight, guided by the soft glow from gas lamps and the brighter, flickering light from carbon-arc electric lamps, Winston explored the West End.

Though it wasn't his intention, he found himself standing once again outside the home of Melodia Spectre. He stood at the base of her front steps, just outside a puddle of light from the nearby gas lamp, considering whether to knock. Mrs. Bradley was right. It was late, and considerably later than most would admit an unexpected guest. But Melodia was not like most; she made her own rules. And something had drawn him to her home. Still, he didn't want to disturb her. He'd turned back to the sidewalk when he heard her door crack open.

"Jack. I've just opened a bottle of whisky. It's cold out there. Stop being foolish."

He shook aside his surprise at her knowing he was there. The suggestion of whisky turned his stomach even as his mouth watered. The

Scotch he'd used earlier—an attempt to fortify his confidence to send a message to his family—still clouded his head. "I had better not, Melodia. I need to wake early tomorrow."

"The whisky will keep until another time." She held the door open wider. "Come in anyway. We'll have a cup of tea instead."

He climbed the steps and followed her into the house. She showed him to the front sitting room and left to prepare the tea. Books occupied most of the seats in the room. He gathered the smallest pile and placed them on an empty shelf, arranging them in alphabetical order. The task settled his restless mind. She hadn't yet returned with the tea, so he continued with another stack of books. As he slid one onto the shelf, he heard Melodia's footsteps. His cheeks burned as he realized what he'd been doing. "Sorry," he muttered when she entered the room.

Melodia waved his apology away. "No matter. I'll know where to find them. Now, what has brought you to my door again, Detective?"

Their previous conversations ran through his mind. She knew about Riley. She knew of his family. He knew so little about her. And yet he sensed she wouldn't answer any questions about herself. He settled on what he thought she might answer. "Tell me more about the journal. How would you describe how it works?" He swallowed, his mouth suddenly dry. "Are you . . . a. . . ." The final word stuck in his throat.

"I'm a woman, Detective." She spooned sugar into her tea. "There are things in this world that are knowable. And there are things that are not." She clinked the spoon against her cup. Jack inched forward in his seat. "Know that the journal works. Know that there is no need to understand how or why. Rest in the comfort of not needing to know." She sat against the back of her seat.

"I don't think that I can do that, Melodia. I worry sometimes that it will cease working." Where would that leave him? Winston couldn't bear the thought.

A slow smile crept across her face. "It will cease working when you no longer need it."

The woman was infuriating with her roundabout answers. "I cannot imagine that ever happening." When he picked up his teacup, it shook in his hand. "Will it?"

"I cannot say, Jack." Her voice was soft, reassuring. "If I knew, I would tell you."

"And if she tells me something that will impact the future? What will happen then?"

"It's best not to let that happen, Jack. Her caution is warranted."

Their conversation shifted to lies—the harm, the raw pain that they caused. "I see much pain in you, Jack."

He looked away. How did this woman see so deeply? What did she see? "Deceit causes pain everywhere, Melodia. What sort of lie does a person tell themselves to justify taking a life?"

"Everyone perpetuates lies. Most have many." She sipped her tea. "They might not be big lies, and they might tell them only to themselves. The lies that let us harm others, those are born from hurt. From anger. From pain. Watch for those lies, Jack."

They finished their tea and Winston bid her good night. Outside, he breathed deep of the cool night air on his way back to Mrs. Bradley's house. He slipped through the door and turned the lock as quietly as he could.

CHAPTER 26

Jack

WHEN WINSTON ARRIVED at the station the next day, his mind still hummed from his conversation with Melodia the night before. But he'd slept better than he had in many nights. The only other person at the station, apart from the overnight jail occupants, was the desk constable. He was a quiet man and occupied himself with reading the previous night's newspaper. Confident he would be alone for at least a little while longer, Winston settled into the chief constable's office and pulled the journal from his bag to check for a response from Riley.

Winston paused before opening its pages. He'd been thinking about the missing necklace. If he were to find it and return it to Shuttleworth once he'd solved the present case, what would be the implications for the future? They were impossible to predict. In Riley's time, would it mean Lucy would not have been gifted it? Would it suddenly disappear and all who had seen it be mystified? Would they have no memory of the jewellery? It confounded him trying to understand the limits and possibilities of a single act like this.

But even the correspondence he had with Riley effectively altered his choices, and therefore his future. Winston shook his head. It would take him some time to articulate his thoughts on this matter. And the matter felt more appropriate to discuss in person, when emotion could be conveyed through facial expressions and not just words on a page. He rested his hand on the book, knowing they would have to confine the conversation to paper. He opened to the spot his ribbon marked.

Dear Jack,

Thank you for the information about your murder victims. Although the cause of Lucy's illness is not the necklace, her condition is unchanged. I'm left searching for the true source. But thank you for narrowing the search with your news.

The hospital ran more tests and the results are expected tomorrow. I can only hope that they will reveal why Lucy is sick. They have decided to limit treatment until they know the source for fear of causing further damage.

As for the necklace, I've been considering whether to tell you more about where it was found. If I reveal that information, what will change as a result? There is something wonderful about finding a piece of history lost for decades. If I tell you where to find it, the discovery will not be made. How will it impact your case if it's retrieved?

I'll leave my musings here.

Best,

Riley

Tension in Winston's shoulders eased as he read Riley's response. She wrestled with the same questions as he did.

Dear Riley,

I am hopeful that the physicians treating your sister will find answers soon. While I enjoy our written correspondence, I must admit that there are times when I wish we could sit across from each other and decide upon the parrameters of our exchanges. Or test the impacts of sharing information. I recognize that will never happen, and we simply have to navigate the blurred lines that connect us by writing these words.

He picked up his pencil to add another line when Miller appeared. His eyes twinkled with excitement, and Winston's heart leaped. Some good news, finally. Winston shut the journal and pushed himself away from the chief constable's desk.

"Sir, I have some news."

Winston gestured toward the chair in front of his uncle's desk. "Go on."

"The other case you gave me. I spoke to the suspects last night, and it didn't take much: they confessed almost immediately. It was as if they were relieved." Across the desk, Miller's leg bounced.

"That's welcome news. And a job well done, Thomas."

"I didn't really do anything, sir. Even if they hadn't confessed, the stolen goods were right there, with them. They didn't even try to come up with an excuse."

"I suppose a criminal's life isn't for everyone," Winston said as he extended his hand to shake Miller's. "Did you go alone? It might be better to have another officer accompany you on such visits. You never know what a suspect might do." Winston recalled being trapped by a murder suspect when he'd entered the man's house alone.

Miller nodded, and some of the smile faded from his eyes.

"Still, you should be pleased, Thomas. Now let us turn our attention back to the Shuttleworth and Block murders. What did you learn from Block's colleagues?"

Miller pulled his notepad from his pocket. "They didn't know him well, sir. He's only been working with them for a few weeks. But they said he was pleasant enough, happy about his wedding, making plans for the future."

"Those don't sound like the actions of someone about to murder his wife, or who had murdered her employer a few weeks earlier."

"I agree. I don't think Block is the killer."

"Still, he had—and lost—the necklace," Winston said. He pulled his hand down his face. "Susie Pegg took the bed linens and her sister's clothing from the apartment. She'd snuck in before we arrived." He stood and approached the board they'd created earlier. What was he missing? "Let's consider the scenarios. Could she have killed her sister?" Winston asked.

"The timing doesn't work. She killed her sister, left, returned to supposedly find her dead, then came here to report her sister's death?" Miller asked.

"You're right. That doesn't make sense." Winston crossed Block's and Susie's names from their suspect list.

Miller stood at the board, arms crossed. "I've been thinking about Mrs. Plum. Do you think she's really a suspect?"

Winston paused. None of the names on the board were the key suspect, Bobbie Lyon. But he couldn't tell Miller that. He'd rifled through the records in the storage room—an easier task since Miller's reorganization—looking for any reference to the name but turned up nothing. He'd sent one of the new constables to check city records, instructing him to report back to him only. Nothing. He stroked his moustache and answered Miller's question. "She had easy access to Mrs. Shuttleworth, but she speaks highly of the family. And she's been working there for years. If she killed Mrs. Shuttleworth, why now?"

"Unless something changed. But then why kill the maid?"

"Precisely." Winston rolled a piece of chalk in his fingers. "I'll admit that I did have a passing thought about Mrs. Plum, however. What if she was fond of Shuttleworth and she thought he would marry her once his wife was dead?"

"Mrs. Plum would have to believe he shared her affection." Miller turned back to the board and tilted his head. "Why would she think that, and why now? Perhaps something he'd said?" He took his own piece of chalk and wrote *affection for Mr. S?* beside Mrs. Plum's name.

"Her affection—however strong—for Mr. Shuttleworth doesn't explain why she would kill Kate Block."

Miller scratched at his jaw. "Unless Kate knew what Mrs. Plum had done. She killed Kate to ensure she didn't tell anyone."

"Fair enough, Thomas. How did she do it?"

"Maybe she visited Kate and slipped her something," His face paled. "We gave Kate those scones from Mrs. Plum."

"You're right. But we ate them with no ill effect." Winston shook his head. "Let's move on, Thomas." He tapped the board. "Who else?"

"Shuttleworth? Isn't the husband the most likely culprit?"

"Ordinarily, Thomas. But we also have Mrs. Block's death. Why would he kill her?"

Miller shrugged. "She knew what Mr. Shuttleworth had done. What better way to ensure your deed remains a secret than to kill anyone who knew about it?"

"How did he do it?" Winston surveyed the board. "Besides, he didn't even know her name."

"Would he know where she lived?"

"Doubtful. Especially since she'd moved to live with her new husband." Winston blew a slow breath through pursed lips. "I'm tempted to cross his name off the list. I can't consider him responsible for both deaths, so I don't think we can consider him for either."

"Is that true, sir? Eliminating him as a suspect in the maid's death does not eliminate him from his wife's. He could still be responsible for that."

"So. . ." Winston spread his hands out. "We're back to thinking of two different killers?"

"Why not?"

"Very well." Winston pointed to Susie Pegg's name. "And Miss Pegg? Is she in a similar situation to Mr. Shuttleworth?"

"How so?"

"It's easier to associate her with her sister's death than Mrs. Shuttleworth's. Sure, she had access to her, but why kill her employer?"

"For her sister? Was Kate feeling trapped in how Mrs. Shuttleworth used her?"

"Why go on to kill Kate after freeing her? And we agreed the timing doesn't work. Unless she's lying about when she last saw Kate."

"Did she not appreciate what Susie had done for her? Was Susie jealous of Kate's new life as a married woman?"

Winston wrinkled his nose. This train of thought was too forced. "She claims she didn't know her sister was married. And she doesn't have an easy life filled with people to take Kate's place. She seems genuinely upset for her loss."

Miller ran his hand through his hair. "Susie didn't kill Kate but might have killed Mrs. Shuttleworth. Mr. Shuttleworth and Mrs. Plum didn't kill Kate either. Our suspects have plausible reasons to kill Mrs. Shuttleworth, and none have good reasons to also kill Kate Block. Where does that leave us?"

Winston pursed his lips. "With two victims and no killer in common." He slammed his palm on the chalkboard, releasing a cloud of dust. "What are we missing?"

Miller cleared his throat. "What did the doctor say about the poison? We know it was administered orally. Is it slow- or quick-acting?"

Winston recalled the doctor's note. "It didn't provide those details. But I expect him to report to us with more information this afternoon."

"After we speak to him, we might have a clearer path."

"You're right, Thomas. Before I speak to Evans, I'm off to see Mr. Shuttleworth. Time to uncover who's lying. While I'm gone, write up your investigation report while it's fresh in your memory. At least we can cross one thing off our list."

CHAPTER 27

Jack

THOUGH WINSTON ENJOYED travelling through the city using the public streetcars, he flagged a cab when he left the station, opting for speed. Frustration churned in his chest. He forced his breathing to slow, though it did little to set him at ease.

The driver made good time to Mount Pleasant, and the hustle of the downtown streets opened into quieter boulevards, where the occasional carriage rolled by. Winston alighted outside the Shuttleworth house and knocked on the door.

Edward Shuttleworth opened the door, looking better rested than when Winston had seen him last. His eyes widened when he saw Winston, hat in hand.

"Detective Winston, I wasn't expecting to see you today."

"Mr. Shuttleworth. I have a rather delicate piece of news to share. Might I come in?" Winston stepped over the threshold before Shuttleworth answered.

"No constable today?"

"I've asked him to look at other evidence."

"You're making progress on the case?"

"Can we sit down?" Winston let Shuttleworth lead him into the sitting room.

"Mrs. Plum is working in the kitchen, but I haven't any maids at present, as you know. Shall I ask her to prepare tea, Detective?"

Winston pressed his hand against his leg to feel the outline of his stone. "That won't be necessary. I hope you'll forgive me, but I must start with unsettling news."

Shuttleworth lowered himself into a chair, gripping the arms. "I'm ready."

"I have reason to believe your wife was murdered, Mr. Shuttleworth. Further, I believe she died the same way as your former maid, Kate Pegg—though she was known at the time of her death as Kate Block, having married since leaving your employment."

Shuttleworth's face grew pale. "Penelope was murdered?" He let his mouth drop open. "By whom?" He seemed to be searching for words, then recovered himself, tugging at his waistcoat. "She died from an illness. At least that's what the doctor said."

"That's what the doctor believed at the time. Our medical examiner, Doctor Evans, shared the same belief. But he has re-evaluated that opinion based on some recent findings."

Shuttleworth brought his hands to his head. "If it wasn't illness, what was it?"

Winston leaned closer, softening his voice. "We believe your wife was poisoned."

Shock crossed Shuttleworth's face as he lowered his hands. "Who would do that? To my Penny? How?"

"That's what I am investigating," Winston said gently. "Can you think of anyone who may have wanted to kill your wife?"

Shuttleworth's face froze in a mask of utter bewilderment. "Not a soul," he said at last.

"With whom did she keep company, other than you? Were there any recent new acquaintances that you can think of?"

"I wasn't with her every waking moment, Detective, but to my knowledge, she spent much of her afternoons paying visits, as women typically do. She also worked with some women from our circle of friends to create a hospital auxiliary."

"Would you be able to provide me with their names?" If he couldn't find answers, Winston would need to expand the circle of people to speak to.

"Yes. Let me think."

Winston opened his notepad, jotted down the names, then threw another question at Shuttleworth. "Who gave her the necklace?"

The man flushed and sat straighter in his chair. "The one that was stolen? I gave it to her." He dropped his gaze and turned to pour himself a glass of water from a pitcher on the table beside him. "Why do you ask?"

Winston cocked his head. "Mr. Shuttleworth, is there something that you're not telling me? I implore you. Anything may be relevant to this investigation. I must know the truth."

Shuttleworth licked his lips. Winston sensed the man weighing what to say next. He collapsed against the back of the chair and let his head hang. "I don't see how this is relevant." Shuttleworth pointed at the furniture and books in the room. "I came from rather humble beginnings." His gaze landed on a bookshelf behind Winston. "I have created a life that suggests money is nothing new to me. In truth, fortune shone her light on me and granted me a small success through my game."

"Your game led to all of this?"

"It did. I was working on another game, which I had hoped would bring us even more success, but with Penny's death. . . It's been a setback." He raked his hands through his hair. "I don't know how I will continue."

Something poked at the edge of Winston's memory—an image, an idea. He pushed it away to gain focus and stayed quiet. Shuttleworth had more to say, and people were often moved to fill a silence.

"I gave her the necklace to celebrate our success," Shuttleworth said. "With the game, I mean."

What had Kate said about Mr. Shuttleworth's game? *There was more to it.* "Your success?"

Shuttleworth shifted in his chair. "Well, yes. She inspired me. Put up with my late nights working on ideas for the game. You know how it is. Your wife must be patient with your detective's hours."

Winston ignored the comment. "When I spoke with your wife's former maid, she hinted that your wife had given her the necklace."

Shuttleworth paled. "Why would Penny do that?"

"Others I spoke with suggested your wife was generous. Giving gifts was in her nature."

"This is true." Shuttleworth smiled at a memory. "But the necklace. . . I thought that one held meaning for her. . ." His voice trailed off. "And if it wasn't stolen, I fired that maid for no reason."

"And her sister, Susie Pegg, also worked here. Susie quit when you fired Kate," Winston said.

"Not that I would have needed them." Shuttleworth slumped. "I've lost my way without Penny." He pulled his hand down his face. "She would never have let me accuse that maid. I must apologize to her." He started to rise. "Oh, but you said she was dead too. Also murdered? Poisoned?" He dropped back into the chair.

"It looks that way, yes."

"Who?"

"That's what we are investigating, sir."

"And she had the necklace? Will you return it to me?"

"If it is confirmed that your wife gave it to the maid, you'll need to prepare yourself for the reality that it no longer belongs to you." Winston spoke gently.

Shuttleworth stood, a signal that he considered the interview to have reached its natural conclusion.

"Before I go, Mr. Shuttleworth, I have two more questions."

The man sighed and gestured for Winston to continue.

"How have you been feeling yourself? I mean after your wife took poorly. Did you share any of her symptoms at any stage?"

Shuttleworth clapped his hands on his rib cage. "Very fit, Detective. No physical ailments." He suddenly frowned. "Other than sleeplessness, after Penny. . ." He raised his eyes to meet Winston's. "You had a second question?"

"Yes. Now that we know the women were poisoned, we need to search for the source. Might I have a look around your garden?"

Shuttleworth's mouth gaped at the request. "Whatever for? It's not yet spring. Nothing is in bloom. And surely you don't think the poison came from there?"

Winston held up his hands. "We need to consider all possibilities."

Shuttleworth stepped back. "What are you suggesting? I poisoned my wife? And her maid?"

"I merely want to take a look, Mr. Shuttleworth. I cannot rule out anything at this point."

"Very well. I'll show you." Shuttleworth led Winston through the kitchen door at the rear of the house. Mrs. Plum was elsewhere, but the aroma of her recent baking lingered.

Shuttleworth slipped into a pair of well-worn boots at the door and held it open for Winston to follow. He led him to a shed at the furthest corner of the garden. The door of the shed opened easily to reveal neatly stacked pots on a workbench and unlabelled sacks on the floor. Winston squeezed past the narrow door and brushed past the sacks as he entered the shed. A cursory look revealed nothing out of the ordinary.

Outside the tiny building, Shuttleworth was bent over a bush, pruning its branches. "Might as well do a little trimming now that you've got me out here, Detective," he said, rising.

"May I trouble you to take me on a little tour of what grows in your garden, Mr. Shuttleworth?"

Shuttleworth scowled, a message that yes, he did consider it a bother. But he took Winston from bed to bed, pointing out those that were dedicated to ornamental displays and those closer to the kitchen door, which were reserved for growing vegetables and herbs. He warmed to his subject as he moved around the garden, and Winston jotted any plant names he was unfamiliar with in his notepad.

When they stood at the perennial border, Shuttleworth went into greater detail. Delphiniums were a favourite of his, apparently. As Shuttleworth described his anticipation of the blooming season, Winston noted it was the most at peace he'd seen him since making his acquaintance. He let the man wind down to a natural stopping point, then thanked him for the tour.

"Will that be all, Detective?"

"Another question, Mr. Shuttleworth. What about your valet? You didn't mention him when I asked about staff earlier."

"Tom Cullen. He is my former valet. He left shortly after Penelope died."

"No hard feelings between you? Do you know where he is working now?"

"I don't, I'm afraid. I gave him a good reference but haven't heard from him since he left."

"I have one final question. Do you employ anyone named Bobbie Lyon?"

Shuttleworth's eyes narrowed and his body stiffened. "No."

"Did you?"

Shuttleworth squared his shoulders. "I have never employed anyone named Bobbie Lyon. I hope I have satisfied your questions for today." His tone was clipped, terse.

Winston wasn't sure what to make of Shuttleworth's reaction. Was he just fatigued, tired of all the questions after receiving such upsetting news? Or did he know more? "Thank you, Mr. Shuttleworth," Winston said.

He left Shuttleworth plucking at the bush and took the path around the side yard to the street. He still hadn't discovered who

Bobbie Lyon was, but perhaps Tom Cullen could answer that question.

CHAPTER 28

Riley

RILEY LET HERSELF into her sister's apartment. Without Lucy or Alex to greet her, the place felt empty. Soulless. "She'll be back soon," Riley said to fill the silence.

With a few short strides, she entered the bathroom. Lucy's side of the vanity looked untouched since the last time Riley had been there. The bright labels on the bottles and jars, which had looked cheerful before, now looked out of place among the muted tones of the towels and other objects in the room. The first bottle's contents rattled when Riley picked it up to read the label. *UFOCUS. Think Better.* She took a photo of both sides of the label. Despite its promise to contain only pure ingredients, she didn't recognize most of the names. She sent the photos to Jules. When she untwisted the cap, a handful of pink tablets remained at the bottom of the bottle. She knocked one into the lid and snapped another picture, also destined for Jules.

The next bottle, this one labelled *ULITE*, appeared to be from the same manufacturer. She repeated the same steps she'd followed with the first bottle. The third bottle, *BOOSTED*, had a different company name, though the ingredient list was equally incomprehensible. Claims of "all natural" and "only clean" rang hollow when she removed the cap and a cloud of green dust escaped. She dabbed at the dust with her pinky and rubbed it against her thumb. The smooth, chalky powder coated her fingers in a silky film. Maybe it mixed well with liquids because it was so fine.

The final bottle had a much smaller label than the others did. It simply read *FRVR*. When she opened it, a fruity smell set her mouth watering. She'd never actually wanted to take a vitamin before, but this one promised to taste as good as it was for you. For the briefest of moments, she considered popping one into her mouth, but then she remembered why she was here. What if this was the one making Lucy so sick?

After she sent the last photo to Jules, she swept the bottles into a clear plastic bag to take to the hospital. On the street, she hailed the ride-share she'd ordered and climbed into the back seat, where she immediately began looking up the manufacturers of the supplements on her phone. The website for the manufacturer of the first two items had the stock photos of happy and healthy people Riley had been expecting. The manufacturer of the powder sold "health-focused tinctures," supported by five-star endorsements. She skimmed through the accompanying results and a discussion forum where people confirmed increased energy after adding the powder to their morning smoothies. She rolled her eyes. Oh really? Was it the powder or the smoothies that improved their energy?

The lone result for the manufacturer of the smaller, sweet-smelling pills was a website that published nothing but glowing reviews from people enthusiastically sharing their results after using the product for only a few weeks. The tight ball of worry lodged in Riley's chest became even tighter when she noted that none of the reviews were older than three months. The website had no contact information or address for the manufacturer. How had Lucy ordered them? Or had they simply arrived one day so Lucy could promote them?

She opened her sister's social media page and scrolled through several posts to find one from three months earlier. Under a post titled "New Regime," Riley found her answer. Just as she was about to dial Alex, her phone rang.

"Jules?"

"Riley, hey. Thanks for sending those pictures over. I can't find much about the companies, but that doesn't surprise me. They can be pretty fly by night. I looked up their domain name registrations, and none are more than twelve months old."

"Thanks. That confirms what I'd figured—they weren't well established."

"Listen, that's not all." His voice had taken on an edge.

Riley's breath caught.

"Alone, these supplements are pretty harmless. But combined, they're bad news." Her stomach clenched as he explained.

The ride-share driver had hardly slowed down in front of the hospital before Riley jumped from the car.

*

RILEY BURST INTO her sister's room, ignoring a shout from a nurse as she ran by the station. Lucy was positioned on her side facing the door, propped by a stack of pillows behind her. Her eyes widened when she saw the bag of bottles in Riley's hand. "Thank you for bringing those," she said, reaching for the bag.

"Are you kidding, Lucy? These are making you sick." Riley held the bag firmly in front of her, clasped with both hands.

Lucy blinked. "What do you mean? They're good for me."

"Have you been taking all of these together?" Riley shook the bag so the bottles knocked against each other. A nurse approached the bed. Riley held up her hand to stop her. "Lucy. Have you been taking these together?"

Lucy looked down at the bedsheets. "Maybe."

"Did you talk to your doctor before taking any of them?"

"Doctors make you sick," Lucy said. Behind Riley, the nurse scoffed.

Riley fought an impulse to throw the bag at her sister. How could she be so foolish? "Lucy. Doctors have been trying to figure out what's making you sick. And you know what it was?" She wiggled the bag again. "These. You did it." Out of the corner of her eye, Riley noticed the nurse turn to leave the room. She hoped it was to get a doctor.

Lucy reached for the bag. "Are you sure? They say they're healthy."

"Where did you get them?" Riley's voice was strained with the effort of remaining calm.

"They arrived with a note from someone who saw me on social media." Lucy gestured at the bag. "They're healthy."

"No. They're not. I just spoke with Jules. He looked them up." Riley pointed to one bottle. "Not all the ingredients are listed. Did you do any research? Or did you just start taking something that came from a stranger? Why would you do that? What were you thinking?" The flurry of questions bubbled out along with her frustration.

Lucy shrank into the bank of pillows, recoiling from Riley's words. Riley took a calming breath and smoothed out a place at the end of the bed. "Lucy, you can't just . . . take random pills."

"I looked at their websites."

"Which have basically no information. That's not research."

"Except the sites say they're healthy. And the people look so happy." Doubt had crept into Lucy's voice. "But you're saying it's not true. Aren't you?"

"Maybe taking just one of them would have been fine. But all of them? Jules said the ingredients have a history of dangerous interactions." Riley grabbed for Lucy's hand. "You could have died."

"I didn't know. I started taking the first one. And I felt fine. So I took the others. They're for energy, long life, wrinkles, and. . ." Lucy's voice had grown quiet.

"And?" Riley matched her sister's tone.

"And. . ." Lucy gripped the sheet. "And I started taking extra doses. Because after a while, I wasn't feeling as good. I thought. . ."

Riley waited while her sister searched for the words, biting back her own.

"I thought if I took more. . . I didn't know what was going on. I tried not taking them for a few days."

"Did that help?"

"A little, but those ones," Lucy said as she pointed at the thinner of the bottles, "I liked how they made me feel the best. Like, almost right away."

"So you took more than the directions said to?"

Lucy nodded. Riley could see in her sister's eyes that even now, if given the chance, she would take more. Potent stuff. "You can't. Not anymore." Riley leaned in closer and softened her tone. "Just eat healthy. Or exercise. Whatever you do, do it in moderation." She pulled from her pocket the package of gummy bears that she'd found still sitting on the counter at her sister's apartment. "And you can eat these. Honestly, a few won't hu—" Riley didn't finish the word. "Just stop being so silly." She set the package on the nightstand beside the bed.

She pushed herself from the bed and scooped the bag of supplements into her arm.

"What are you doing with those?" Lucy asked.

Riley winced at the desperation in her sister's voice. "I'll give them to your doctor. She can dispose of them or test them. Or whatever. But you can't have any more. And I'll make sure Alex knows to deal with any that just show up." Riley took two steps then turned back to her sister. "I'm glad you're okay. I love you, Luce."

Lucy's doctor was waiting with Alex outside the room. "How much of that did you hear?" Riley asked as she handed the doctor the bag of supplements.

"Most of it." The doctor took the package. "Thanks. I'll see if we can get these tested. Supplements are unregulated. These could contain already banned ingredients, but if they're not labelled, you'd never know."

"Unless you ended up here," Riley said.

Riley's mother rushed toward her, panic pinching her features. "Has something happened?"

"I think I've figured out what was hurting Lucy. She was taking a toxic combination of supplements."

"We'll test them to identify the specific culprits, but your daughter will be okay, Mrs. Finch," the doctor said. She moved toward the elevator with a purposeful step, the bag of supplements swinging from one hand.

"You should go talk to Lucy," Riley said to her mother. "I think she's realized just how stupid she's been, keeping secrets."

"And that's never a nice feeling, is it, dear?" her mother said, patting Riley's arm.

CHAPTER 29

Jack

Tom Cullen was at the first shipyard Winston inquired at. With only a few minutes until lunch, they arranged to meet at the pub where Cullen ate his midday meal. The former valet was a popular man, judging by the greetings he garnered from the other patrons as he entered. He exchanged a laugh with a few, promising that he'd see them later.

"I'm afraid I have some news, Mr. Cullen," Winston said. He went on to tell Cullen of Kate's death.

As he listened to the story, first of Kate's hasty wedding and then of her recent death, Cullen paled. "Dead? How?"

Winston studied the man's reaction as he told him she'd been murdered. Cullen's face showed genuine astonishment to learn of the manner of his friend's death. "I have to ask. Where were you when Kate died?"

"I was returning from Victoria. I was sent to pick up some tools from an iron works over there. The new guy gets the grunt work, you know?"

It would be easy enough for Miller to verify Cullen's story, and if true, it confirmed Winston's theory that the man was not involved in Kate's death. And it was unlikely that the two women were killed by different people who used the same method. "How well did you know Mrs. Block?"

"Well enough. We worked together at that house for nearly two years. Mrs. Plum, she's my mother's cousin. She got me the position." He wiped an eye with his finger. "How's Susie doing?"

"She's grieving, as you might imagine."

"Those sisters were close. They seemed to be able to communicate without using words. Like, one could tell what the other was thinking. They'd look at each other, then they'd both giggle."

"I never saw them together, but what you're telling me is consistent with what I've heard." Winston thought of his own brothers. Even though Ellis was older, he'd always made time for Winston and George. He would tell them stories about made-up worlds where trees talked and animals changed shape. He dropped his hand below the table and squeezed the rock.

Ellis.

He looked across the table to Cullen, who still had a pained look on his face, lost in his own remembrances. "I'd like a little information, if you don't mind."

Cullen furrowed his brow. Winston's request was not what he'd been expecting to hear.

"With the death of a second person from your former household, we are looking at everyone."

"I thought Mrs. Shuttleworth died from an illness."

Winston shook his head.

Cullen's jaw tensed as a sudden realization flashed on his face. He pushed his plate away. "Well, I didn't do it. I haven't seen Kate since I left." He held up his hands in defence. "And why would I kill Mrs. Shuttleworth?"

"In truth, I don't think you did," said Winston. "I was hoping you might have some information to help me understand who may have committed these murders."

Cullen looked down at his hands, seeming to study his nails. "I knew Susie better than Kate. I'll stop by her house and let her know I'm thinking of her." Winston noted the man's avoidance of his appeal. Cullen reached for a morsel of bread. "Do you think she'll talk to me?"

Winston stayed quiet, observing the man. From the way Cullen spooned stew into his mouth, it was clear he'd been taught polite behaviour. Winston noted the new calluses forming on his fingers, still red. "Why did you leave the Shuttleworth household?"

"After Mrs. Shuttleworth died, Mr. Shuttleworth agreed there was no need for me to stay. He paid me for an extra month."

Was Shuttleworth paying Tom Cullen for his silence? "When did you agree on those terms? The extra month, I mean."

"When I told him I was leaving."

"And you told him? It wasn't him asking you to leave?"

"Not at all. I told him I thought it was time I find something else to do. I had heard about the shipyard hiring more men. I thought, Why not give it a try? Mr. Shuttleworth wasn't going to need me to do much, and I didn't want to sit around all day. I think he wanted me to stay, but he said he understood."

"Didn't you want to find a job in a shop?"

Cullen massaged his palm. "Something that didn't use my hands, you mean?" He stretched out his fingers. "I liked the household, but there's something about building something. Creating something that didn't exist before. I can polish a pair of shoes or fix a tear in a seam, but that's not as satisfying." Cullen's smile reflected the gratification his new work brought him. "Mr. Shuttleworth is the same, you know. He spends a lot of time in his garden. I had to work to get mud out of a cuff once after he'd tended to some plant or other in a dinner jacket."

"You weren't disappointed to leave Mr. Shuttleworth's employment?"

"Not at all. Like I said, he gave me a fair sum and he let me go on my way." Cullen seemed earnest in his replies. "Besides, the money's better at the shipyard."

"What was your impression of how Mr. Shuttleworth felt about his wife?"

"He loved her." The words came easily.

"What about Kate? Did he love her, too?"

Cullen looked away. "I never saw him speaking to her. But I did walk in on him and Susie once. They were in his study. Not embracing or anything, but standing maybe a little too close together, if you know what I mean. I pretended I hadn't seen anything. As a valet, you have to be discreet."

Winston wrote this in his notepad. "Had he spoken to you of intending to take a trip with Mrs. Shuttleworth before she died?"

Cullen looked at the table and considered the question. "Mr. Shuttleworth travelled for his business occasionally. I often joined him if the trip was longer than a few days. I'd have never gone anywhere else if it wasn't for him. But he didn't have any trips planned that I knew of. And Mrs. S., she didn't like to travel on the steamers. The sea didn't agree with her." He wiped his hands on a napkin. "But I wasn't preparing for him to be away before she died. No. No trips."

Was Mrs. Shuttleworth planning to travel without her husband, then? Why would she have told Kate about this? "And had she been ill before she died? Mrs. Shuttleworth, I mean."

"For a few days. Not long."

"And before that?" Winston asked.

"Not that I recall." He tore off another piece of bread and dipped it in the stew. "Though, now that I think of it, I heard Kate tell Mrs. Plum once that Mrs. Shuttleworth had seemed to have less energy."

"Do you recall when that was?"

Cullen shrugged. "A month before she died, maybe? I don't remember exactly."

Winston made another notation. "Thank you for speaking to me. And yes, do speak to Susie. She'd probably appreciate a friend right now."

*

As JACK RETURNED from his lunch with Tom Cullen, he met Doctor Evans outside the station's entrance. "Doctor Evans." Winston extended his hand to greet him. "I hope you come with news about the poison that killed Mrs. Block and Mrs. Shuttleworth."

Evans shook Winston's hand and gestured to the door. "Let's speak in the morgue, if you don't mind."

Winston spoke to the desk officer as he passed. "Can you please send Constable Miller to meet us?" The officer nodded.

Winston and Evans made their way to the cold, stark room. Winston closed his eyes, holding his breath as he pushed the door open. He appreciated the meticulousness that Evans applied to cleaning the room after his procedures, but the stench of decomposing bodies would never be masked by vinegar, citrus, or any of the other scents he used to make the space more accommodating. Winston swung the door wide to let Evans enter.

Behind him, Winston heard Miller's breath catch in his throat. He turned to find the constable holding a handkerchief to his nose. He had his own squeamishness about the morgue, but Miller's reaction seemed exceptionally dramatic. "Come now, Thomas. It isn't quite that awful. Let's hear what Doctor Evans has to say about the dead women." He ushered the constable ahead of him.

Evans cleared his throat. "I understand this isn't the most pleasant place, Detective, Constable, but you'll benefit from what I will show you today." He motioned for the policemen to stand behind the low table on which he performed his examinations. Evans unlatched the handle on the cooling cupboard in which Mrs. Block's body lay on a wheeled table. He pulled the body from the chamber and backed himself toward the table, then moved to relatch the cupboard door. He looked from Winston's face to Miller's, waiting for their signal.

When they nodded, Evans unrolled the blanket covering the body, stopping when he reached the chest.

"I will focus my lecture here." He gestured at the body and his own chest. "As you know, I believe Mrs. Block was killed in the same manner as Mrs. Shuttleworth, though without Mrs. Shuttleworth's body, I cannot say this for certain. What I can say is that Mrs. Block suffered an agonizing death, despite the serene look on her face. Were I spiritual, I would claim that her look is one of relief at meeting God in her final moments of life. But I am a scientific man, and I will say that her expression is one of relief due to the pain finally subsiding."

Miller shifted his weight. "How can you tell she was in pain, Doctor?"

"Poison, especially if it is slow to act, often brings with it pain."

"Be that as it may, Doctor Evans, perhaps you could speak to what you do have evidence of," Winston suggested, quieting Miller's question with a hand on the younger man's shoulder.

"Thank you, Detective." He exhaled. "I've performed a test known as the Marsh test. It appears that Mrs. Block died from arsenic poisoning."

"Could it have been administered using the necklace?" Winston asked. They'd more or less ruled out the possibility, but he wanted to be certain.

Evans shook his head. "No. The evidence points to ingestion as the means of administration." Relief flooded Winston. He could confirm—based on scientific evidence now—that Doctor Evans had ruled out the necklace as the source of poison. Even if it was the one Riley's sister had been given, it was not responsible for the harm she endured. Discovering the location of the necklace was no longer a matter of urgency.

"Doctor, your note suggested that you'd found evidence of both acute and chronic poisoning when you examined Mrs. Block's stomach." Winston swallowed against the dryness of his throat as he formed his question. "Can you tell us more about that?"

"As you know, chronic poisoning would point to incremental dosing over a longer period. Acute would point to a critical concentration administered at the end, maybe in a final dose meant to be fatal. I see evidence of both in Mrs. Block's body. Arsenic explains this damage."

"For chronic poisoning, the killer would need to have consistent access to the victim, wouldn't they?" Miller asked.

"Precisely, Constable."

"That moves Block further down our list, I should think," Winston said to Miller. "Leaving Shuttleworth and Mrs. Plum." He turned his attention to Evans. "Doctor, this has been most enlightening. Earlier you had concluded it was ingested rather than absorbed through touch. Now you've given us the type of poison." Winston paused. "Do you believe both women were killed in the same manner?"

Evans held his hands up as if to defend himself. "On this, I cannot say. I didn't perform the same examination on Mrs. Shuttleworth. There was no need to."

"I understand." Winston continued in a quiet voice. "We believe, although we cannot prove, that the women were killed in the same manner." He dropped a hand and reached into his pocket. His mind calmed as his finger brushed the smooth stone. "How might we feel surer of this conclusion?"

Evans rubbed the bridge of his nose. "I read of a test that can be conducted using hair." He tugged at his own. "Do you think you can find a sample of hers? I may be able to test that," Evans said. "Of course, the test won't reveal whether the poisoning was intentional. That is your area, gentlemen."

"Yes, you are correct. Only discovering motive will lead us to the poisoner." Winston stroked his moustache. "Doctor, what are the common sources of arsenic?"

Evans consulted his notes. "Tobacco, rat poison. There are other sources like contaminated water, but I think you can rule that out."

"Rat poison might make sense for Kate Block. As a maid, she might have had to deal with it. But Mrs. Shuttleworth was unlikely to have encountered it regularly," Miller said.

"We will go back to the Shuttleworth house. Is there anything else we should look out for, Doctor?" Winston asked.

"That's all I can offer at the moment, Detective. I wish I could point you in a clearer direction."

"We'll learn what we need." Winston extended his hand. "Thank you. You've been most helpful."

"Be careful, Jack."

"Understood."

Winston and Miller withdrew to Philpott's office. "Miller, with the doctor's conclusion about Kate Block, I'd like to confirm our theory about Mrs. Shuttleworth. Tomorrow, go to the house and see if there are strands of her hair in her dressing room. On a brush or an ornamental comb, even an article of clothing. Perhaps Evans can perform his test on them."

"Yes, sir."

Miller left the office, and Winston drew the journal from his desk drawer.

Dear Riley,

Doctor Evans has confirmed that the necklace is not the source of poison for Kate Block, Mrs. Shuttleworth's maid. She was killed by oral administration of arsenic. I have sent my constable to search for Mrs. Shuttleworth's hair so the doctor may perform a test on it to confirm that she was killed in the same manner. If we assume arsenic poisoned both women, he believes they suffered from ingesting steadily increasing doses over a period of time. This is not to say that arsenic is the offending toxin in your sister's case, but whatever is making her ill, there is now scientific evidence to confirm that it is not the necklace.

I trust that this information brings you some comfort, though I realize it does not provide any clarity about the true cause of her ailment.

Winston licked at his dry lips. Recovering the necklace was not a priority. He believed Kate received it as a gift, as imprecise as her disclosure had been on the subject; Shuttleworth had no claim to it. It could rest, undisturbed in its hiding place, until Riley's time.

I have decided to do nothing with the information you shared about where your sister's necklace was found.

With concern,

Jack

CHAPTER 30

Riley

ON HER WAY home, Riley called Johnny and asked him to meet her for coffee. "Lucy's going to be fine," she assured him.

When he arrived at the coffee shop, she handed him a coffee and scooted down the bench so he could sit beside her. She wrapped her hands around the mug of tea that she'd ordered for herself.

"What's up, Riley? You look pretty sullen for someone who's just figured out what's making her sister sick."

"I just wanted to say thanks," she said. She stared forward, not daring to look at him.

"I'm so relieved Lucy's going to be okay." He set down his coffee. "Should we celebrate? Maybe a nice dinner?"

Tension crept into her neck. She kneaded it with one knuckle. "My mom is still here. She and I need to talk about her plans. When she's going to move."

"What about our plans?" Johnny's voice was nearly a whisper.

"Our plans?" She bit her lip at the shakiness of her voice. Why had she asked him to meet her if she didn't want to talk about exactly this? She'd been avoiding it, using Lucy's illness as an excuse.

"Can we make some plans?" He reached for her chin, giving it a gentle nudge so he could meet her eyes. "We never seem to be able to plan any further out than a week or so." The earnestness in his eyes tugged at Riley's heart. "I like spending time with you. I want to spend more." He swallowed, leaning in to brush a strand of hair from her face. "Don't you?"

Didn't she? Johnny was so perfect, so kind, so warm. Riley shimmied away. A half shimmy. Why was she putting distance between them? "I do. I just need a little space right now. With my mom moving here, my sister, the changes at the museum. . . It feels like a lot. And I can't ask you to wait."

"But we're not in the right time."

What an unusual way for him to phrase the sentence. Her stomach clenched. "You've been so great while Lucy has been sick. Letting Alex stay at your place. Sitting with us at the hospital."

He set his hand on hers. "It's what you do for someone when you—"

"Not yet," she said. A lump lodged itself in Riley's throat when she saw the pain on his face. She squeezed his hand. "Can we just sit here? Have our drinks? We don't have to say anything."

Johnny shook his head. "I don't think so." He stood.

"Wait." She rose and threw her arms around him. "I'm just not ready yet," she whispered into his ear. He squeezed her briefly, then released her.

"I should go. Thanks for the coffee."

She watched him cross the street, a knot of uncertainty pulling tighter in her stomach.

*

Dear Riley,

I am reluctant to bother you when you must be consumed with worry for your dear sister. Read the following only if you have time and energy to do so.

I write this to you after a final conversation with Mr. Clayton Block. His wife, Kate, was Mrs. Shuttleworth's maid. She died in the same manner as her employer, and it is her death that pointed to Mrs. Shuttleworth's being unnatural. I have ruled out Mr. Block as a suspect. He had no motive to kill Mrs. Shuttleworth and little opportunity. I am letting him return to Ontario as this city holds only the memory of loss for him.

Regarding the necklace, Mr. Block claims not to know where he lost it after finding it around his dead wife's neck. He reports that she was asked to keep it safe, though to what end remains unclear. One theory is that Mrs. Shuttleworth was planning to use its value to fund a secret trip, though where or for what purpose, I do not know.

Ruling out Mr. Block leaves me with three suspects for the murders: Mr. Shuttleworth himself, though he had little opportunity to kill Kate after he dismissed her some weeks ago; Mrs. Plum, the Shuttleworths' cook; and Susie Pegg, sister to Kate and also a former maid in the Shuttleworth house. I've included her name in the interest of thoroughness, although I have my own misgivings about her having any meaningful motive.

I am at a loss. Do you think I'm overlooking anything obvious? Have you any suggestions? On the matter of the name you shared, Bobbie Lyon, I've been unable to uncover anything about this person.

Has your sister's health improved? I really should have asked before sharing my trivial case. I take comfort think-

ing my situation serves as a distraction from your own. If this is not true, please let me know and I will refrain from sharing further details of my investigation.

With concern,

Jack

Jack was right: working on his case was a welcome distraction from worrying about Lucy. Now that they knew what was making Lucy sick, how long would it take for her to recover? Riley shook the thought away and set the journal on her bedside table. She moved to the bathroom to run a bath.

Her mother had not yet returned from the hospital, and she hoped to soak away the physical aches from unforgiving hospital chairs. And the weight of her lingering remorse after seeing Johnny. She climbed into the tub and slipped down until her shoulders were submerged in the warm, fragrant water.

After her soak, Riley felt refreshed. She sat at her kitchen table and wrote the names of Jack's suspects on a large piece of paper before typing them into the search bar of the city's online archives. Mrs. Plum proved difficult as Riley didn't know the woman's first name. She made a note to ask Jack. "Susie Pegg" yielded a single photo of a young woman taken at the end of the nineteenth century, before Kate Block died. Susie likely married and took her husband's name, so unless Riley could find a record of the marriage licence, she was a dead end. Finally, Edward Shuttleworth. She found no new results about him except for the mention of his wife's death in a newspaper article. Maybe he left town after she died.

Broader online results were unlikely to be fruitful, given how many people might share the names Riley was researching. Still, she tried Edward Shuttleworth's name, expecting little when she clicked

"Search." Instead, on the second page of the results she found a link to a family tree created by a Shuttleworth descendant, complete with pictures of Penelope and Edward, and a wedding photograph of the couple. Riley searched their stern expressions for a signal showing how they felt about each other. Mrs. Shuttleworth's mouth hinted at a smile, while her husband's was more firmly set. According to the family tree, Mr. Shuttleworth remarried, and this union led to several children and grandchildren, a descendant of whom created this online homage to her forebears.

Riley let her mouse hover over Susan Shuttleworth's picture—the second Mrs. Shuttleworth. She appeared several years younger than her husband, but it wouldn't have been uncommon at the turn of the century for an older man to select a younger wife, particularly if he hoped to have children. The first Mrs. Shuttleworth is acknowledged as having died after a short illness. No mention of her having been poisoned, but perhaps that wasn't a detail to boast about on a family tree.

She was about to close the page when her breath caught. Was Susan Shuttleworth the same person as Susie Pegg? Had Mr. Shuttleworth married his former maid? Riley tried her name again, this time entering "Susan Pegg," and an announcement of her marriage to Mr. Edward Shuttleworth appeared, one year after Penelope Shuttleworth's death.

The cursor shook on the screen as Riley reopened the image of Susie Pegg and compared it with that of Susan Shuttleworth. Susie's photo was fuzzier, taken from further away. It was hard to be certain, but the women seemed to have the same facial features.

Riley held her hand over the journal and closed her eyes. What would be the implications of sharing this information with Jack? The Shuttleworths remained in Vancouver, so Jack would likely hear about Mr. Shuttleworth's second marriage within a few months. If Riley told him about it now, she was simply accelerating what was going to happen anyway. Would the Shuttleworth family tree also change as a result? She opened her eyes and began to write.

Dear Jack,

I'm looking into Mr. Shuttleworth. Has he shown any interest in Susie Pegg? Has she said anything to suggest she has strong feelings for her former employer? Would they be strong enough that she might kill his wife? Even as I write this, I can't believe she would kill her own sister, though. Certainly not if they were close, which they must have been to be able to work so closely together. Who else can confirm how close the Pegg sisters were?

It may be nothing, but according to a document I found, Mr. Shuttleworth and Susie are connected in the future. I'm reluctant to explain how, but your conversations with them may hint at their feelings for each other.

Also, what is the first name of the cook, Mrs. Plum?

Lucy's condition is unchanged, but the doctors say that is a good thing. At least she is stable and not getting worse. And earlier today, I discovered the source of the toxin that is responsible for her illness.

Riley paused. How could she explain supplements to Jack?

She'd mistakenly taken some medicines that were incompatible, believing both to be beneficial. And as I'd hoped, and as you'd given me reason to expect, the tests the hospital ran on the necklace revealed there were no surface tox-

*ins on it. So we continue to wait for Lucy to recover. I will
spend as much time as I can with her as she does.*

Keep well,

Riley

Suddenly exhausted by the past few days, Riley prepared for bed.
She climbed under the covers and fell into a fitful sleep.

CHAPTER 31

Jack

WINSTON ARRIVED AT the police station early. Again he found the quiet conducive to clear thinking. While he waited for Constable Miller to arrive, he reread his notes, finding nothing in his observations about Susie Pegg's feelings for Mr. Shuttleworth. How would he explain to Miller that he wanted to look deeper into their relationship without revealing Riley as the source of his theory?

Miller entered Chief Philpott's office with a cheerful smile. "Thomas, please tell me you've got some good news to share. I'd dearly love some, as we haven't made any progress worth smiling about on this case." Winston rose and pointed to the chalkboard adorned with their earlier scribbles.

"It's nothing to do with work, sir. I've just persuaded my younger brother to move into a house with me. To spread out, move away from our family home. It's time I took some responsibility."

For the briefest of moments, Winston pictured himself as destined to forever live at Mrs. Bradley's house. Then he remembered it was his own choice. And he was happy enough for now. "That is worth smiling about. Have you a house in mind?"

"The one next door to my parents is available. I thought it might be a good place to start."

Winston clapped Miller on the shoulder. "Why bother," he said with a chuckle, "if you're only likely to trouble your mother for food and clean laundry?"

"It will be much easier if she's so close," Miller admitted. "Though I will be living separately from her."

"I suppose that's true. Well done, Thomas. It sounds like this is what you want."

"Thank you, sir."

"Now that we have your home situation sorted out, let's turn our attention to our case." Winston returned to his desk. "I have been thinking. . ." He recalled the conversation with Cullen and thumbed through his notes. "Here it is. Cullen saw Susie standing close to Shuttleworth, looking more intimate than he thought proper. What if Susie and Shuttleworth had a secret relationship?"

"And either Susie or Shuttleworth killed Mrs. Shuttleworth so they could be together." Miller picked up the thread of Winston's theory. "And then Kate, because she knew something."

Winston considered this for a beat. They had virtually eliminated Susie as a suspect, thinking she had no motive. If she and Shuttleworth were having a secret relationship, that gave her motive. "Even if she and Shuttleworth were romantically entangled, Susie seemed genuinely distraught about her sister." Winston steepled his fingers. "I don't think it was her. What about Shuttleworth? His guilt would explain why he is so distraught. Before we settle on this, let's review. What do we know?" Winston asked.

"About the two dead women?"

"Right. Let's start with Kate Block." Winston eased back into his chair.

"She was accused of stealing the necklace."

"And in truth, Mrs. Shuttleworth gave Kate the necklace as a gift. Her husband said he found her with it and has since lost it. But we don't know where it is now."

"Are you certain she didn't take it?" A hint of frustration crept into Miller's voice.

"Kate said she didn't. And in our conversation with Polly, the kitchen maid, she said that Mrs. Shuttleworth frequently gave things to Kate."

Miller nodded. "But why would she give Kate that necklace?"

"Why indeed? Shuttleworth gave it to his wife. If she then gave it away, it clearly didn't hold for her the meaning that he'd hoped it would. Learning about a secret relationship with a maid might do that. What if after Mrs. Shuttleworth learned of the relationship between Susie and her husband, she was going to sell it and use the money to leave him?" He pulled the pages he'd taken from the Blocks' apartment from the pile of notes in front of him. "If Mrs. Shuttleworth gave Kate the necklace, can we assume she also gave her these notes? We know that Kate was only learning to read, so she didn't write them herself."

"The game instructions?" asked Miller.

"Yes. Why would Mrs. Shuttleworth have them? Her husband is the inventor." He examined the pages again. "I don't see anything that suggests they might be anything other than game instructions." Players were to be dealt cards that they then played to traverse a board. The instructions suggested it was a game of strategy: certain cards advanced the player's journey or impeded another's.

Miller walked to the blackboard. "Do we know for certain that Shuttleworth and Susie have a relationship? All we know is they were seen standing too close once."

Winston couldn't share that they would eventually be "connected in the future," as Riley had written in her note. Miller was correct; they didn't know whether the relationship had started yet. "It did have me wondering if the occasion when Cullen saw them wasn't the first. Mrs. Shuttleworth could have observed another, or one of the other household staff," Winston said.

Miller circled Shuttleworth's name with Susie's. "How did they kill Kate, though? If Susie hadn't seen her sister?"

Winston joined Miller at the chalkboard. "Susie claimed not to have seen her sister." Winston's fingers tingled with excitement at the hint of a breakthrough. But along with the promise of progress, a sense of disappointment that the friendly woman might be the killer settled in his chest. "Evans has confirmed the poison is arsenic. It's used to kill rats. I visited Shuttleworth's gardening shed, and it contained unmarked sacks." He tapped the board. "Easy enough to sprinkle some onto their food."

"With a final dose just before Kate died."

But Susie was not Bobbie Lyon if she goes on to marry Shuttleworth. Winston stared at the board for inspiration, his gaze resting on Mrs. Plum's name. Riley had asked for her first name. "Miller, I know you like her, but we need to take a closer look at Mrs. Plum."

Miller's face fell. "Why?"

"She may be the key." Winston straightened himself. "But first, we need to visit Doctor Evans. He should know more about the poison by now."

*

WINSTON AND MILLER sat in silence as they rode a streetcar in the direction of the doctor's house. The noises of the bustling city carried Winston's thoughts to the regular routines of the people around them, living their lives on this damp day—shopkeepers displaying their wares, boys making deliveries, women darting from shop to shop with raised umbrellas, out to view the latest fashions. Soon enough, people would welcome spring, waking from the dark and wet winter to enjoy the return of brighter days and cheerful flowers. Did this same pattern continue in Riley's time?

The streetcar had hardly slowed at the stop nearest Doctor Evans's house before Winston leaped off. He set a hurried pace to the doctor's house, using the side entrance for patients. The small room Evans's patients waited in contained only a worried mother holding her baby to her chest. Minutes after the officers arrived, Evans appeared, eyebrows rising when he saw Winston and Miller. Winston shook his head, nodding toward the mother and child whose needs were more urgent than those of two dead women. Evans nodded his thanks and ushered the mother deeper into the house.

Winston passed the time by reviewing his notepad. His thoughts drifted back to his conversation with Melodia. What lies might the suspects be telling themselves? Shuttleworth and Susie Pegg. His fingers tingled as he thought of them. The truth they may be hiding was critical to this case. Were they more than employer and maid? And Mrs. Plum. Did she know about Susie and Shuttleworth?

His thoughts were disrupted by the young mother exiting the examining room. Winston and Miller stood and nodded politely in her direction as she passed.

Evans said goodbye to his patient then turned, searching the policemen's faces. "Detective. I assume you're here about the Shuttleworth case."

"I have some questions and hoped you might have time to answer them." The men exchanged handshakes.

"Of course. I'm still writing my report, but I'll answer whatever I can."

Evans led Winston and Miller into his office. Rows of books lined the walls, and a large desk took up one corner of the room. Evans settled into a chair behind the desk and gestured to the pair of chairs that faced him.

"You conducted a test on Kate Block's body to isolate the type of poison used. Could you perform it on something else?" Winston reached into his satchel and withdrew two wrapped packages. He unwrapped the first one and slid it toward Evans. "This is a scone given to me by Mrs. Plum."

Evans pointed to the partially eaten section. "You ate some? Did you experience any ill effects when you ate it?"

"Nothing of note."

"And the other?" Evans reached for the second package.

"From my clothing. I rubbed against something that left a residue on my trouser leg."

"And you sacrificed it for the investigation?"

"It's important to find the truth."

Beside him, Miller stifled a look of surprise. Winston hadn't shared what he was going to ask Evans. Miller leaned toward Winston. "That's clever, sir. The experiments. Could be useful in investigations."

"I think so too, Thomas."

"Let's see what we can do," Evans said. Winston and Miller followed him into his garden, where he had several scientific instruments set up under a canopy. "The test requires good ventilation," Evans explained. "I prefer to do it outside."

Evans added a solution to a small glass vessel. He then scraped particles from the section of trouser into a beaker, then broke a small piece from a shiny rock and added it. He poured the solution into the beaker and closed it using a stopper that had a rubber tube connected to it. He touched the flame from a match to the other end of the rubber tube. The smell of burned rubber stung Winston's nostrils. Evans was wise to perform this test outdoors. With a careful hand, Evans directed the tube toward a small plate. A jolt of excitement passed through Winston as tiny dark droplets formed on the plate. Evans extinguished the flame and turned to Winston and Miller. "Arsenic."

"Evans, this is remarkable. Show me again." Winston watched, fascinated by the doctor's methodical movements. As before, the dark droplets appeared. They had discovered the source of the poison.

"Where did you encounter this, Jack?"

"In Shuttleworth's garden shed. Can you test the scone?"

Evans repeated the procedure, but this time no droplets appeared. "There is no arsenic in the scones."

"Thomas, you must be pleased that the scones are safe." He gave Miller a wink. "Thank you for showing this to us, Evans."

Winston had his answer.

CHAPTER 32

Jack

THOUGH THE CRISP air still held a bite, the sun now peeked through the clouds, hinting at warmer days to come. The optimistic thought matched Winston's mood as he and Miller approached the Shuttleworth house. The sound of someone humming came from the backyard.

"Miller, I think it's best if you wait here, near the front." Winston had made the mistake in the past of entering the home of a suspect without having another officer nearby. He bypassed the door for the gate, which closed silently behind him. Not wanting to surprise the person humming in the yard, Winston reopened the gate and swung it shut to signal his presence. Shuttleworth, dressed in work clothes, appeared from behind the house with a spade in his hand. He greeted Winston with a wave and led him to the back garden. "Hello, Detective. I am taking advantage of this sun and getting an early start on spring planting. Well, not planting today, but preparing to."

"Are you an avid gardener, Mr. Shuttleworth?" Winston asked.

"All my life. I think my father was rather disappointed that I didn't remain on the farm." He mopped his brow with a handkerchief he pulled from a back pocket. "But the work is hard, the hours are long, and you're at the mercy of the weather. Still, I like to spend time out here, and perhaps I enjoy it more because my livelihood doesn't depend on it."

"Yesterday you showed me the bed where you grow vegetables. What do you like to grow there?"

"A little of everything. Mrs. Plum uses produce from it in our meals, and I must say I find it immensely satisfying to enjoy what we've grown right here."

"Is that where the inspiration for your game came from? Digging in the garden, I mean. It's like digging for treasure."

"My game?" Shuttleworth stepped back. "Oh yes." He mopped his brow again. He set down his spade and circled the perimeter of the yard. Winston watched as the man paced slowly, pausing in front of a cluster of skeletal-looking shrubs. After several seconds, he returned to Winston, looking as though he had reached a decision. "Actually, Detective, there's something I should tell you about that," he said and looked over both shoulders. His voice was quiet but unshaken. "It was my wife."

"Your wife?" Winston repeated.

"Yes." He raked both hands through his hair, setting it on its ends. "She invented Finders."

"And you took credit for it?" Winston's pulse quickened at this new information. Mrs. Shuttleworth had given Kate the game instructions they had found in the Block's apartment. Had Mrs. Shuttleworth realized that she was being poisoned?

"We agreed that it made more sense for me to be the inventor." He looked at the house. "She didn't want the attention. And the truth is, a game invented by a woman would not be taken seriously."

This logic was sound. Even though there were many women—he thought of Melodia and even Mrs. Bradley—who successfully operated their own businesses in the city, they would never be invited into the Vancouver Gentlemen's Club or the other venues where men of influence gathered and made decisions. "And she felt no resentment?"

"None at all. I think it rather suited her to be silent about the partnership." Shuttleworth pressed a thumb into his cheek, leaving behind a smear of dirt. "She was brilliant." He pulled his hand down his face. "She told me she'd been working on a new idea. One she thought would be even more popular."

"Will you continue to develop it?"

"This is a problem. She didn't share her ideas with anyone. I don't even know where she wrote them down. Nowhere I have found. I don't know what I'll do without her."

"You didn't discuss it at all?" Winston turned the idea over.

Shuttleworth shook his head silently. "No," he whispered.

Winston reached into his satchel and pulled out the game rules they'd found after searching Kate Block's apartment. "Might these be your wife's notes?" he asked.

Shuttleworth wiped his hands on a handkerchief before taking the pages from Winston. As he read them, a smile grew on his face. "Where did you find these, Detective?"

"They were found in the home of Kate Block, your former maid."

"How did she get them? Did she steal them when she stole the necklace?" Bitterness seeped into Shuttleworth's voice.

"As I mentioned yesterday, Mr. Shuttleworth, I don't think she stole the necklace. I think your wife gave it to her, along with these pages and the game piece," Winston said.

Shuttleworth rocked back on his heels. "Why? Why would she do that?"

"I think she knew someone was trying to kill her, and she didn't know whom to trust." He removed the pages from Shuttleworth's hand.

Winston led Shuttleworth to a bench nestled between two trees. In the summer it would be a shady spot to read or think, with leaves rustling overhead. He sat beside the shaken man and let his own mind swim with the full impact of what Shuttleworth had shared. If his very livelihood and success depended on his wife's brilliance in her role as game inventor, then it made no sense that he would kill her. He'd effectively just struck his own name off the list. Winston gathered his thoughts and asked, "Is there anyone else who might have known about the game? Perhaps a close friend of hers?"

"Nobody knew the truth. She never would have told someone without first discussing it with me."

And yet she'd given their maid a copy of the rules for her next game. Did she suspect her husband was behind her illness? Or someone else in their house—Bobbie Lyon? A bird landed on the arm of the bench. "Tell me about Bobbie Lyon. Who is this?"

Shuttleworth blinked. "That woman no longer exists."

A woman. One question answered. "What does that mean? You know her?"

"I knew her." Shuttleworth pressed his lips together. "She cannot have killed my wife. Or. . ." His voice trailed off. "It wasn't her."

He pushed himself from the bench and returned to where he'd been working when Winston had arrived. This time he picked up a hand trowel he'd left beside the path. He lowered himself to the ground and twisted to offer Winston another trowel. "Get your hands dirty, Detective. It helps me think."

Winston accepted the tool and looked down at his shoes. They were already dirty. If it would help Shuttleworth feel calm and encourage him to answer more, he could sacrifice another suit as well. He knelt where Shuttleworth pointed. "Who is she?"

"Someone from my past." Shuttleworth stuck his trowel into the bed and demonstrated for Winston, pushing deep and lifting a full scoop of soil. He turned it over, dumping the contents onto the surface of the bed. "Like this," he said. "We're giving the soil some air. We all need it."

Shuttleworth repeated the trowel work in a small section until the soil in that area looked loose and took on the deeper brown of the rich loam beneath the bed's surface. Winston grasped his trowel and mimicked his work, unsure whether he was doing it right. Shuttleworth said nothing, so he continued turning the soil over. "Did Bobbie Lyon know about your fondness for Susie Pegg?"

Shuttleworth's trowel fell to the ground. "Fondness? For Susie? Our former maid? What fondness?"

"You were seen. At least once, possibly multiple times, by different people. One person I spoke with thought you might have been embracing."

A beat passed as Shuttleworth tried to remember. "Ah—Tom, you mean? I recall the moment. But he didn't see what he thought he saw." The man had recovered himself; he spoke with confidence. "I loved my wife, Detective. We were a team. Nothing was going to change that."

"Did you embrace Susie?" Winston pressed the point, although if Shuttleworth had embraced the maid, what did that have to do with her sister dying? Had Kate known about a secret relationship between Susie and Shuttleworth? Or the true identity of the game's inventor? And had she died to keep that secret?

Shuttleworth shook his head. "Never." He dug in the dirt again. "If you're referring to Tom walking in on Susie and me discussing something, it was a surprise I was planning for my wife. Susie had agreed to help me, and I grasped her arms in a moment of thanks." Shuttleworth faced Winston and clasped his hands around his upper arms. "Like this. It was the only time I ever touched her. Tom happened to walk in at that time. I can see how he thought it was the end of an embrace, but truly, it was not." Shuttleworth released Winston's arms. "Susie, the maid, she is pleasant. But I assure you, as long as my wife was alive, I never pursued another woman."

Shuttleworth's story matched Susie's, and he was inclined to believe it. Had Tom told someone else about the embrace? "Mr. Shuttleworth, you say you used to know Bobbie Lyon. Where is she now? I really must speak with her."

Shuttleworth picked up his tool and thrust it into the ground. "That person no longer exists. I loved her once. And she me. But she would never have hurt Penelope."

"Did your wife know her?"

"She did. And they thought highly of each other."

"How can I speak to her?"

"You can't, Detective. Bobbie Lyon no longer exists."

Shuttleworth's words spun through Winston's mind. How could Bobbie Lyon be dead if she will be named as the woman who is ultimately convicted of Mrs. Shuttleworth's murder? And how could Winston tell anyone what he knew about her? "You're certain? Bobbie Lyon is dead? And she cannot harm you?"

"She would never."

Winston mulled over Shuttleworth's responses. His choice of words was peculiar. Twice he'd said "no longer exists" instead of "has passed" or "is deceased." And he'd sidestepped the direct question "Bobbie Lyon is dead?" It seemed too painful for the man to even contemplate.

Winston shifted position and shifted his thoughts. If Shuttleworth's wife had been behind the success of Finders, his killing her made no sense, especially if she had been working on another game that might prove to be equally successful. This certainly argued against Shuttleworth finding any advantage in the death of his wife.

"Do you use rat poison in your garden, Mr. Shuttleworth?"

The man shook his head emphatically. "Never. I worry that it will get into the soil. Then into our food." He paled. "Is that what killed Penny? Rat poison? Mrs. Plum used some once in the kitchen. But I told her I'd rather she used another method to deal with them."

"I encountered what I later learned to be rat poison in your shed," Winston said.

"Perhaps Mrs. Plum put it there when I asked her not to use it any longer."

The trowel slipped in Winston's hands. He picked it up again and turned another pile of dirt as his pulse quickened.

That person no longer exists. Shuttleworth's words swirled in Winston's mind. He drew in a sharp breath. Because she's taken on a new identity? An image returned to Winston—Mrs. Plum fumbling a package of scones on hearing the name Bobbie Lyon. Mrs. Plum and Bobbie Lyon. Could they be the same woman?

CHAPTER 33

Jack

"I MUST SPEAK with Mrs. Plum." Winston had returned to the back garden after confirming with Miller at the front of the house that he'd seen no one leave.

A shadow clouded Shuttleworth's face. "You were just here, Detective."

"After our conversation, I took a little walk to think."

"Do you seriously think she killed my wife?" Shuttleworth laughed as if it were an absurd notion. "I have known her my entire life. Her father's farm was beside ours."

"You gave me the impression earlier that she joined your household only a few years ago, Mr. Shuttleworth."

"And that is the truth. But I knew her before."

"How did she end up working for you?" Winston asked.

Shuttleworth wiped his hands on his coveralls. "I needed a cook. She needed work."

"Did you find it awkward? Did she?"

"She's worked for us for a few years now, and I imagine if she found our arrangement uncomfortable, she would have left or said something to me. She has had much loss. Working here gave her a family of sorts."

"How did your wife feel about your inviting Mrs. Plum into your home?"

Shuttleworth dismissed the thought. "She treated Roberta—I mean Mrs. Plum—like a sister."

Roberta. Bobbie. That was it. "A sister who manages your kitchen. And has access to rat poison."

Shuttleworth paled. "I don't know what you're saying."

"It's time for answers."

"Indeed it is." Shuttleworth croaked the words.

Winston gave a short whistle and Miller entered the yard. As Winston walked to meet Miller, Shuttleworth began to follow. "I must insist on hearing what you are asking her," Shuttleworth pleaded.

Winston held up a hand to stop him. "And I must insist that you remain outside. Please be patient. Go back to your garden. I will brief you afterwards."

Shuttleworth hesitated, then offered a small nod.

Winston turned back to meet Miller, and they entered the house from the kitchen door.

Mrs. Plum greeted them with a warm smile. "I'll just put on the kettle. Can I offer you a scone, Detective? I've just pulled some from the oven."

"Thank you, but not today." He patted his stomach. "I doubt you'll be able to persuade Constable Miller either. We had a decent meal earlier." Beside him, Miller started to protest, which Winston quieted with a quick shake of his head.

"How can I help you?" she asked.

Winston and Miller made their way to the kitchen table. Gesturing to the chair opposite, Winston asked, "Do you have time to answer a few questions? We'll keep it brief." He kept his tone light.

She placed glasses of water in front of Winston and Miller and sat down. "I have a few minutes before I need to start on lunch. Mr. Shuttleworth will need a hearty soup after his work in the garden today."

"Does he spend a lot of time in the garden?" As Winston asked the question, Miller arranged his notepad and began taking notes.

"We grow as much as we can. I was raised on a farm, so if Mr. Shuttleworth is unable to tend to the plot, I get out there."

"Your father is a farmer?"

"He was." She looked away. "It feels like a long time ago. Another life."

"How do you feel about working for Mr. Shuttleworth? I understand he is your former playmate. Does that make you at all uncomfortable?"

A flicker of fear pinched her eyes. "Never. He treats me like family. What else could I ask for?"

"And when he told you he was no longer going to need your services?"

Colour drained from her face. "He said no such thing. Poor Edward needs someone to care for him, especially now with Mrs. Shuttleworth gone."

Winston noted her use of Shuttleworth's given name. "Let's return to gardening. You mention that you spend some time in the garden. And I noticed some rat poison in the shed. Do you have a problem with the creatures?"

"Not anymore." Her gaze flicked toward the pantry, where shelves held containers of various ingredients. "Really, what are you talking about?"

"My theory is that you weren't as content to be the cook as you let on," Winston said.

"I've been the cook for two years."

"That may be the case, but I think something happened to make you feel uncertain in your position. Perhaps you learned Mrs. Shuttleworth was looking to replace you?"

"She had no such plans." Mrs. Plum pushed a strand of hair from her face. "I have been loyal to the Shuttleworth family."

"Which is why I think you were upset when you thought that Mrs. Shuttleworth wanted to replace you."

"How would I have learned that?" She locked eyes with Winston and squared her shoulders.

"Kate Block told you," he said, holding her gaze. "She was Mrs. Shuttleworth's maid, and she overheard a conversation between the Shuttleworths. Were they planning to move? Or just look for a new cook?"

Mrs. Plum licked her lips and set them into a sneer. "Penelope tolerated me. She knew my family and Edward's family had long histories, and she resented me reminding her husband of home. He loves me, you know."

"As a sister?" Winston pressed her. "And Plum is not your real surname, is it?"

"I think you know the answer to that question, Detective." She brushed her hands together, wiping away the idea. "I should be his wife. We were in love."

"Yet he chose another woman over you." Winston kept his voice soft. The words were harsh enough and inflicted pain.

Mrs. Plum squared her jaw, her gaze still fixed on Winston. "His ambition led him down a path he shouldn't have taken."

"What path is that?"

"The one that led him away from me. We would have been happy."

"Why now, Mrs. Plum?" Winston leaned toward the woman. Beside him, Miller continued with his note-taking. "Were you not satisfied running this kitchen? Your baking, certainly, is delicious."

Mrs. Plum settled into her chair. She let out a breath and looked at her hands, now folded in front of her. "I've always loved working in a kitchen." Her voice shook as she spoke. "From as soon as I could stand, I worked alongside my mother, preparing our family's meals. When she grew ill, I took over for her. Not long after that, when we were sixteen, Eddie professed his love for me. He wanted to buy the next farm over and start a family. We would have been happy. Until he got it into his head that his fortune would be found out West. I couldn't leave my family, not with my mother unable to cook for them. Eddie said he would wait, but he didn't."

Her eyes glistened with the memory, and Mrs. Plum paused to wipe them with her thumbs. "My mother was the first to go. It was easy, really. I mixed some of what we used to deal with the rats into the flour when I baked bread and gave it to my mother. Sent her to her bed for several days."

Her words sent a jolt through Winston. She'd done this before. He stole a glance at Miller, who had dropped his pencil onto his notepad.

Mrs. Plum continued her tale. "She didn't recover. She wasn't upset. She'd been poorly for so long. My mother was ready to die, and she did with a smile on her face."

Was she justifying this murder? Winston suppressed a shudder. Miller's knee began to bounce. Winston motioned with his hand beside his hip to calm the constable.

"It was so easy with her, and I couldn't be blamed. I didn't tell anyone, and I convinced myself it was for the best. It was only later when I realized that if the rest of my family was no longer a burden, I'd be free to travel west and be reunited with Eddie."

Winston sat forward, unable to hold back his question. "How long did you wait until you killed the rest of your family?"

"Too long. If I'd done it sooner, perhaps I would have already been his wife."

Winston let the impact of her words hang in the room. He refrained from looking toward Miller.

"So you came here, but found him married," Winston continued. "He let you join his household. Is that when you changed your name?"

"I'm getting there, Detective. You will only get this story from me once, so you'd better not rush me. I had no reason to be reminded of my past. And Eddie understood my heartache at losing my family, so tragically, to bad water. I was lucky I survived." Her voice had taken on a sing-song.

Miller pushed his water glass away.

"Why didn't you kill Mrs. Shuttleworth right away?" asked Winston.

"I won't pretend that I wasn't disappointed that he'd married Penelope. But she had such a brilliant mind. Those games. . ." She swept another strand of her hair behind an ear. "Pretending to invent that game gave Eddie such joy. I couldn't take that from him."

"Yet you did kill her."

"And Kate Block," added Miller.

"One evening, after he had too much to drink . . . this wasn't too long ago . . . he became my old Eddie for the night. He found me in the kitchen. I think he wanted to reminisce." She waved the thought away. "We shared a kiss. Nothing more. But Penelope knew. Somehow, she knew. And she insisted it was time to let me go. I couldn't let her do that." Mrs. Plum stared into the distance.

Winston leaned forward. "So you killed his wife? What about Kate Block? Why involve her?"

"Kate suspected Mrs. Shuttleworth's death wasn't natural, and though she didn't accuse me outright, she hinted at it. I started treating her to some of my special baking." Mrs. Plum gave Winston a chilling smile. "And you two were so helpful, delivering the last package of scones for me."

Miller shot Winston a horrified look. Winston shook his head almost imperceptibly and closed his eyes briefly. The message: don't react.

Miller recovered and, without skipping a beat, asked the cook, "Did you give Kate the necklace?"

Mrs. Plum shifted her focus toward the constable. "Mrs. Shuttleworth gave it to her before she died. Kate showed me." She massaged her palm with her thumb. "When Mrs. Shuttleworth died, Kate asked me what she should do with it."

Miller's chair legs scraped against the floor as he moved forward. "What did you tell her?

"I told her to hang on to it."

"Did Kate see it as payment for staying quiet about her suspicions? How did you know she hadn't told her sister? Or the man she married?"

"What could she say? She didn't have any proof or even know for certain I killed Mrs. Shuttleworth. Who would believe a silly maid over me anyway?" Suddenly her face contorted into an expression of grief. She wrung her hands and put on a desperate voice. "I was as concerned for Mrs. Shuttleworth as the rest of them, making her soup and scones until the day she died." She dabbed at dry eyes with an imaginary handkerchief. "It was so tragic, such a loss." She gave an exaggerated sniff.

Winston held up his hand to put an end to her dramatics. "And the game piece?"

Mrs. Plum smiled, waving her hand. "I tossed it into the stove. I wanted to throw suspicion from Kate. Maybe the thief thought the piece was valuable."

"The necklace certainly was," Miller said. He had resumed taking notes.

"It's a lovely piece. I imagine Kate's husband can sell the pearls for a neat sum."

"You aren't interested in the money, Mrs. Plum?"

"I've never been interested in the money, Detective. This is what you don't understand. I simply wanted to be Eddie's wife. My bumbling Eddie, for all his flaws, is a lovely man. When he became Mr. Shuttleworth, he grew into someone I didn't recognize, with his fine fabrics and grand house."

Winston stroked his moustache. "Thank you, Mrs. Plum. You'll need to accompany us now to the station."

"Whatever for, Detective?" She patted her hair. "I need to put on Mr. Shuttleworth's lunch."

"He'll have to help himself." Winston stood. "I'm placing you under arrest for the murders of Penelope Shuttleworth and Kate Block, formerly Kate Pegg." In a fluid motion, he circled the table and grasped Mrs. Plum's elbow to lead her from the house.

CHAPTER 34

Riley

RILEY LEANED AGAINST the door frame, letting a wave of exhaustion sweep through her. She bent to pull off her boots and grabbed her bag from where she'd dropped it when she'd stumbled into her apartment. Her mother had stayed at the hospital with Lucy, so she had a few moments to herself. She pulled the journal out of her bag and began reading on her way to the couch.

Dear Riley,

I arrested a woman today for the murders of Penelope Shuttleworth and her maid, Kate Block. The murderess was the Shuttleworths' cook—known to us as Mrs. Plum, but her true name is Roberta Lyon. She had known Edward Shuttleworth her entire life, their families working on neighbouring farms in Ontario. Before she followed Mr. Shuttleworth west, she poisoned and killed her entire family to gain the freedom to leave. She believed Shuttleworth was in love with her and intended to marry her until he met the woman who became his wife. So this was her motive: to remove Penelope so she could take her place. Kate became her target when she became suspicious that the cook had killed her employer. I will get additional details from Mr. Shuttleworth later this afternoon.

How much love for one man could drive a woman to murder—multiple times? This was obsessive love. Off the scale. Riley couldn't wrap her mind around it.

I shared previously that her method of poisoning was arsenic, a known lethal toxin. Mrs. Shuttleworth and the maid were both slight of stature, meaning they became gravely ill. Mrs. Plum, or Bobbie Lyon, was careful not to use it in the food of other members of the household. When she killed her family, she ingested some of the poisoned food herself to avoid suspicion.

Thank you for your help with the case, especially the information about Bobbie Lyon. Shuttleworth responded with genuine surprise when, in the course of my inquiries, I asked if he had any feelings for Susie Pegg. But I'm not surprised to learn they will turn to each other for comfort.

I trust your sister continues to be in good hands and her health will improve.

With concern,

Jack

A swell of pride warmed Riley's chest. Jack had solved his case—again with her help. And Lucy was going to be okay. She was reaching for her pencil to respond when her phone buzzed.

Hey. I emailed some places Steve and I haven't visited yet. Pick one (or two) to explore with us. xx

> Will do. But not until tomorrow. I
> need some rest.

She turned off her phone and set aside the journal. Responding to Jack could wait.

∗

EARLY THE NEXT morning, after a deep and reviving sleep, Riley opened the journal.

> *Dear Jack,*
>
> *Congratulations on your arrest. It must be a great relief to solve the case.*
>
> *I should have written to you yesterday evening, but I was so tired after the events of the last day that I fell directly into bed when I got home from the hospital. Lucy is still there, but her condition is much improved. She has already texted me this morning.*

Riley replaced "texted" with "sent me a message" and continued.

> *I can't quite believe the hospital staff are letting her be so active so soon after the worst of her illness, but Lucy is very persuasive. She probably promised to promote the nurse. People are keen to be recognized.*
>
> *I'm thrilled you've solved your case and thrilled my sister is getting better. Now I need to go to work and impress Nick, who is going to be my boss for the next few months.*

*I'm less than thrilled about that, but everything can't be
perfect, right?*

R.

"Less than thrilled" didn't adequately describe how Riley felt
about Nick's new position, even if it was temporary. She needed to
meet the challenge head on. She grabbed her cozy robe from the foot
of the bed and headed for the kitchen.

As she waited for the kettle to boil, she let her thoughts turn to her
conversation with Johnny. He hadn't sent a message last night, but
neither had she. She would send him one later, maybe invite him to
an event in a month's time. Baby steps toward a longer-term commitment. If he hadn't completely closed the door to that idea. The
thought made her heave a deep sigh.

Tea in hand, she returned to her bedroom. The journal lay open
and showed a new message from Jack.

Dear Riley,

*I'm pleased to hear your sister is recovering. I'm confused
about her promoting the nurse, however. I thought Lucy
worked in a store. Is she working in a hospital now?*

Jack

Riley giggled at Jack's response. How could she explain social
media to him without making her sister, and the twenty-first century,
sound absurd? She settled on explaining that Lucy would praise the
nurse and make sure others heard of this praise.

She tossed the journal in her bag and looked under the bed for her
shoe, mulling over how to handle Nick. She heard her mother's voice

in her head, scolding her not to start the day worrying about something that hadn't yet happened.

✳

RILEY ARRIVED ON time for work, but the museum hallways were empty as she descended to the archive. She checked her watch, making sure she hadn't misread it. She swiped her card on the reader by the door and let herself in.

She was at work before Nick, though this was typical for her. And it would stay that way. He might be the boss, but she would direct things. Let him think ideas were his. One idea to pursue was naming her the head of the archive room. It was a job she could easily do, and he was sure to support it; he'd be based with other members of the museum's senior team and seldom have reason to frequent the archive room. As head of the room, she would set the schedule and ensure that she had plenty of time alone with these documents.

Riley fished her phone out of her bag and smiled when it lit up at her touch. Her mom had sent another heart emoji. She must have just gotten out of bed to start her morning. It surprised Riley how much her mother's decision to return to the city now made her heart sing. This was truly the silver lining to Lucy's illness.

Lucy. An easily influenced influencer. She had agreed to take a pause on the social media circus and focus on growing her boutique business. How long that pause lasted remained to be seen. With her mother, Alex, and Riley on the alert, Riley felt hopeful there'd be no repeat of this experience.

Riley's footsteps echoed as she crossed the floor. She set down her bag and settled in, ready to take on the exhibit.

CHAPTER 35

Jack

WINSTON HUNG HIS hat on the coat tree in the corner of his small sitting room. It had been quite a day. He'd identified the murderer in this baffling case, and not just any murderer—one who'd admitted to causing several additional deaths. He would send a telegraph tomorrow to the police in Ontario about reopening the investigations of the deaths of Roberta—Bobbie—Lyon's family members. Tonight he would relax with some whisky, possibly even ask William Fisher to join him.

He cast his gaze toward the bottle on his desk and spotted the stack of unopened letters beside it. His throat tightened. In two quick strides, he crossed the room to the desk. His hand lashed out, knocking the letters to the floor.

With shaking hands, he poured himself a drink, downing it in one painful gulp. He poured another. And another. As the liquid burned through him, he recalled the night before George's wedding. The brothers had stayed up late into the night, reminiscing about their childhoods. "What do you remember about Ellis?" Winston had finally asked. His stomach soured at the memory.

George had sipped his whisky and taken a few minutes to collect his thoughts. "Impressions. A shape. Looking up at him. Laughter," he'd said. "Mother with a smile on her face."

Winston had sharper memories of their brother. George, a few years younger, had spent less time with Ellis. "Those are good memories. Keep them, George," he'd said. The mention of their mother's smile had been unexpected. Winston had forgotten that she hadn't always been the severe woman she was now.

"It's hard. Nobody ever speaks of him. As if he never existed." George had reached for the bottle but decided against refilling his glass. "I need to have a clear head tomorrow," he had said with a chuckle. "Why do you ask, Jack?"

"Do you ever wonder why that is? Why nobody speaks of him?" Winston had asked.

"No. I'm sure the memory is too painful. Mother would not thank me to speak of him." He'd gripped Winston's arm. "You're not going to say something tomorrow, are you? When the family gathers for the wedding?"

What would Winston say? And what would he gain by doing so? He'd shaken his head. "No. Tomorrow is your day. And your fine bride's."

He knelt to retrieve the letters and began sorting them according to their postmark. It was a calming exercise, like organizing Melodia's books. For a moment, he cradled the envelope with the earliest date, then tore it open.

My dear Jack,

I will not insult you by beginning this letter with a plea for forgiveness or understanding. Instead, I will begin by saying that I was wrong to withhold the truth from you. In so doing, I discovered that I could avoid feeling the unspeakable pain that comes when someone dies. I protected myself from that pain and believed I was also protecting you and George. I realize now that a mother cannot close one part of her heart—the part that loves one son—without closing the parts that love her other sons. My heart has been closed for so long that I know it will never reopen

completely. However, I find that in writing these words,
it may be possible to soften ever so slowly.

The letter shook in Winston's hand. He pushed himself from the floor and sat at his desk, pouring himself another measure of whisky.

It pleases me tremendously that you attended George's wedding. Family is important to him, and I believe the same to be true for you. Which is why I have decided to send you this letter. I cannot undo your pain. But I can tell you about your brother Ellis.

When Jack and Riley attend festivals that turn sinister, can they solve the crimes before tragedy strikes again? Book 4, *The Bodies in the Boundary*, will be released in 2024.

Read More

For a sneak peek into Jack's and Riley's lives before they met and to receive early notice of upcoming books, visit Sarah's website: https://sarahmstephen.ca/newsletter-book/ to sign up for regular dispatches.

Books in the Journal Through Time Mysteries:
The Dead of False Creek
The Hanging at the Hollow Tree
Murder in Mount Pleasant
Bodies in the Boundary (available 2024)

He chases crooks in the nineteenth century. She researches the past in the twenty-first. When both attend festivals that turn sinister, can they solve the crimes threatening the events?

Vancouver, 1898. Detective Jack Winston is sent to police a spectacle that turns into a murder investigation.

Vancouver, 2018. Riley Finch joins her sister at a music festival and uncovers a threat to the good vibes.

Jack and Riley team up through their journal to uncover the truth behind the events. Can the pair solve the mysteries before it's too late? *Bodies in the Boundary* is the fourth book in the Journal Through Time historical mystery series. If you like time-bending mysteries, you'll love this winding tale.

With each book in this series, I learn more about the world that Jack and Riley share and the city we call home. More than once I have found myself somewhere in Vancouver and wondered what Jack would have seen or thought while standing in the same place.

While I am not a historian, I draw inspiration from pieces of history. For example, while writing this book, I learned that in 1903, Elizabeth Magie patented a board game she'd invented. That game eventually became Monopoly, but her early contributions have been largely forgotten. Like the fictional Finders that Jack plays in this book, Elizabeth Magie's version had two sets of rules, where players could co-operate and all succeed or compete and a single player win. I'm sure that Elizabeth Magie is not the only woman to have invented something and have her contribution erased. Though I don't feature her as a character (she was in Washington, D.C. and patented her game a few years after Finders), her story is worth reading about, which you can do in *The Monopolists: Obsession, Fury, and the Scandal Behind the World's Favorite Board Game* by Mary Pilon.

I use the modern names of streets in my books, though Jack would have known them with different names. I found maps in the City of Vancouver Archives to be helpful with understanding the young city's transit network. I'll share one of my favourite maps on social media and in my newsletter, but you can also find it by searching online for "Vancouver Tourist Map 1898".

If you enjoyed this book, please consider leaving a review, recommending it to a friend, or requesting that your library order a copy. These little gestures are so meaningful to authors.

Finally, I love hearing from readers. You can reach me at sarah@sarahmstephen.ca or follow me on social media to share your comments.

Warmly,
Sarah M Stephen
Vancouver, 2023

Acknowledgements

Many people contribute to creating a book, and though I'm bound to overlook someone, there are a few people I'd like to specifically acknowledge. First, and always, my family, for their continued support. My husband, my son, my parents, my siblings, and my many aunts, uncles, and cousins. I love you all. My editor, Janet Fretter, for her thoughtful guidance. My podcast partner, Brook Peterson, for helping me puzzle out ideas. If you haven't, you should read her books! My proofreader, Shelley Hudson, for ensuring that no sentence is left unpunctuated. And my early readers, for providing thoughtful ideas that strengthened the story. To all of you, thank you. I look forward to working with you on the next one!

And finally, as ever, I am thankful for you, my reader. I appreciate you spending time in the little world I created and hope you found your visit worthwhile. Thank you.

About the Author

Sarah M Stephen started writing at an early age, first scribbling pages of notes while pretending to be a journalist before she could print. After mastering the alphabet, she moved into poetry and short stories. Following a few successes in grade school (a regional poetry prize) and university (a short story published), she traded her creative tales for corporate ones. A graduate of The Writer's Studio at Simon Fraser University, Sarah also co-hosts the *Clued in Mystery* podcast, where listeners can hear about her love of the mystery genre. She lives in Vancouver, Canada, with her family.

Contact Sarah:
Instagram: https://www.instagram.com/sarahmstephenauthor/
Facebook: https://www.facebook.com/sarahmstephenauthor/
Website: https://sarahmstephen.ca/
Podcast: https://www.cluedinmystery.com

www.ingramcontent.com/pod-product-compliance
Lightning Source LLC
Chambersburg PA
CBHW061655190726
48289CB00006B/1891